CRAZY FOR YOU

S.B. ALEXANDER

DEDICATION

To my husband of twenty-two years who is the most courageous, honorable, moral, and wonderful man I have ever met. His battle with amyotrophic lateral sclerosis, ALS, has been a challenging journey for the last five years. But through the ups and downs and twists and turns, he always has a smile on his face. He's the love of my life and my soulmate, and I'm honored to call him my hero.
With all the love in my heart.
Susan

"The greatest pleasure of life is love."

— EURIPIDES

FOREWORD

J.A. OWENBY, INTERNATIONAL BESTSELLING AUTHOR

"Every now and then there comes a story that will rip your heart out and piece it back together. This is that story."

PROLOGUE

I pressed the button on my Fitbit as sweat trickled down my temples. The summer heat had been off the charts with high humidity that, according to the weatherman, would last well into next week. I usually didn't mind sweltering temps as long as I was either on my skateboard, swimming in the ocean, or in an air-conditioned place.

Sadly, our AC had been on the blink, and I suspected it was broken. Dad liked to keep the electric bill as low as he could, which meant the indoor temp was high and not as cold as my bestie's place. Georgia's parents both worked at the local hospital. Her mom was a nurse, and her dad was an ER doctor, so they could afford to keep her home cool.

Still, I was tempted to grab my skateboard and hit the park, but Dad wouldn't like me traipsing out at three in the morning. Not only that, but my junior year was starting the next day, and while I would love to do anything but sit in a classroom with students I didn't care to know, I'd promised Dad I would do well my upcoming year.

High school sucked the big one. Drama galore, and then there was Grady Dyson. He was the ass of all asses, despite his good looks—tall, football beefy, thick blond hair that curled around his ears, and blue eyes. Most girls in school bowed down to him like he was a rock star. But I wasn't one of them. The dude had hated me since the seventh grade. He'd stuck his tongue practically down my throat on a dare, and in turn, I'd kicked him in the balls. Then I'd spread a rumor about how awful his kiss had been. Girls had giggled and whispered about him that year. Since then, I'd been on his radar.

Oh, he was making me pay with the crap he'd said about me. I'd ignored the gossip my freshman year, but sophomore year, and one rumor in particular, had been a different story.

"Stay away from Lawson. She's a terrible lay," Grady had told his friends and anyone who would listen.

After that, guys looked at me funny or not at all. But I wasn't one to back down. I'd stormed onto the football field during one of his practices and kneed him in the balls. I'd gotten suspended, but I considered it worth it.

I had no idea how I would keep my cool or bite my tongue, but if I didn't want to sit in detention or get suspended again, I had to. Aside from Grady, I also had to pay more attention in class. My mind wandered too much. While the teachers lectured, I daydreamed, mostly about nothing or skateboarding—anything but math, English, and science.

My mom had died in a car accident two years ago, and neither Dad nor I had been the same since. It was hard to be happy after we'd lost the glue who held us together. Dad and I had tried to get our lives back to something resembling normal. We'd moved out of our old four-thousand-square-foot mansion that Mom had designed. Too many memories, although it was hard to forget the day we'd moved in. She'd been the happiest I'd ever seen her. Her bright blue eyes sparkled like the ocean on a clear summer day. Her smile had been infectious, and she couldn't wait to show me my room. She'd had the entire house decorated with new furniture before we stepped into the grand foyer.

"We're starting anew," she'd said as she draped her arm around me. "You're going to love this place, Skye."

A tear escaped as I planted my feet on the scuffed wooden floor and rose. I missed the plush white carpet I'd had in my former bedroom. Hell, I missed so much, and memory after memory suddenly bombarded me. I sat down on the edge of the mattress and cradled my head in my hands. Every time I thought of Mom, another piece of my soul was ripped away.

Taking a deep breath, I got up once again. I couldn't keep crying. I couldn't keep making myself miserable. But it was hard not to shed a tear any time I thought of Mom.

Stella, my Maine Coon, purred from her perch on my chair in the corner.

"It's okay, girl. Just thinking about Mom."

She meowed as if she, too, was still mourning Mom. After we'd buried her, Stella looked for her everywhere. It had broken my heart to see her wandering aimlessly around for weeks.

"I know, girl. I'm still grieving too." I turned on my nightstand lamp, and the soft glow shined on the dirty clothes piled on the floor near Stella.

I wasn't the cleanest person. That award went to my BFF. Her room was immaculate, but then again, I didn't have a maid who picked up after me.

I ambled over to Stella, then rubbed her head. "Go back to sleep. I'm just going to crack the window." Maybe the air wasn't so stifling outside.

A car door slammed as I was about to raise the blinds. I didn't have to look out to know Mr. Caldwell, our next-door neighbor, was stumbling up his driveway.

Regardless, I peeked. Sure enough, he was swaying as he walked. The man had a drinking problem. I'd overheard his wife, Bonnie, telling Dad one day that, after his thirteen-year-old son drowned, Mr. Caldwell hadn't been the same. "He drinks to drown the misery," she'd said.

Dad and I could sympathize with their sorrow, but alcohol wasn't the answer. Or at least that was what Dad had said to Bonnie.

The therapist Dad and I were seeing explained that everyone dealt with problems differently.

For sure. I daydreamed and cried. But I also read a ton. When I wasn't skateboarding, I was reading. I devoured books like a hungry animal, from romantic comedies to political thrillers or anything to keep my mind from wandering down a deep, dark hole that I couldn't get out of.

Dad, on the other hand, tinkered in the garage during his free time. He liked to fix golf clubs for some of his friends. And every Saturday, he played eighteen holes with his buddies. If he drank, it was never more than one beer.

Once Mr. Caldwell was out of sight, I lifted the window higher, hoping a brisk wind would blow in. Sadly, the humidity was too thick for anything to cool down.

I picked up my Stella. "How about we check the thermostat and then sit outside?"

We had one of those large wraparound porches, which was what had drawn Dad to our modest eighteen-hundred-square-foot home. He'd grown up in the deep South in a similar two-story with lots of land. We didn't have a large yard, but the neighborhood was decent, and I liked the moss trees and the azalea bushes that decorated properties up and down our street.

I loved sitting in one of the rockers, watching

cars and people walk by. I'd practically lived on the porch only to get a glimpse of the boy next door. Colton Caldwell was dreamy in every sense of the word. He had wavy brown hair, almost the color of mine sans the blond streaks. Colton was tall, with eyes the color of warm melted chocolate, and a sexy grin that made my belly swarm with butterflies.

Stella jumped out of my arms, then took off the moment my feet hit the cool tile at the bottom of the stairs.

The moonlight filtered in through the large transom window in the family room, highlighting a path for me as I headed into the kitchen.

As my feet slapped on the tiled floor, I heard faint crying. I held my breath as I sharpened my hearing.

The deep-baritone sob grew louder.

Dad? The last time Dad had shed tears was at Mom's funeral.

I hurried down the short hall to his room. The closer I got, the louder his cry became.

My heart split in half, and I fought hard not to let my own tears fall. Seeing Dad sob twisted my insides like a violent storm.

Our therapist had said that time would help

ease the grief, which was total bull crap. Anytime I thought of Mom, that empty, hollow feeling came back as strongly as the day the social worker had called to tell us that Mom had died on the way to the hospital.

I knocked softly. "Dad?" Then I opened the door and faltered.

Dad was on the floor with his back against his dresser as though he'd fallen and couldn't get up.

I ran like a sprinter, hoping my legs wouldn't give out. "What is it? Are you having a heart attack? A stroke?" I dropped to my knees.

He shook his head, blinking several times, his blue eyes clouded with tears. "Why are you up? You have school in the morning."

"Don't worry about me. What is it?" I felt his carotid artery as if I knew what I was doing.

His fingers wound around my wrists. "I'm fine."

"You're crying. So you're not fine."

He patted a spot next to him. "Sit with me."

Once I did, I grabbed his hand. "Are you sure you're okay?" Dad was my anchor, my saint, my world, and if he died, I would die a thousand deaths. I rested my head on his shoulder. "Are you thinking of Mom?"

"No, sweetheart." He took a huge breath. "I need to tell you something."

I stiffened at the despair weaving through his voice. I knew that what he was about to tell me was bad, not only by his tone, but also by how hard he was squeezing my hand.

"Do you remember what Lou Gehrig died of?" he asked so softly that I almost didn't hear him.

I nodded. "He lost the ability to control his muscles." Dad and I were big baseball fans. In the South, we rooted for the Atlanta Braves. Truth was, I didn't like them that much. My team was the Chicago Cubs.

"Well," he whispered.

I shook my head violently. "No. No. No. Please don't tell me that's what you have." I knew a little bit about the disease, mainly from watching *The Big Bang Theory*. Sheldon was a gigantic fan of Stephen Hawking, who'd lived with ALS for many years, which was very rare. Lou Gehrig had died within two years of diagnosis.

Dad shuddered. "Skye, I'm so sorry. I don't want to believe it myself." Tears streamed down his unshaven face.

"Did a doctor diagnose you already?" I knew he'd had his yearly physical last week.

He cried. "I have some very revealing symptoms. Remember a few weeks ago when you asked if I'd been drinking because I was slurring my speech? Well, I'm finding it's hard to say certain words. And one of the guys asked me the other day if I was drunk when we walked off the golf course."

In my head, I replayed what he'd just said, trying to detect any sort of stumbling in his speech. "But you're not slurring now."

"True, but it comes and goes."

"Maybe it's just stress." He'd been under a ton with his job at the local chemical plant, and Mom's death hadn't helped.

He dragged his fingers through his thinning blond hair. "I wish it were."

"So the doctor knows this for sure?" I refused to believe it.

He wrapped me in his arms. "I want you to know I'm going to do everything I can to make sure you're taken care of."

My tear ducts burst open, and I sobbed. "I can't lose you, Daddy. I can't." My stomach hurt. My heart splintered and my world went black.

1

―――――

ONE YEAR LATER

"Dad," I called as I wound my way into the family room from the kitchen. In the year since finding out he had ALS, or Lou Gehrig's disease, he had severely declined.

I was blown away by how quickly the disease had taken hold of him. I was blown away by how our life had changed in a blink of an eye. I was blown away by how Dad was on the fast track to another life. And as crazy as it might sound, I often wondered if Mom wanted him to join her in heaven.

I squeezed my eyes shut as I shook off the thoughts of death, of losing another parent, of being alone. I couldn't sleep at night, I could hardly eat, and if I sat and stared at Dad, I ended up crying like a newborn.

I was only seventeen, and if he died before I became an adult, I would end up with his sister. I'd only met her maybe three times when she visited for a holiday here and there. She and Dad had a strained relationship, a falling out when she was in college over some dude Dad didn't like. He hadn't shared the whole story. Over the years, they'd reconciled, but they still didn't keep in touch on a regular basis.

Despite that, I didn't want to move to California, and I sure as hell didn't want to live with my aunt. The last time she'd visited, a year before Mom passed, Aunt Clara was snooty to me. Maybe she'd changed. Maybe she was a nice lady. I'd gotten the feeling she didn't like kids, and to my knowledge, she didn't have any.

My mom had been an only child, and her parents had died years before, so that was out.

Even if Dad passed after my eighteenth birthday, I had no idea how I would survive. He'd tried to talk to me about what was to come, but I always ran out of the room in tears. I just couldn't bring myself to even think about the future without him.

Regardless, watching him decline tore my

heart right out of my chest. He'd gone from walking one day to a wheelchair the next and from speaking one day to having no voice the next.

I wished upon a star that I could hear his voice, his laugh, or even a reprimand if the need arose. I missed him calling me "sweet pea" or "sweetheart." I missed carrying on a conversation with him about anything and everything. He had a computer to relay his thoughts for him, but its robotic voice wasn't the same.

Dad sat in his wheelchair in front of the TV, wearing a large blue bib over a hospital gown, while Nan, his caregiver of six months, fed him breakfast. Dad had been through three caregivers before finding Nan. I was praying she would work out and stay for the long haul.

She had a great personality, soft and patient. She had a big heart and a caring soul. She reminded me of Mom in some ways.

She and Dad had hit it off from the moment she'd walked through our front door with her easy smile and gentle touch. In a different time, I was certain they could've been more than friends. They weren't that far apart in age. Dad was approaching fifty, and Nan was in her mid-forties.

Above all else, she never complained when

Dad was moody or burst into tears, and with ALS, instant emotional changes were the norm, particularly for Bulbar ALS, the rare form that started at the neck and took his voice first.

Tears threatened as I settled behind the leather couch that faced the fireplace, holding in the mountain of emotion that was ready to explode.

Nan pushed her gold-rimmed glasses up on her nose. "Good morning, Skye. Are you ready for your first day of senior year?"

I put on the most genuine smile I could. I didn't want to show Dad I was unhappy about leaving him all day or how much I hated school in general. High school was a petri dish of drama. The only saving grace for me was hanging with my BFF, Georgia, and our new friend Mia, who'd moved into our sleepy, North Carolina beach town last year.

A laugh broke out in my head. I had to hand it to Mia. She was super comfortable with her body and her sexuality. Me, not so much.

Nan shoved a spoonful of yogurt and oatmeal into Dad's mouth. "I like the outfit, and your new haircut brings out your pretty features."

I blushed. "Thanks." I wasn't wearing anything special—a pair of jean shorts, a new V-neck that

I'd gotten at the Jonas Brothers concert on my birthday last month, and my Vans. I'd also chopped off my long, light-brown hair the day before. I needed a change, something to pick me up and make me feel like I wasn't being weighed down. Anything to change the sour mood I'd been in for the last year. The change was helping so far. I did feel lighter, and I loved my new style, which I'd found on Instagram.

Even Georgia thought my new look fit me perfectly. "That A-line bob is so skater-girl-esque for you."

Dad's blue gaze glistened as he gave me an infectious smile. Then he turned to his computer screen, which was attached to a pole on his wheelchair, and typed with his eyes.

He had the coolest gadgets, compliments of his medical insurance. The infrared bar below the screen tracked his eye movement and allowed him to blink once on a letter, and then it would show up on the screen.

I had a love-hate relationship with technology. In one breath, I was glad he had the tools. His high-powered wheelchair got him from room to room and even outside to enjoy the warm Southern sunshine. I had been ecstatic when he received his computer so he could communicate easily. Before that, he'd had to type with his hands, but he'd struggled with his fingers giving out quickly.

Nan set the spoon down and dipped into the pocket of her scrubs. She had just about every color. That day, she was dressed in a flowered top that hung over dark purple bottoms. She pulled out a hair clip, wound her brown hair into a bun, and secured it while Dad typed.

The sound from the TV over the fireplace floated in the room. We'd eliminated the bulky furniture so Dad could get around in his wheel-chair. Aside from the TV and the couch, a table lined the window that peeked out to our porch, with a hand-carved wooden lamp on top Dad had made, and that was it.

The newscaster said something Nan didn't like —she shook her head. I'd learned to tune her and Dad out when the news was on. They were into politics, which was not my jam.

All I needed was my skateboard, the wind, my earbuds, and music, and I was more than happy.

My therapist had said I should find an outlet to take my mind away from my troubles. After Mom died, Dad had bought me the skateboard, and ever since, the sport had been my salvation, at least in those moments when I was catching air or doing acid drops at the local skate park.

"Skye," Nan said. "Did you hear your dad?"

I blinked once then twice. "I'm sorry."

Dad briefly looked at his screen before the computer-generated male voice he'd chosen spoke. "You look beautiful. Nan's right, the new cut makes your big brown eyes pop. Your mom would love it too."

I gave him a picture-perfect grin. Otherwise, he might start sobbing if we talked about Mom.

Nan resumed feeding Dad. The spoon clinked against the glass bowl. "Are you nervous about your first day of senior year?"

I had no reason to be. "I'm good." My goal was to graduate, plain and simple. But I had to do a better job than I had the year before. I'd barely passed my classes because my mind had been on Dad, and I knew I was in for another challenge that year with Dad getting worse. I wasn't planning on attending college, though. All I had to do was listen, do my homework, and study for tests.

Dad typed again, and after a minute, the computer voice spoke. "I want you to have the best year of school, sweetheart." Dad's warm expression was thin at best, and deep within, I could see the sadness oozing out. No doubt he was wishing and praying that he would be around to see me graduate.

Don't cry, girl. Just don't cry. You don't want swollen eyes on your first day. I didn't want to give Grady Dyson a reason to spread another rumor about me. Still, I wasn't the perfect student and didn't toe the line. The only rules I followed were given out by Dad.

I mostly kept to myself, except for Georgia and Mia. We were the three amigos when Mia wasn't spreading her legs for some guy. She had an appetite for sex, which worked for her. I had yet to go down that road. Georgia hadn't, either. We weren't as forward as Mia.

I wanted my first time to be with someone I liked, not someone who would drop me for his next conquest with big breasts and long legs. In my opinion, most guys in high school were on the prowl, searching for an easy time.

My phone pinged as I skirted the couch to give Dad a peck on the cheek. "I'll see you this afternoon." Without a backward glance, I answered.

"Where are you?" Georgia screamed. "I've been waiting for, like, ever for you to get here."

Crap. I'd forgotten we were meeting at the local coffee hangout near school. "I'm on my way."

"Drive. Do not take your skateboard," she ordered in the high-pitched tone she used when she was frustrated.

"I'll be there in ten." Grabbing my backpack and skateboard, I waved to Nan and Dad and walked out into the late-August sunshine.

"Skyler Lawson," she said. "Drive for Pete's sake."

"Yes, ma'am." Then I hung up, put my earbuds in, turned on my music, and hopped on my skateboard.

Again, I didn't listen well, and for as much as I loved Georgia, I wasn't in a hurry to get to the coffee shop. We had plenty of time before school started. But I knew my BFF. She wanted to discuss the day and gossip about the year, goals, and boys.

"We are seniors. We are the queens of the school. We need to come up with a plan for how we're going to make this year fun and exciting. And I'm going to start by having a party." She'd told me all this while I'd been getting my locks chopped off. "Besides, we need you to have some fun. Last year sucked the big one for you, and it hurt me to see you so sad."

Georgia had the best intentions for me, and she loved my dad almost as much as she loved hers. In some way, I thought she was masking her own sadness about my dad.

Still, I couldn't have fun knowing that he was withering away.

2

I cruised into a packed parking lot and gritted my teeth. It seemed the entire school was at the Latte House. I spotted Grady's souped-up black truck, which reminded me of those vehicles in *Transformers*. My evil mind wanted to scratch the pristine paint or deflate a tire or two, but I believed in karma, and I wasn't exactly the malicious type.

However, in all fairness to Grady, he hadn't been as vocal in our junior year. We'd both ignored each other, even at the parties he'd thrown. Maybe he had a heart and felt bad when he'd heard about Dad. Either way, I wasn't letting my shields down.

I coasted around a row of cars, and just as I was about to jump off my board, someone shouted, "Watch out!"

The next few seconds were a blur. The only thing I registered was pain in my hip before I fell hard, my right arm taking the brunt of the impact against the scorching pavement. *What the hell?*

A mob of people ran over to me as my mind scrambled to figure out what had happened.

"Holy shit!" a girl screamed. "Do you not watch where you're going?"

It took me a minute to register the girl's voice as Mia's.

Georgia came into view, her big green eyes wide as she squatted down. "That schmuck hit you. Are you alright?"

I winced, blowing out a breath as my elbow burned and throbbed. "Schmuck as in Grady?" I vowed to kill the star QB of Blue Oaks High if it were him, even if I was at fault for not looking where I was going.

"I can't see who it is. The perv drives a gray truck. So no, not asswipe Grady." Georgia helped me up, her small hands gentle as she brushed off the pebbles from my bleeding elbow.

I glanced around, trying to look at who'd hit me, but the crowd was in the way.

Georgia waved off the people. "Give her some breathing room."

The kids scattered like rats.

"You're an ass," Mia shouted in her deep and scary voice. Anytime she got mad, her temper came out in Oscar-worthy form. According to Mia, it was the Italian in her.

I righted my backpack and collected my skateboard. Then I homed in on Mia, who was wagging her finger at a boy.

Suddenly, my knees went weak, my heart sped up, and sweat beaded on my neck.

Georgia nudged me. "Is that who I think it is?"

Mia shook her dark head of hair as she stomped toward us in her wedge sandals. "The dude is gorgeous, but he's a jerk."

He was definitely drool-worthy and hotter than I remembered.

Mia snapped her fingers, zapping Georgia and me out of our trances. "Ladies, focus. Do you know him?" She stuck her hands on her hips, her white jersey top lifting above her black shorts to expose her belly ring.

I bobbed my head. "Yep."

"Well," she said. "Who is he?"

He's the boy next door who makes my palms clammy, my belly tingle, and my brain a pile of mush.

Colton Caldwell stood with his brown eyes wide, frozen in place as though someone had stopped time. He looked like a Greek god, taller, brawnier, and dreamier than I remembered. His wavy brown hair was longer than before and skirted his shoulders. His thighs were thicker, his arms more muscular. Instantly, the butterflies in my stomach took flight, flapping their wings, wild and crazy.

Holy cow!

Georgia was telling Mia all about Colton as he strutted up to me, his swagger screaming hot.

"Skye?" My name rolling off his tongue was pure heaven, and he smelled like sandalwood as he towered over me.

I considered myself tall for a female at five foot seven, but Colton was well over six feet.

I was going to faint.

With his long fingers, he took my right hand. "I'm so sorry. I didn't see you. Can I take a look?"

He could do whatever the hell he wanted to me.

My chest rose and fell as I struggled for air. At

any moment, I was afraid I might throw myself at him or run my hands through his thick, damp hair.

Breathe, a quiet voice in my head urged.

Mia and Georgia's voices were muted even though they were tittering and chatting about the statue state I was in.

"You should get this cleaned up," Colton said in his smooth, delectable Southern accent. "I think I have a first-aid kit in the truck."

I sighed. I would need more than a first-aid kit to break the magical spell he had on me.

"Are you back for your senior year?" Georgia asked Colton.

"Something like that," Colton replied, not looking at Georgia but at me.

I was hypnotized by the one guy who could tell me the Earth wasn't round, and I would believe him.

Locks of his hair fell forward, creating a curtain around his strong, angular jaw, shielding us from everyone near us. Suddenly, I felt as though he and I had been transported to a secluded place, where it was just the two of us.

My heart pitter-pattered at a rapid rate.

"Come with me," he said.

Georgia grabbed my skateboard, her pink painted lips splitting into a brilliant smile, her eyes alight with mischief. If anyone knew how I felt about Colton, it was my bestie. She and I used to sit on my porch and watch him cut the grass. We were lowly freshmen then, as was Colton, but man, he'd been the hottest guy in school.

Mia said something, but I tuned her out as I followed Colton like a puppy. He led me to the passenger side of his truck.

Most guys in school drove trucks—in the South, souped-up trucks were like Mercedes cars. The girls in school—the rich girls, anyway—drove expensive convertibles. I didn't keep track. Dad had an old Toyota that was officially mine since he couldn't drive anymore, but frankly, I preferred to get around on my skateboard.

I finally swallowed the dryness in my throat and attempted to speak. "So..."

Colton opened the glove compartment and took out a first-aid kit. "I stopped at your house earlier. Sorry to hear about your dad."

And just like that, the lust tethering me to him snapped. A rush of sadness blanketed me.

Georgia bounced up, her blond curls swaying with her jean-clad hips. Like Mia and me, she was wearing shorts, soft blue to be exact. We didn't switch our summer wardrobe until late December or January, when the weather cooled down. "We should get going."

I didn't want to leave. I wanted to stay and talk to Colton. He'd never given me the time of day before.

He hit you with his car. He's feeling guilty.

It was best if I left, though. I didn't want to talk about Dad, and I didn't want Colton's pity.

"Are you sure you're okay, Skyler?" Colton's eyes swam with concern—maybe he worried that I would press charges.

The ache was stronger in my shoulder than my hip. "I'm cool." I was anything but. My emotions were all over the place. "I'm sorry too. I probably whizzed by too fast, and you couldn't track me."

"You need to get that elbow looked at," he said, his gaze melting me into gooey and warm saltwater taffy.

"I'll get a Band-Aid from the school nurse."

"Colton, is that you?" Grady Dyson's gruff voice scraped every nerve along my arms. Then, like a hurricane, he barreled through, pushing poor Georgia out of the way.

Definitely my cue to leave. I couldn't be responsible for what happened if he so much as glanced at me in front of Colton.

My BFF's feistiness blossomed as she pushed the beefy guy back. "Watch where the fuck you're going!" She snarled up at him.

He laughed, ignoring her as he all but swatted me out of the way.

I didn't take shit from anyone, either. "Asswipe." I kicked him in the calf when I wanted to punch him in the jaw. That would probably have broken the bones in my hand, and I already had an elbow to heal and a shoulder to nurse.

Grady spun around, his ice-blue eyes glaring daggers. "Did you just kick me, Lawson?"

I snorted, puffing out my chest. "Is your dick small?"

His pudgy cheeks burned red as his gaze dropped to my average-sized breasts. "Want to see for yourself?" He grabbed his crotch.

Colton mumbled something I couldn't make out, and Georgia full-on laughed.

"You're lucky I didn't use your balls as my punching bag this time."

His wince was fleeting, but it was there, nonetheless. "Are you trying to look like a boy, Lawson?" Grady continued to scrutinize me. "Why did you cut your hair?"

I threw him the middle finger as my stomach dropped to my feet. I guess I shouldn't have been surprised that Grady didn't like my new look. Then again, rumors about my hair were far better than him telling boys I was bad in bed.

Mia came running up like she was about to save the day, her ponytail swishing behind her. "Back the fuck off, Grady, or I will blast pics of your small dick around school."

"You, of all people, know my heat-seeking missile isn't small," Grady shot back.

Georgia and I snorted at his metaphor—of course Grady had named his third leg. Colton didn't react at all. Actually, I couldn't get a read on him, in stark contrast to Grady's flamboyance.

Petite and fiery, Mia rolled her hazel eyes, brushing off Grady's bravado. "Well, if you want to get laid again"—she poked him in the chest—"step off."

Grady squinted at Mia, a muscle ticking in his jaw. Then he turned to Colton, who had just closed the door to his truck. "Welcome home, bro. Are you ready to play football?"

They exchanged a quick manly hug.

It was my turn to roll my eyes. I didn't remember Colton being friends with Grady. Then again, I couldn't recall much of my freshman year after Mom's death.

Colton's head dipped, his hair falling forward. "For sure."

Georgia took hold of my arm. "Let's get out of here. I had Mia put your skateboard in my car."

Mia flanked me on the other side as we left the guys talking about football and games and the upcoming season.

Whatever.

When we were finally in Georgia's VW convertible, she asked, "Did you know Colton was home?"

I pushed out a shoulder. "No clue." His mom came over to see Dad on occasion, but hardly talked about her son, and I had no reason to ask.

"You think he got kicked out of that private school?" Georgia asked, starting the engine.

Mia flipped down the visor in the passenger seat and checked her red lipstick. "Who cares? Have you seen him? His hair. I want to run my fingers through it."

Sighing, I rested back against the seat, glancing up at the clear blue sky. "Get in line."

Georgia wheeled out of the lot behind a long line of cars. "It will be an interesting year."

"Why? Because Colton is back?" I asked, even though I knew what she was thinking.

Georgia eyed me through the rearview mirror. "Um. Yeah. He's the only guy who stole your heart. So you need to make sure no girl gets her paws on him." Then she whipped her attention to Mia. "He's off-limits."

I had to love my BFF. She always had my back.

Mia propped her arm on the passenger door. "It's not me you have to worry about. You both know Amanda will be brushing her big tits against him and marking her territory when she sees him."

Every damn girl in school would be doing the same. Colton was, for all intents and purposes, fresh meat, and I had no doubt he would have groupies hovering.

"He's his own person," I said. I didn't have time to swoon or get caught up in a love affair. Dad was my responsibility, and I had to spend every free minute I had with him.

3

___

The cafeteria was brimming with students, and the noise level was so loud, I could barely hear Georgia. Her lips moved as she leaned in across from me, but the thunderous drone was masking her high-pitched voice. It didn't help that I wasn't really paying attention.

I was laser-focused on Colton, who was sitting with dickwad Grady. They seemed to be best buds as they laughed and ogled girls who were giggling and flirting with them.

I rolled my eyes as my stomach churned. Jealousy was new for me, and I wanted to trip each hussy as she waved at Colton. Or maybe they were waving at Grady. He was a good-looking guy, but his bully attitude blackened his soul and handsome features.

Georgia banged on the table. "Wake up, woman."

I sighed heavily. "Why did he come back?" Not that I wasn't happy. But my world was already upside down. Colton had seemed nice enough when he'd come to my rescue at the Latte House. But he was hanging with Grady, and that wasn't a good sign.

She shrugged. "Ask him. Ooo, you could sneak next door. Doesn't your bedroom face his?"

I narrowed my eyes at my BFF. "That's his mother's office now." Mrs. Caldwell worked from home, doing billing for a couple of medical companies.

Georgia tossed a quick look over her shoulder. "Maybe his mom gave him back his room." She sighed, her shoulders sagging. "I don't remember him being that studly. He was lanky, if I recall."

Lanky or not, his body wasn't the part I was attracted to. I was drawn to his eyes—smooth, brown, and belly-flipping. He had a haunting, quiet, endearing, sexy look about him. She was right, though. Colton's body was, in my words, hunky, and for me that was icing on the cake. "It doesn't matter. He's out of my league," I mumbled. "And he's chumming with that asshole, Grady."

I didn't see Colton and me together. I didn't have long hair like ninety-nine percent of the female students. I didn't flaunt my body like them, either, or at least not like the ones sashaying by him like models on a runway.

Guys liked long hair, big tits, and shapely curves. The list went on. I didn't fit the mold.

My breasts were a B cup, I hardly had curves, and I was slowly regretting cutting my hair. I wasn't dissing myself, and I didn't have low self-esteem. I'd just noticed how guys lusted over the girls with those attributes, and I'd never had reason to want a guy to notice me.

Georgia waved her hand, snapping me out of my pity party. "Skyler Lawson, stop already. You're beautiful. What you have going for you is not only your looks but your heart, which makes you a force to be reckoned with. And fuck Grady. He's going down this year if he so much as farts in our direction."

I snorted. "I love you, too, chica." Without her, I would be holed up in my room, under the blankets and sucking my thumb.

"Besides, you don't know what Colton likes."

She played with the gold necklace that hung down over her cream-and-peach polka-dot blouse. "He could very well not care about girls who look like Amanda Gelling."

I clenched my teeth at the mention of her name. I hadn't seen Amanda yet. I was sure she would be rubbing her large breasts all over Colton the moment she had the chance.

Suddenly the voices died, as none other than Amanda Gelling, aka Bitch Extraordinaire, glided into the cafeteria. It felt like she had glued everyone's lips together with a snap of her fingers.

I couldn't figure out what in the hell she had that made people stop and look—I didn't see much. Mom had always said, "Beauty is in your heart," but Amanda Gelling didn't have one. If she did, I suspected it was black as night.

She flipped her thick auburn hair behind her, searching the room, seemingly eager to find the person she was looking for. One of the three girls on her heels stuck her burgundy-painted nail in the direction of Colton and Grady.

I flicked my chin at Amanda. "Here we go."

Georgia swiveled in her seat, as did most of the other kids who had their backs to Amanda.

Colton and Grady whispered to each other before Grady belted out a laugh.

Amanda's heels clicked on the vinyl floor, the only sound in the room other than the clang of silverware as kids stepped into the food line with trays in hand.

She slapped her hands on her hips and stopped at Grady and Colton's table. Her posse waited a few feet away as Amanda bent over and whispered something in Colton's ear.

Grady watched intently, as did every other person in the room, including me. Frankly, I wanted to pluck her by the hair and toss her out with the trash. But that wouldn't serve anything other than to reveal my jealousy to the entire student body. Besides, I promised Dad I would behave this year, and I couldn't have him worrying about me.

Other guys at Colton's table sized up Amanda's groupies, hunger swimming in their gazes.

Colton listened to Amanda as his shoulders lifted, seemingly tense until Amanda laughed. Then Colton's arm snaked around her, and he seated his hand on her lower back, grinning at her.

I growled under my breath.

Georgia snorted. "Want to start a fight?"

I swallowed thickly. "As much as I would, it would only get me in a ton of trouble."

"It would be fun."

The excitement in her tone was infectious, and I couldn't help but smirk. "Let's go. The bell is about to ring, anyway." I needed to get out of that suffocating space.

Georgia grabbed her tray. "Mia wants us to meet her in the library."

The three of us had a study period after lunch, which made me happy. If I'd had a class, I wouldn't have been able to concentrate. Then again, the day had been one big blur. All I kept thinking about was Colton, his delicious cologne, the way he'd touched me that morning, and the way he'd looked at me with awe in his eyes. I was toast if I couldn't get my head on straight.

I stomped over and deposited my tray and trash before walking out, trying hard not to look over my shoulder. I was afraid that if I did, I would do something I would regret. I also didn't want to torture myself more than I already had.

I didn't have time for Colton or dating. It was best I forgot about him. My heart and mind belonged with Dad. With time ticking away, he deserved all of my attention.

Yet somehow, it was going to take an army to prevent me from not thinking about Colton. After all, he lived next door. And if the day was proving how I would react to him, my senior year was going to be hell on wheels.

Once Georgia and I were out in the hall, I let out a humongous breath and almost screamed at the top of my lungs.

A handful of kids followed us out and scattered down one of two halls.

She curled her hair around her ear. "You have to show him you're interested."

We headed down an empty hall toward the library.

I was about to volley back a barb of some sort when Colton called my name.

Every fiber in me tingled at the sound of his Southern drawl. His voice was like a balm to my frayed nerves.

"Now's your chance," Georgia whispered in my ear. "I'll see you in the library." Then she hurried off.

I went to stop her when Colton sidled up to me. "How's the elbow and the hip? Again, I'm so sorry."

My heart pounded even harder when he

placed his hand on my lower back. The most delightful shivers blanketed me, and I was a goner. I knew I wouldn't make it out of school in one piece that day or ever as long as Colton was anywhere in the vicinity.

"Can I take a look?" he asked sweetly.

His sandalwood fragrance was messing with my head, and any second, I was about to pass out. "I'm fine." Well, my elbow was, but my mind wasn't. Still, as soon as I'd gotten into school that morning, I'd gone to see the nurse. She'd bandaged me up and said she didn't think anything was broken. Her orders were to take some over-the-counter pain meds if I needed to.

Colton arched a brow, his gaze circumspect. "You don't look fine."

My face scrunched. I knew what he meant, but a small part of my brain was heading in a different direction.

He shook his head as though he wanted to take those words back. "What I mean is you look hot—I mean flushed." His cheeks were turning a light shade of red.

"Which is it?" My voice cracked. "Don't answer that." I didn't want to hear his explanation. It was clear to me he was feeling guilty for hitting me with his truck and nothing more. "I gotta run." But my legs wouldn't move.

The guy who'd wrangled my heart in that parking lot earlier sized me up, slowly and surely. *What was I saying?* Colton had taken my breath away when I'd first moved in next door. Granted, he hadn't been as godlike then, and the feelings coursing through my body hadn't been as strong.

The more he casually took his time checking me out, the more my face burned like an inferno. Question after question hit me. *Does he think I'm pretty? Does he like me? Is he only paying attention to me out of pity?* One thing was certain—the way he was looking at me was starkly different than when Grady sized me up.

Grady always wore a disgusted look, as if I was the scum of the earth. Colton was giving me the vibe that he was trying to get inside my head.

Footsteps clamored nearby, breaking our connection.

I stabbed a thumb down the hall. "My friends are waiting. See you around."

He caught my arm just as I took a step. "Skyler, would you do me a favor?"

Please say "come over after school and hang out." Shut up, brain. "Depends." I had to be careful. As much as I would probably bow at his feet, I couldn't just open myself up. Colton was friends with Grady, and my weird thoughts went to a dark place—Grady could've put him up to something. The football team had a thing with initiating new players. And with my luck, Grady would spew more untrue rumors about me.

Colton looked both ways down the somewhat empty hall. "Can you not say anything to my mom or even your dad that I hit you with my truck?"

The way I was feeling about Colton, I would do just about anything for him, but lying to Dad was not an option. "I don't lie to my dad."

He combed his long fingers through his hair, and I almost whimpered. "I get that. But please." His brown eyes softened to silk.

I craned my neck up at him. I wasn't breaking my moral code no matter how handsome he was. "I'm sorry. I can't lie. Have a good rest of your day." I started for the library.

He growled, muttering swear words.

He probably hated me, but I couldn't worry about that.

"Wait," he called. "I said please."

I pivoted on my heel and shrugged. "Please

isn't enough, Colton. Like I said, I don't lie to my dad."

His jaw went slack. I got the feeling girls didn't say no to Colton Caldwell.

I didn't fall into that category, even though I might be tempted, given the way my belly was doing somersaults.

Nevertheless, I lifted my chin, mentally giving myself a high five for not caving. But the day was still young.

4

____

I flopped on the bed, relieved that my first day of school was over. After I'd left Colton standing dumbfounded in the hall, I'd had a stomachache for like an hour, analyzing our exchange as if I was figuring out a complicated calculus problem.

The questions I'd formed as he drank me in had plagued me all day. Not only that, but I kicked myself for saying "have a good rest of your day." I sounded like... I didn't know.

Georgia and Mia had given me their two cents.

"He likes you," Georgia had said.

"I agree, but you should test our theory," Mia had added. "I think you should wear a sexy outfit like a miniskirt or a dress and do up your face."

"You mean like Amanda?" I'd asked. The girl was a clothes whore, and I didn't have the money nor the interest for wearing skirts or dresses. My shorts, tank tops, T-shirts, and Vans were it for me. The last time I'd worn a dress was to Mom's funeral.

Nan poked her head in, severing my thoughts. "Your dad's awake now if you want to see him."

I lifted up to rest on my elbows. "I need to use the bathroom first." I'd checked on Dad when I'd gotten home, and he'd been fast asleep. He didn't spend much time in his wheelchair anymore. I imagined that before long, he would be in his bed twenty-four-seven.

She stepped deeper into my room, glancing around as she fiddled with some of the wispy brown strands that had fallen out of her hair clip.

My room wasn't as cluttered with dirty clothes as it used to be. Since Nan moved in, I'd done a better job at picking up after myself. As part of her caregiving role, she did laundry for us twice a week.

She swung her gaze from my desk, which held a stack of my math and English books, to me before she sat on the edge of my bed.

I adjusted myself, hugging my knees to my chest.

Her gaze flicked to my elbow. "What happened?" She sounded deeply concerned, which only served to poke an old wound.

Mom had been just like her, always doting on me or afraid of me getting hurt when she would take me to the park. Mom hated when I went too high on the swings. "Skyler Lawson, you're going to get hurt," she would say.

I'd always giggled. "But Mom, it's so much fun."

I covered my elbow with my hand. "Fell off my board. It's fine."

"You're going to break a limb one day," she said.

"Possible. But it comes with the sport."

She mashed her lips into a thin line. "Do you wear a helmet?"

I shrugged. "Sometimes." I wasn't a fan. Dad had ordered me to wear one several times, but it was too confining.

"You should all the time. Can I see? I want to make sure it's clean."

I scooted closer to her. "The school nurse took

care of me." But now that I wasn't obsessing over Colton, a smidge of pain registered.

Gently removing the Band-Aid, she felt along the bone. "It's swollen but doesn't seem broken. Does it hurt?"

Nan was super caring and treated me like I was her daughter. She didn't have any kids. When Dad had interviewed her, she'd told us her patients were her children. Then she'd laughed.

I didn't doubt it. She had her hands full with Dad. I helped any chance I could. There were some hygiene tasks that Dad refused to let me do. Still, the lift system over Dad's bed had been the best thing ever. Nan raved about it every time she got Dad ready in the mornings.

"Just a tad. Nan, please don't tell Dad."

She gently placed the bandage on. "He's going to notice."

She was right. Dad had a keen eye for everything. I made a mental note to swap out the large bandage for a small one before I went in to see him. "I don't want him to stress."

"Skye, he worries about you regardless."

"I know. I hate to add one more thing to his plate. Any new developments with Dad?" It seemed like ALS sapped his physical abilities further and further every day.

"He's just sleeping a lot more," she whispered as if trying to keep her emotions tucked away.

"You care for him?" It wasn't really a question. It wasn't hard to see that Nan had developed feelings for Dad, and in part for me too.

She gave me a sad smile. "He's a wonderful man. I wish I would've known him before his ALS."

I grumbled. "ALS sucks the big one. Why can't they find a cure?" It was a rhetorical question. According to Dad's neurologist, the medical industry was studying and trialing different drugs. However, expecting a miracle was a tall order. For the time being, Dad was on special meds to slow the progression, which in my book wasn't doing crap. His journey with ALS was on a bullet train, even with medication.

"Maybe one day they will," she said.

I didn't want to be Debbie Downer, but I knew they wouldn't in Dad's lifetime. The average life span for a person with ALS was three to five years. But every person's journey was different. Case in point: Lou Gehrig barely made it to his second year, and others I'd read about died sooner than that.

Nan rubbed my arm. "I'm here for you, Skye."

My eyes began to fill with angry tears. I didn't think I could cry anymore. I'd bawled endlessly when Dad first told me he had ALS, and I hadn't really stopped. Each day was a challenge to stay positive and not get so raging mad or depressed.

"What do you always say to your dad? No-Crying Monday or whatever day it is." Her voice was light.

Excessive laughing and crying were symptoms of Bulbar ALS, which Dad had in spades. Hence, my mantra of No-Crying Monday. I laughed weakly as the tears flowed. "I hope at least he gets to see me graduate."

Silence dangled.

I blew out a breath. "I ran into a guy today." It was time to change the subject.

"Oh? Tell me about him."

I wiped my nose with my hand as I straightened. "He's"—I didn't quite know how to describe Colton without sounding like I was in love already —"off-the-charts hot."

Her pink lips split into a smile. "Does this boy have a name?"

Tingles broke out along my arms as I thought of him. "Colton."

One thick eyebrow lifted. "You mean Bonnie's son?"

My mouth fell open a tad. "You know him?"

"He stopped by this morning."

Oh, yeah. Colton had mentioned that. "Why?"

"Bonnie made your dad her famous peach cobbler. He dropped it off. But you're right. He's handsome. Not many boys have shoulder-length hair."

"Well, he's got girls at his feet. So…"

Her head tipped to the side. "You weren't about to say you're not pretty enough, I hope."

I considered myself nice looking, but I wasn't beautiful like Amanda Gelling. Maybe Grady was right. Maybe I did look like a boy.

Nan rose and took my hand. "Come with me."

I had no idea where we were going until something hit me. Maybe she was taking me next door to Colton.

I tugged my hand away. "I should go see Dad."

"This will only take a minute." She crossed the hall and went into the bathroom. "Come here, please."

My shoulders slumped as I joined her in front of the sink.

She flicked on the lighted mirror. "I want you to tell me what you see."

"Why? I know what I look like." Short brown, streaked with blond and cut above my ears. Brown eyes that were red around the edges, and a nose as red as Rudolph's.

She gripped my shoulders from behind. "Do you?"

We locked eyes through the mirror.

"I sense a bit of low self-esteem. And for as long as I've known you, I have yet to see someone who thinks they're not good enough."

I was strong and feisty when I had to be. But I was also quiet and reserved. It all depended on the situation. But maybe she was right. Since I'd laid eyes on Colton, I'd been a little out of sorts. "I just feel... I haven't been interested in a guy before now."

"I understand. They can bring out emotions in you that you never knew you had."

Colton definitely did that. Since that morning, I'd experienced tingles, butterflies, heart-pounding nerves, and even sweating.

"Well," she said, "if you need to talk, I'm a good

listener. But please do me a favor. Never, ever think you're not beautiful. Because you are."

"What if he doesn't see me as such?"

"Then he's an idiot and not right for you."

I frowned because I should have been talking about boys with Mom.

Nan rested her delicate fingers under my chin and lifted. "Smile."

I didn't want this to morph into a depressing convo about Mom, so I turned and hugged her. "Thank you." In some ways, I needed her as much as Dad did. She was becoming a light in our darkness. "Nan, when that time comes, can I live with you?"

She moved strands of my hair out of my eyes. "I don't think that's possible. Don't get me wrong— I would love for you to—but I think your dad has other plans."

I shoved down the need to cry again. I didn't want to live with his sister in California. Above all else, I couldn't leave my friends behind. "I can talk to him." Not that I wanted to talk about life after Dad.

"You'll be eighteen in what, eleven months, right?"

"Yeah. End of July next year." I'd just turned

seventeen a month before. Nan had baked me a lemon cake.

"Let's take one moment at a time. I know that doesn't help, but we can't look that far out. If we do, we'll make ourselves sick. Enjoy the time with your dad as much as possible. But I also want you to have fun with your friends. It's your senior year, after all."

Dad grunted loudly, the sound coming through the baby monitor she had in her scrubs. That was his way of saying he needed help or wanted something.

She started for the door, pushing her glasses higher up on her nose.

"Nan, thank you for all that you do for Dad and me."

She blinked several times, no doubt trying not to cry. "I'm so glad I took this job. I'm here anytime for you. Okay?"

"Yeah. I'll be in to see him in a minute." It was time to put on a happy face and get myself together, but that was becoming more and more of a challenge.

5

Twenty minutes later, I walked into our modest kitchen, the aroma of roasted chicken heavy in the air. I plucked a piece of meat off the carving board that was sitting on the small island fit for two. When we moved in, Dad had given the room a makeover—fresh coat of paint, new white cabinets, black appliances, and a sprinkle of red in the curtains I'd hung in the corner window above the sink.

I savored the juicy chicken as I glanced out our sliding glass door. Pinecones littered the grass from the trees climbing to the sky at the far end of our backyard. Azalea bushes decorated the perimeter of our fence on both sides, with several rosebushes nestled between them.

I was ready to grab another piece of the juicy meat when I heard yelling.

"I hate you." It was Colton's voice.

My heartbeat tripped. I inched over to the window that I realized was cracked. Nan often opened it to let out the heat from the oven.

From where I stood, part of my view landed right on Colton's deck. The other part looked out into our yard.

"Why did you pull me out of Deer Run Academy?" Colton practically shouted. "So I could endure your shit? News flash, old man. I'm not living here if you're going to lash out every time you get an ounce of liquor in you."

Colton's dad, who resembled Colton with his brown eyes and thick hair, jumped out of his chair so quickly that I couldn't track him. The next thing I knew, the elder Caldwell had his hand around his son's neck, almost bending Colton's back over the railing. "Respect your elders, son. And let's not forget: my house, my rules."

Mrs. Caldwell ran out, trying hard to wedge her petite frame in-between father and son, but she failed. "Mike, what are you doing?"

Colton shoved his dad, baring his teeth. "Touch me again and I'll make sure you regret it."

My eyes almost popped out of their sockets.

Mr. Caldwell slammed his beer bottle on the deck and closed his hands into fists. "You're threatening me?"

My pulse became unsteady as I watched father and son practically tear each other apart.

I couldn't quite see Mr. Caldwell's face, but I didn't have to, given the rage dripping in his tone.

Mrs. Caldwell swept her hand up the back of her brown bun. "Mike, stop this right now."

Her husband wasn't listening. Colton stood tall, his features pinched hard.

I knew I shouldn't be eavesdropping or watching, but I couldn't look away. Our neighbors were privy to Mr. Caldwell's drunken outbursts even when Colton wasn't home. At times, the whole neighborhood could hear him yelling at his wife.

"Son," Mrs. Caldwell said to Colton. "Please."

Colton regarded his mom, his eyes softening. "No. I didn't come home to be attacked by my father or to put up with his shit."

Mr. Caldwell raised his fist.

"Go ahead, old man. You won't win this round."

Mr. Caldwell retreated a few steps.

"If you weren't drinking, you still might have a job, and I would be at the academy instead of in this dump of a town."

In a mere second, Mr. Caldwell was throwing a punch at Colton.

I gasped and slapped a hand over my mouth, hoping they didn't hear me.

Mrs. Caldwell cried, "Mike, stop right now! The neighbors are probably watching."

I didn't know if she'd seen me, but she knew we could see her deck from our kitchen.

Colton touched his bleeding lip. "I'm out of here."

"Colton," Mrs. Caldwell pleaded. "Please."

Her plea fell on deaf ears as Colton stormed into the house. In a matter of seconds, I heard his truck fire to life. Tires screeched before the sound of the engine faded.

Nan came in. "Are you listening to the commotion?" She pointed to the window.

"I now know why Colton is finishing his senior year at Blue Oaks. His dad lost his job."

"It's none of our business," she said. "And your dad is asking for you."

I understood that I shouldn't get involved, and

I wouldn't. But it was difficult when neighbors aired their dirty laundry outdoors.

After wiping my hands, I waltzed into Dad's bedroom, complete with a hospital bed, lift system, two rolling carts filled with medical supplies, a stand with his eye-gaze computer, and a big-screen TV on wheels situated at the foot of his bed.

Dad's smile brightened my day. "There you are! How was school?" the robotic male voice from the computer asked.

I bent over and kissed him on the cheek. "Fine. Teachers explaining the upcoming year mostly."

He typed again.

As I waited, I glanced at one of many framed pictures of Mom and me that Dad had on the walls. The images were his way of feeling like he had us at his side.

"Did you see Colton today? He came by this morning. Maybe you can ask him to help you change the oil in the Toyota. Bonnie says Colton has been tinkering with cars up at the academy."

I'd heard him, but I read the words on the screen anyway, more to collect my thoughts than anything else. I felt as though I'd been sideswiped by an oncoming car. I mean, Colton had been on my mind since he'd hit me that morning, but I wasn't prepared to hear Dad bring him up. "I'm sure I can take the car to one of those oil places or change it myself. You did teach me how." I hadn't done it yet, but I was sure I could.

After Dad was diagnosed with ALS, he'd begun a list of things to teach me, such as car maintenance, how to use the collection of tools he had, and other things that didn't seem important. He'd been preparing me for when he wasn't here anymore.

"Do you remember how?" Dad asked.

"I have my notes."

"Let Colton help you. At least this one time."

I gave him a thumbs-up. If Dad wanted me to solicit Colton's help, then I would. I couldn't or wouldn't disappoint my dad. Besides, maybe it was a way to break the ice between Colton and me. "I'll ask him."

Hell, him ramming his truck into you broke the ice.

Dad's blue eyes brightened before he returned to typing. "Skye, Aunt Clara will be flying out to get reacquainted with you. I think it's important to discuss some of the details of guardianship before it's too late."

My stomach hollowed. "I want to live with

Nan." The words rushed out like a fast-moving current after a hard rain.

His eyes filled with tears.

Way to go, Skyler. Hurt your dad's feelings. I leaned in so my head touched his. "I'm sorry." I shuddered. "Aunt Clara is nice." I couldn't bring myself to tell him I didn't like her. Or maybe it was more the idea of moving over three thousand miles away. "I don't want to leave my friends. And you're not dying anytime soon." I had to believe that.

"We need to be prepared, and my sister is family," the computer voice said.

Nan was more family than my aunt. But with his emotions all over the place, I debated whether to continue to push the subject.

He typed, "I know Aunt Clara and I have been at odds, but since she found out I had ALS, we're building back the relationship we once had. We're putting our past behind us."

In my opinion, it was a little too late. "Dad, I want to graduate here with my friends, not in California." I figured one last-ditch effort wouldn't hurt.

More tears leaked down his face as he typed once again.

"Please, Dad. Don't send me to California. Mom is buried here. You'll be buried next to her. I can't leave you guys. I won't." It was my turn to cry as I bit my thumbnail.

Dad sobbed like a baby.

I felt like a schmuck as my heart broke a thousand times over.

Nan came in with a tray of food. "I thought it was no-crying Monday."

Dad and I both laughed.

As Nan set his food down on the table, the computer said, "Aunt Clara will be here this weekend, Skye."

My aunt was only visiting. Still, my stomach dropped to my Vans. Reality was quickly setting in. "She's just visiting?" I asked, just to be sure. I didn't think Dad would send me away before he passed. If he did, they would have to drag me out of North Carolina. I was not leaving Dad alone to die.

Nan nodded. "Yes. Only visiting."

The blood began to flow through my veins again. I had time to convince Dad that Nan was the better option.

Still, the conversation was too much. I wanted my dad to live for the next fifty years. I wanted him to see me flourish into a woman, get married, and play with his grandchildren. I wanted him to teach me the things he hadn't had a chance to, and above all else, for him to be there for me when I needed him.

As much as I didn't want to disappoint Dad, I labored for air. I needed to get out of the house.

"Skye," Nan called as I ran out of the room.

I grabbed my skateboard and backpack on my way out the front door. I felt like I was pulling a Colton, but I had to clear my head.

6

———

"Beautiful Pain" by Andy Black blared in my ears as I skated through my neighborhood, letting the tears fall.

It was hard not to feel sorry for myself. It was hard to be strong, to laugh, to act like everything was okay. It wasn't.

A boulder sat in my stomach. I felt alone and broken. I had no one anymore. Mom was gone, and Dad... I couldn't think that far ahead. I squeezed my eyes shut for a brief moment, wringing out my sorrow. My heart hurt more than ever before, which I wouldn't have thought possible.

My pity party came to an abrupt halt when a

vehicle whizzed by, narrowly missing me. One beat passed before I realized it wasn't just any car. Then shock stung me worse than a bee. *What is Grady doing in my neck of the woods?* Rich kids like him stuck to their big mansions on the ocean and hung out at the ritzy golf club my dad couldn't afford to play at.

He slowed before his reverse lights illuminated. His disgusting signature truck nuts dangled from the trailer hitch.

I was tempted to head the other way but knew that Grady would probably chase me down.

I hopped off my board, snapped it up, and beelined for the sidewalk. Maybe he hadn't seen me. Maybe I could duck down behind one of the many cars parked along the street.

"Lawson!" Grady shouted in his grating voice.

Too late. "Fuck off." I threw him the finger as I walked at a fast pace.

His truck rolled along with the speed of my legs. "Is that any way to act? I was being nice," he shouted over the rap music blaring from inside his cab.

I rolled my eyes and tapped my ear, even though I'd heard him. I wasn't about to scream at him. I didn't want to disturb the neighbors.

Then the music died. "Did you hear me?"

"What are you doing in my neighborhood, anyway?"

"Looking for Colton. Have you seen him? He was supposed to meet me an hour ago. You do live next door to him, right?"

"I'm not his babysitter." I wouldn't have told Grady shit even if I had known where Colton was.

A stop sign loomed ahead, which meant he had to stop—but I didn't. I could turn right at the end of the block. The skate park wasn't that way, but I could take a detour.

When we reached the corner, he asked, "Where are you headed? I can give you a ride."

A wild laugh escaped me, my middle finger flying in the air. "I'm not getting in a car with you."

I wasn't worried about what he might do to me, but rather what I would do to him—I wanted to claw out his eyes. After all, he and I had a mutual hatred for each other, especially after he'd called me a boy and dissed my haircut.

I banked right without even batting an eye, willing and praying that Grady wouldn't follow me.

He peeled out, and within a second the sound of his engine began to fade. I tossed a look behind me, catching the last glimpse of those nasty truck nuts as he turned a corner.

I sighed as I got back on my skateboard. Georgia's house wasn't that far, and I suddenly didn't want to be around a crowd of people. I needed my BFF's shoulder to cry on. Besides, if I did end up at the skate park, the minute I did a vert—a skate term for vertical—down one of the bowls, I would probably faceplant.

I stuck my earbuds in my ears just as "Rollercoaster" by the Jonas Brothers, a perfect song to describe my emotions, began to play. I probably shouldn't have been wearing my earbuds. Safety and all. Dad had reprimanded me for that very thing a few times. But I was on the sidewalk, and I wasn't in any danger of getting hit by anything, other than maybe running into a person.

A warm breeze blew in my face and the music blasted as I passed homes and crossed streets. A sense of calm washed over me, as it always did when I rode. I didn't skateboard to compete—I wasn't that good—but to relax.

With Grady not in my face, my pulse began to slow until I thought of Colton and wondered where he had gone when he tore out of his driveway. He probably had a girlfriend. Or maybe he was going to see Amanda. After all, they'd seemed chummy at lunch.

I killed the music and pulled out my earbuds as I darted into a shopping center, a shortcut to Georgia's house. I paid attention to traffic. I didn't need another mishap.

Once on the other side, the coast was clear, devoid of any cars.

When I reached Crane Plantation, I hopped off my board, admiring the manicured shrubs and flowers in front of the brick walls on either side of the entrance. It was a ritual for me whenever I went to Georgia's. In a way, I felt like Mom was there with me. She'd been on the homeowner's association when we lived a block down from Georgia and had always made sure that the gold-plated name tacked to the brick wall had been spit-shined and glistened.

I briefly closed my eyes, inhaled the salt air—the ocean wasn't far from there—collected my skateboard, then headed into the upscale property. In addition to the beautiful homes, the place boasted a golf course, a recreation area with a pool, tennis courts, and a small park.

I walked by Craftsman-style homes and brick mansions with columns and large porticos that fit in with the Southern charm. When I reached Pony Circle, my pulse quickened as it always did when I went to see Georgia.

A nice couple from the North had purchased Mom's dream home on that street. I inhaled deeply as I made the turn onto Pony Circle, pushing down the memories of days long past. But it was useless when the bluish-green siding with high-angled peaks came into view.

I skidded to a halt when I laid eyes on a For Sale sign, my memories vanishing as my heart raced. I wasn't sure why. It was just a stupid sign. I really wished Dad could afford to buy the house back. That thought evaporated when I zeroed in on the two cars in the driveway and gasped. Sure, a family lived there, but Colton Caldwell sure as heck didn't. I knew his truck well and not because he'd hit me with it. I knew his license plate. Yep, I had the darn thing memorized. Then again, it was rather easy to remember when "Hang Ten" was stamped on it.

I riffled through my brain, digging deep into why he would be sitting in my old driveway of all places. If the same family we'd sold the place to still lived there, then the children were definitely not of age to date. But my answer came swiftly when Amanda fucking Gelling glided ethereally out the front door with her auburn hair flowing behind her, tanned legs that I was jealous of, and a flirty smile that screamed she was getting laid or something. That last part made me clench my hands into fists.

She bounced up to the passenger window of Colton's truck. I suddenly hated Amanda more than even when Colton was whispering in her ear or had his hand on her lower back like she was his pride and joy.

"Amanda," an older version of Amanda called as she came out with her Louis Vuitton bag and gold-rimmed sunglasses that probably cost more than the Toyota I drove. "My clients are going to be late."

Amanda stuck her hands on her hips. "I got things to do, Mom."

Her mom owned Gelling and Associates, one of the top real estate companies in town, as the For Sale sign announced.

I growled under my breath as Amanda said something to her mom before she jumped into Colton's truck.

I should leave before they see me, or Colton might think I'm stalking him. I placed my skateboard down and was about to get on it when the universe stepped in. My board sailed right toward Colton's truck as he was backing onto the street.

The word "fuck" dropped from my lips, and not because he or Amanda would notice me, but my board was about to get smashed. I couldn't lose my one outlet, the one salvation that kept my demons at bay. Sure, I could buy a new one when money wasn't so tight. But even so, I didn't want a new one. That skateboard was a gift from Dad. I had to cherish it forever.

I ran like I was about to save a person from getting hit by a car, the word "idiot" coming to mind. I couldn't tell if Colton could see me or not. His back window was lightly tinted.

My horror-movie scream fell on deaf ears as Colton ran over my board.

Well, fuck.

The truck stopped, as did my heart. Colton got out and darted to his tailgate. He glanced at his tire before those molten-brown eyes drank me in. "Skyler? What in the world?"

Amanda graced us with her presence. "What the fuck are you doing here?"

Ignoring the bitch, I grabbed my mangled board. Okay, maybe it wasn't so bad, but one of the front wheels was bent. Inwardly, I yelled at myself. I usually wasn't an airhead. It was all Colton's fault. He was making my mind a glob of goo.

"Skyler," Colton said in that Southern drawl that made my goose bumps fire to life.

Damn him. My pride was as crumpled as my board. I couldn't deal with him, and especially not Amanda or both of them together. Shaking my head, I walked away. Otherwise I would punch the smug look off Amanda's delicate face or say something I would regret. Above all else, I was ready to burst into tears.

"Wait," Colton said in a loud, deep, and dreamy voice.

Keep walking, Skyler.

"Leave her." Amanda's voice was like that cringy sound of nails on a chalkboard. "We're going to be late."

"Skyler," Colton called again. "At least let me give you a ride home."

I was not getting into Colton's truck, not with her in it. That was a recipe for disaster. It was bad enough that my hormones were soaring into outer space just from hearing him say my name, and on the other spectrum, my jealousy was at an all-time high.

I stuck a hand in the air and waved without turning around. "I'm good."

"Her bestie lives at the end of the street," I heard Amanda say.

She would know. She'd hung out with us a few times in middle school, mostly at Georgia's birthday parties, which her mom was famous for throwing for her only child.

I sharpened my hearing the farther I got from them, praying Colton would listen to Amanda and just get the hell out of there. I had only three more houses to hurry by before I was in the safe zone. Then a wild laugh broke free in my head. Safe zone—it wasn't as if he would hurt me.

But as much as I didn't want to look, my curiosity got the better of me. Colton stood in the street, watching me as Amanda hooked her arm into his. Then she flattened her hand on his chest and said something to him.

He threaded his fingers through his shoulder-length hair, and I swore a whimper came out of my mouth. I was so screwed. I wouldn't make it through the first week of senior year. Either Colton would destroy me in a delightful way, or I was going to cave and just pull a Grady and stick my tongue down Colton's throat. Maybe if I did, I would get him out of my system.

Other than Grady and his gross antics in the seventh grade, I'd only locked lips with one other dude, and that was in my sophomore year. Bruce Maddox had asked me to dance at the spring fling. He was nice and cute, but not someone I'd been interested in dating. Anyway, he'd kissed me that night when the music had ended, all hard lips and teeth. "Awkward" was the way I'd described the moment to Georgia after the dance.

Colton and Amanda finally got back in his truck. When he took off in the opposite direction, I let out the sigh of all sighs as I ran up to Georgia's front door.

7

———————

Georgia and I sat on the bleachers, watching the football team and the cheerleaders practice. After Mia was finished, the three of us were headed to the beach.

Georgia fanned herself with her notebook. "Have you recovered from yesterday?"

"What do you think?" I'd been grumpy all day because of my skateboard. When I'd gotten home from Georgia's the night before, I tried to fix the mangled front wheel, but it was useless. "Sorry. I didn't mean to sound like a bitch."

She patted my leg. "It's just a skateboard. You can buy another one."

I narrowed my eyes at my BFF. "You did not just say that."

She lifted a bare shoulder that was reddening from the orange ball of heat in the sky. "Skye, I'll buy you another one."

I should have hugged her for being the best friend a girl could have. Actually, I'd thrown myself at her the day before, crying in her arms for many reasons, not just my skateboard. "As I told you last night, my dad gave me that board. Sentimental, you know."

She resumed fanning herself as she looked out at the field. "It's scorching today."

Mia and her squad of cheerleaders were practicing one of their high-flying routines while the footballers were huddled in the middle of the field, listening to the coach. I spotted Colton. It was hard not to. He was one of the taller ones among the group, and leaner than most.

I laughed. "We live in the South. You know, you're starting to fry." She was fair and tended to burn easily. Normally, she wasn't one to wear a tank top for that very reason.

"I put on sunscreen. I'll be fine." Her tone was huffy.

I chewed on a nail, feeling like a witch for

taking out my problems on her. "I know you want to help, and I love you for it. But I just want to mourn the loss of my board for now."

She lowered her sunglasses, and her pretty green eyes sparkled beneath two coats of mascara. "I love you too, chica. But seriously, you need to let loose. You're wound tight and I'm worried."

I bumped her shoulder with mine. "I know. It just seems like bad things keep happening. My aunt is coming in this weekend."

She whipped her head in my direction. "You didn't tell me that."

I'd been too amped up about Colton and Amanda and the murder of my skateboard. "That was the original reason I came to see you yesterday. You know my dad is preparing his trust. He wants me to go live with her." The last part, she didn't know. I'd been keeping it from her in the event that Dad changed his mind—and he still could, if I could convince him.

She swiveled in her seat. "No fucking way. Skyler Lawson, you are not leaving me. I'm going to talk to your dad."

I laughed, the act freeing. "You can try. But seriously, I can't blame him for wanting to make sure I'm taken care of when he's gone." I'd thought a lot about it while I snuggled with my cat, Stella, the night before. I couldn't live on my own. Well, I could. But since I was only seventeen, adults would have a problem with that. "I told him I want to live with Nan."

"Isn't the house yours when he..." She couldn't bring herself to say it either.

"It is, but I'm a minor."

She mashed her glossy lips together. "You can live with me. My parents already said you could."

Mr. and Mrs. Branson had offered to talk to Dad, but Dad was adamant about me living with family. "Can we talk about something else now?" I shouldn't have brought it up. It only served to twist my stomach into knots.

Georgia nodded as tears pooled in her green eyes. "I'm organizing a beach party for this weekend. We'll do a bonfire and just let loose. I think I need to take my mind off things as much as you do."

I bumped her arm with mine. "I know you love my dad too."

She wiped a tear away. "He's like a second dad to me."

"Girl, if you get emotional, I will too." And the

football field was the last place to become a blubbering mess, especially with Colton nearby.

"Um... look who's coming our way." As subtle as she could be, Georgia stabbed her blue-painted thumbnail at the field.

Colton strutted toward us, carrying his sports bag in one hand and his helmet in the other. He looked rather beat and definitely sweaty. All that football gear had to be brutal in the Southern heat.

Grady caught up to him, patted him on the back, then darted over to Mia, who was packing up her gear. I didn't get them, except maybe I did. Guys liked sex, and Mia was crazy for it. And yowza, she wasn't one to hold back the details, either. Frankly, I blocked my ears when she was gushing about her latest conquest, which as of late had been Grady.

Mia would always laugh when she found me trying to tune her out. Then she would say, "I like sex, and I'm not ashamed to admit it like you and Georgia."

"It's not sex," I would fire back, though it might have been—I was still a virgin. "You like Grady."

"He's hung like a horse," she would say proudly. "And he's good in bed."

"Ew" would be my response, followed by the need to puke.

Regardless of my sexual inexperience, I admired Mia. She knew who she was, knew what she wanted and liked, and wasn't afraid to admit it.

I, on the other hand, was still trying to find myself. Having gone through one death and getting ready to lose another parent, I felt lost and a little out of sorts, particularly in the guy department, and more so with Colton in the picture.

Georgia waved a hand in front of me. "Where did you go?"

I blinked away the image of Mia throwing herself at Grady. "Nowhere." *Everywhere.*

"I don't get those two," Georgia said as Grady pulled Mia flush against his body.

"Join the club. But we've had this convo many times."

"Do you think we'll be as excited about sex when the time comes?" Georgia sounded frightened.

I couldn't blame her. I was sure my first time would be nerves galore.

Georgia nudged me with her elbow.

My gaze swung from Mia and Grady to the only guy I wouldn't mind giving my virginity to.

Colton crossed the track, his muscular legs eating up the space, and when he climbed the bleachers, my body started to shake, rattle, and roll.

I tucked my hands between my thighs and squeezed, hoping I could get them to stop trembling.

Colton gave me a wolfish grin. "Ladies," he said.

My pulse went into overdrive, the sweat multiplying—and not from the thick humidity hanging in the air.

"Skyler, how's your elbow?" His drawl was electrifying.

"Fine." The swelling had gone down, and except for the occasional throbbing, I didn't even think about my injury.

He gripped the straps of his sports bag as though the item was his lifeline. "You didn't tell your dad, did you?"

I bored a hole into him as we locked eyes. Anger hotter than the Southern sun burned away the nerves and the butterflies, and my hands stopped shaking.

As if Georgia could see the myriad of emotions plaguing me, she said to Colton, "I'm having a bonfire party on the beach behind my house on Saturday. Why don't you come?"

"Grady is having one too," Colton said.

Georgia pursed her lips. "Mmm. Maybe I'll postpone mine. We should have parties every weekend until graduation."

Colton smoothed a large hand over his sweaty helmet hair, which was pulled back into a low ponytail.

I held back a whimper. "Rock star" came to mind. All he needed was a guitar. I could totally see Colton sitting in a chair, strumming a guitar and crooning as his hair fell forward, veiling him and giving him a mysterious vibe.

Amanda's voice pierced the air, calling Colton's name before she all but rushed up the bleachers to stand beside him. "There you are. I've been waiting for you in the parking lot."

Georgia wagged her finger between Amanda and Colton. "Are you two an item or something?"

Colton stiffened.

Amanda snarled at Georgia. "None of your business, Branson." She never called anyone by their first name unless she liked them.

Georgia flipped her off.

Amanda tittered as she slipped her hand into Colton's. "Come on, big guy. We have plans."

I lifted my brows at Colton, who was fixated on me for some odd reason.

Oh, that's right. He wanted to know if I'd told my dad he'd hit me with his truck. I imagined if Dad knew, he would tell Colton's mom, and then his dad would find out. I hadn't forgotten the fight between them.

Amanda tugged Colton. "Let's go." She sounded irritated as she flipped her auburn hair over her shoulder.

I really wanted to cut off her thick locks.

He sighed heavily as darkness washed over his handsome face. Then he tipped his head toward the field. "I need to talk to Grady for a second."

Amanda slid her hand over his butt, then up his back. "Make it quick. We don't have much time before my parents come home."

I clenched my teeth, even though I couldn't blame her for wanting to get Colton alone. I was hoping my facial expression was blank and not showing the ocean of jealousy burning through my veins.

Amanda climbed down in a huff.

Colton's gaze was like molten lava as he regarded me.

"So, you two seem to have hit it off," Georgia blurted out. "I don't know how much you know about Amanda, but once she gets her claws into you, you'll need a surgeon to cut them out."

I snorted.

Colton just grinned, seemingly not caring whether Amanda clung to him or not. Then again, guys loved sex, and maybe that was all he was after. I suddenly wondered if I would have to put out for him to date me. If so, he wasn't the right guy for me. Mia might only want sex, but I wanted more.

Before I could analyze the topic to death, Amanda shouted from the track, "Come on, Colton!"

My nostrils flared. Amanda Gelling had always been an irritating individual, but her liking the same guy I did made it even worse.

Colton started to leave, then stopped. "I'm sorry about your skateboard." He flashed his big brown eyes at me, then trudged down the bleachers, his cleats clicking on the metal benches. Once he joined Amanda, she slipped her hand into his, no doubt marking her territory.

I growled under my breath. "Colton, wait," I

blurted. Dad had mentioned that maybe Colton could help me change the oil in my car, and maybe he could fix my skateboard too. "Can you stop by later? I have a proposition for you."

Grady whistled as he met Colton on the track.

I held back the urge to flip him off, keeping my focus on Colton and no one else.

One side of Colton's mouth turned upward, and a funny feeling pulsed between my legs.

Amanda snarled. "What could you possibly offer Colton with those flat tits of yours?" Her voice was so loud, I was sure the football coach could hear her from his spot on the field.

My middle finger popped up like a jack-in-the-box.

Georgia snorted.

I wasn't the type to start fights, but I would in a heartbeat if it would shut her up. "Wouldn't you like to know?"

Georgia came to my rescue. "At least her tits aren't fake," she fired down to Amanda.

Grady was clearly enjoying himself, wearing his normal irritating smirk.

"I'll see you tonight," Colton said to me.

Then Grady, Colton, and Amanda left.

"I so want to climb Colton like a monkey," I mumbled.

Georgia busted out laughing. "You've been listening to Mia too much, but I agree. I wouldn't mind either. So give me the deets. What's your proposition?"

"My skateboard. Nothing more." Oh yeah. My car too.

"Good plan."

Now to shuck the nervous nellies.

8

I deposited my bag at the door, and for some odd reason, my heart sputtered. I could feel the heaviness in the air. The house was normally quiet, given that Dad was in bed most days. But usually I could at least hear the TV.

I hurried toward Dad's room as Nan's voice floated out. "Breathe."

Afraid to go in, I stopped short, gulping in air as if I were the one who couldn't breathe.

Dad finally grunted out a choking sound and coughed again.

Instantly, tears burned my eyes. The neurologist had told us that choking was a major problem with ALS patients and one of the ways Dad could die.

Please don't let this be the day. Please, God.

I rolled back my shoulders and dug deep for that courage Dad always said I had. No amount of bravery could quiet or stop the turbulent emotions swirling inside me.

Dad coughed hard.

"That's it," Nan said. "One more time." Then the suction machine, a device that had been a life-saver when food got lodged in his throat, whirred.

I flattened my back against the wall outside his door. A tear dropped, followed by another and another.

Dad gagged one last time.

The suction machine continued, and when Nan finally shut it off, she asked, "Better?"

I wiped my face with my shirt. Episodes like that were becoming the norm, no matter how much we pureed his food.

I plastered on a happy face as best I could, then slipped in quietly. As soon as Dad laid eyes on me, he lit up as though he hadn't just hacked up a lung. Suddenly, my heart opened and my stomach settled.

Nan appeared flustered, and I couldn't blame

her. "You're home early. Did you go to the beach with Mia and Georgia?"

"I changed my mind." I wanted to be there when Colton came over. We hadn't discussed a time, and if I knew my friends, they would be at the beach until the sun went down. Plus I wanted to spend time with Dad before Colton made me into a complete bag of nerves.

Nan cleared his table. "I need to tidy up the kitchen." She collected a towel and placed it on top of the dirty plate. Then she left without another word.

I squeezed Dad's toes, which were poking out of the cushioned boots he wore to elevate his legs and reduce the fluid buildup. "Are you good?"

He blinked once, which was our code for yes. Then he eyed his computer, which was tucked off to the side near the window.

I swung the arm of the stand in front of him and hit the power button. "Our old house is up for sale." I'd planned on telling him the night before, but he was asleep when I got home.

He lifted his eyebrows before he focused on the computer screen. Then he blinked as he typed with his eyes. "How much is the house selling for?"

I shrugged. "I'm not sure. I just saw the sign." I

didn't think he had the money to buy it back. "So Colton is stopping by later. I'll ask him to help me with the Toyota."

"Are you and Colton studying? Do you have the same classes?" the computer voice asked.

"No. I busted a wheel on my board," I said. "I'm going to see if he can fix it."

Dad's gaze flicked to my elbow, and within a minute the computer voice said, "You fell. Is that what happened to your arm?"

"Yeah." I nodded, hoping he didn't ask more questions. I didn't want to explain how Colton had rammed his truck into me.

Concern washed over Dad.

"Dad, falling comes with the sport. You know that." I showed him my elbow. I still had a Band-Aid on it. "It's nothing. I'm a tough cookie. Isn't that what you tell me all the time?"

He gave me a proud smile, which I was going to miss. "Do you need money to buy a new wheel?"

"Not yet. I'll see what Colton can do first." I prayed he could fix it. "So did you aspirate earlier?" I wanted to change the subject. The more we talked about Colton, the more my stomach twisted.

"Don't worry about me," he typed.

I huffed. "I will. I don't want to lose you, Dad." I knew that was an odd statement, given that he would die sooner rather than later, but I wanted him around as long as possible. I at least wanted him to see me graduate.

He turned red as he frowned, his bottom lip quivering.

I grabbed his cold hand. "Don't start. It's No-Crying Tuesday." I smiled even though I was gutted inside and ready to bawl again.

He began typing. "My sister sent me a message today. She'll be here on Saturday."

Well, crap. I'd kind of forgotten about her. My stomach tumbled, and a nauseous feeling settled inside.

The doorbell rang. I was tempted to answer it to avoid the subject, but Nan would beat me to it.

My pesky nerves were dancing up a storm as footsteps clamored down the hall. Nan laughed at something Colton said.

His deep voice was smooth as silk and causing all kinds of goosebumps to pop to attention on my arms. When he sauntered in, he seemed taller and bigger than I remembered. Or maybe the ceiling was too low for his height. His tattered jeans hung low on his hips, and his Blue Oaks High T-shirt stretched across his muscled chest. His hair was damp from a recent shower, I imagined, and he had the beginnings of scruff along his jaw.

The word "yum" blared in my head, and I had to stifle a moan.

He ambled up to Dad with his arm extended. "Mr. Lawson, good to see you again."

"My dad can't shake hands."

Colton lowered his arm with a smidge of confusion swimming in his gaze.

I didn't know how much he knew of ALS, or what his mom had told him. "He has no use of his hands anymore."

Colton's features relaxed, and sadness flashed in his eyes. That was a typical reaction when anyone met Dad.

Dad typed in, "Nice to see you too. Are you happy to be home?"

Colton winced at Dad's question. "I miss my friends." Then he regarded me. "I'm sorry I hit your daughter with my truck. She came out of nowhere."

My breath hitched, and I shook my head at Colton.

He bit his bottom lip. "You didn't tell him?"

Nan, who had been quiet up until then, cleared her throat as she pushed off the door. "I need to reposition your dad in bed. I made some iced tea. Why don't you and Colton get some?"

Out of the corner of my eye, I could see Dad's stern look as he entered words into his speaking program.

Nan placed her hand on my shoulder. "Go. You can explain later."

I was grateful for Nan and how she was trying to downplay the situation, but I wasn't moving. I knew better. It was one thing to avoid tough conversations about the future, which I knew Dad understood. But getting hit by a car wasn't something Dad would brush off or take lightly.

"Skye, what is Colton talking about?" Dad asked.

I might as well get this over with. "I'm fine, Dad. It was nothing."

"Is that how you hurt your elbow?" Nan asked, seemingly forgetting that she was trying to come to my rescue.

"Yes, ma'am."

"How many times have I told you to be careful

and pay attention? Did you have your earbuds in?" Dad asked.

I couldn't remember if I did or didn't, so I shrugged. "I don't think so. It's just a scratch, Dad." I kept my voice soft. I didn't want to argue. Normally I would have. Dad and I had had several arguments about skateboard safety.

Dad narrowed his eyes. Even though he couldn't reprimand me in his hard tone, I knew better. Just that fatherly look made me hear his words as if he were speaking. "Young lady, how many times have I told you?"

I hadn't fallen at the skate park or outside in the driveway. I'd gotten hit by a truck—or rather tapped, which was the way I looked at it.

Colton rescued me. "It was my fault, Mr. Lawson."

Dad was busy typing with his eyes. "Admirable, son. But my daughter knows not to skate around traffic or cars."

I hung my head briefly, ashamed that Dad was scolding me in front of Colton. Georgia would have been no big deal, but a boy—and one I had a crush on—was horrifying.

"Randall," Nan said. "Let's get you ready for the night."

That was my cue to leave. I blew Dad a kiss, then eyed Colton, giving him a silent message to follow me.

But he didn't budge.

"Colton," I said.

His six-foot-plus frame seemed frozen like a statue. "I'm sorry, sir." The undertones in his voice led me to believe he was not only sorry for hitting me, but for Dad's ALS.

"Colton," I said again, but the computer voice filled the room.

"Can you help Skye change the oil on her car?" Dad asked.

Colton lowered his shoulders, which had been almost up to his ears. "Yes, sir. Maybe not tonight, though."

"Perfect. Whenever you can," the computer voice said.

Every fiber in me wanted to take that voice and throw it out the window. I should have been used to it, but I wasn't. Not in the freaking least. I wanted to hear Dad's voice. I would give anything for that.

"Go," Nan said to Colton. "I need to take care of Mr. Lawson."

Colton gave them a quick nod before his long

legs ate up the space between us. Then he placed his hand on my lower back, and I thought I would melt as my mouth became bone-dry.

I was about to be alone with Colton Caldwell, and I was sure I would be a blubbering idiot.

9
____

My two-car garage was extremely confining and suffocating even though the space was large. We only had one car, and it was outside.

Colton glanced around as if cataloging what he wanted to steal. I had no clue why I was thinking about him taking stuff. He didn't look like a criminal. Then again, I knew very little about the six-foot-tall hunk of a guy who made my heart race for the darn end zone.

I licked my lips as I shuffled over to my side of the garage. Yep, I had my own area, complete with a locker and skateboard gear and other stuff like a toolbox, which Dad had put together for me.

Yet the small distance between the gorgeous

specimen and me wasn't enough. I was on the verge of hyperventilating.

Colton sauntered up to Dad's workbench, which traveled the length of the garage. "Your dad has a great arsenal of tools here. Was he a mechanic or something?"

I clutched the edge of my own wooden bench, which was small compared to Dad's. "Something like that. He worked in the power industry before he..." I sighed. I didn't want to talk about Dad. I was tired of explaining ALS or even thinking about the awful disease.

Colton whirled around like a hurricane that came out of nowhere. "I thought you told your dad about me hitting you with my truck." He roughed a hand through his long locks, and I badly wanted to be that hand. I liked his hair down rather than tied back, although he was handsome no matter how he wore it. "He's probably going to tell my mom." A muscle ticked in his jaw. "Then she'll tell my old man." Pain blended with something far darker than anger.

"I'll tell him not to."

With his right hand, he grabbed his left triceps, which peeked through the sleeve of his T-shirt. "It doesn't matter." His words definitely didn't match the scowl he was sporting.

I angled my head. "Yeah, it does. I saw the fight with your dad." *Way to go, Skyler. Stick foot in mouth. Now he'll think you're a nosy neighbor.*

He flinched, shock dripping off him for a split second before he banked his emotions. "So as I told your dad, I don't have time to work on your car tonight. Was that your proposition?" His tone was a tad harsh, reminding me of Grady in a way.

I clenched my teeth as I pushed my back into the bench, hoping it would swallow me. Otherwise, I would be tempted to do something that would only serve to break my hand. His abs were made of stone. His jaw was, too. And I wasn't the one making him furious—that medal went to his dad, or so I hoped.

I crossed my arms over my chest so he wouldn't see my hands shaking. Colton unnerved me in a good way. However, I didn't want to be around someone who would take his crap out on me. I didn't put up with Grady's shit, and I certainly wasn't about to tolerate any wrath from Colton, no matter how he stirred the woman inside me to want to climb him like a monkey.

Oh my word! Shut up, Skyler.

"Spending time with your girlfriend?" I held my breath. *Why the heck am I spouting off? Stupid, stupid girl.*

His eyes became slits as fire brimmed in their depths. "Something like that."

My cheeks burned like a house up in flames. I was ready to scream at the top of my lungs.

He strutted toward me like a lion about to attack his prey.

That breath I was holding was making me dizzy. Or maybe it was his cologne or soap. The closer he came, the dizzier I got. Pheromones be damned.

My pulse ramped up and I thought about running. I wasn't afraid of him, but of me. I was afraid I would do something foolish like attack him.

He came to an abrupt halt about a foot from me, as though he was the one who was scared.

I was ready to expel the air in my lungs until he took one step, then another, before he was standing in my personal space. He lowered his head, studying me as if I was a science experiment.

I looked at the shiny floor Dad had painted last year.

Then he leaned in, his muscular arms going around me as though he were caging me in.

Holy hell. I swallowed the desert of sand in my mouth.

His hair tickled my cheek as his broad chest barely kissed mine.

I whimpered, a sound I prayed he didn't hear. I closed my eyes, wanting to disappear. No, scratch that. I wanted to rub my hands all over him.

His warm breath tickled my ear. "Breathe, Skyler." His voice was husky, and I shivered. "I'm just getting your skateboard." As he did, his body brushed mine.

I willed myself to stay still and my lady parts to calm the heck down.

His fingers landed under my chin. "You can open your eyes now."

When I did, he was examining the wheel on my board.

I slid off to the side, letting out the air in my lungs. "Can you fix it?" That was the proposition I had for him, but somehow, all thought escaped me.

"Mmm," he said. "It looks like you'll need a new wheelbase." He continued to examine the shark with jagged teeth, big eyes, and red jaw I'd painted on the bottom. "Cool drawing."

I shook off the myriad of feelings coursing

through me, or tried to, as I zeroed in on my board. "Thanks."

"Are you any good on this thing?" he asked.

"Not Olympic good, but I can hold my own. Why? Do you skate?"

"My younger brother did." His hand began to shake.

Somehow, I found the courage and erased the small space between us. I wasn't sure of what to say or do. I only knew his brother died in a drowning accident. But something told me not to say a word.

"Actions speak louder than any words," Mom had always said.

So I gently placed my hand over his and held it there.

He froze as we locked eyes. We didn't need words. I hoped he saw my empathy and sympathy. I knew what it was like to lose a loved one, and until a person went through a death, they didn't understand.

"I lost my mom," I said on a whisper.

Despair washed over him, sending a zap of pain to my heart. Then his chest heaved, and he withdrew his hand. "I've got to run. Do you mind if

I take this with me? I'll see if I can pick up a new wheelbase for you."

He could take me instead. "Go ahead." I couldn't use it, anyway.

With my most precious possession in his grasp, he headed for the door, when his phone rang, the sound blaring in the carless garage. He stopped to answer. "Yeah."

Amanda's squeaky voice came through loud and clear, as though he had her on speaker.

I ground my back teeth.

He watched me intently as he listened to Amanda prattle on about being on time for something.

I snarled, not caring that I was laying my cards on the table.

A slow, wolfish grin emerged on those thick lips of his, making my freaking heart beat out of control. I had no idea what was happening between us, but whatever it was had to stop. He was dating Amanda, and I wasn't a relationship breaker.

"I'm on my way," he said to Amanda. "Let Grady know I'll bring the beer." Then he pocketed his phone.

One of my eyebrows climbed up to my hairline. "Drinking like your dad?" *Oh, for fuck's sake. Shut up, Skyler.*

He ambled toward me with a sense of purpose. Yeah, that purpose was probably to cut out my tongue. I wouldn't blame him.

Once we were toe-to-toe, he brushed strands of my bangs off my forehead. "Grady thinks you were prettier with long hair."

A gasp lodged in my throat. The word "kill" skipped through my brain like a bubbly child on her way to school. Only I wasn't happy. I was ready to end Grady once and for all.

I lifted my chin, wondering if Colton agreed with Grady or if he even remembered me in our freshman year. "Is that so? Did you know that Grady is a first-class dick? And that if you keep hanging around him, you might fall into that category too?" Those words didn't slip out unexpectedly. I was never more serious, and if he did take after Grady, then good looks or not, he wasn't the guy for me.

One side of his lips turned upward as he leaned into my ear. "Have a good night, Skyler." Then he slowly dragged his scruffy jaw along my smooth one.

I held back a whimper. Damn guy. Damn heart. Damn hormones.

Carrying my skateboard, he strutted out without even a backward glance. His swagger affected me in all the right places... or the wrong ones, if he turned out to be a prick.

10

Stella purred as she settled next to me on my extra pillow. I flipped onto my stomach, trying to get comfortable. Then I turned on my back. "Argh!" Kicking off the covers, I combed my fingers through my short strands.

Grady's comment had been bothering me all night. *I was prettier with long hair.* I growled, when I really wanted to hunt Grady down and give him a piece of my mind.

I couldn't get that line out of my darn head, and I was dying to know if Colton agreed with the asshat.

I puffed out a heavy breath just as Stella pawed

me, as if to say she was there for me. I glanced over at her. "I love you too. You know, guys are maddening."

One in particular. I was approaching the end of the first week of school, and it felt like so much had changed in the blink of an eye. With Dad and now Colton, my emotions were on the precipice of falling off a cliff—a perfect storm was brewing, and I knew that when it hit, I was going to fall hard, and that terrified me.

Still, I couldn't shake the entire convo between Colton and me—or rather what had been left unsaid. He knew he was affecting me.

My hand crept down to my panties. I had a constant ache that needed some form of release. Maybe then I would feel like I wasn't about to explode. I was a virgin, but I wasn't exactly naïve to that pulsing between my legs. I'd slipped my fingers inside my panties when a car door slammed. I checked the time on my ceiling—I had one of those clocks that flashed the neon red numbers in the dark room. Three a.m.

It was probably Colton's dad waltzing in like usual, drunk out of his mind. I'd said I wasn't nosy, but I guessed I was. I had to peek. I climbed out of bed, that pulsing need gone until I ever so lightly pulled down a slat in the blinds. Then the throbbing hit me like a tornado. Colton stood against his truck, shirtless, hair messy around his strong jaw. The spotlight from his garage beamed at him like he was on stage. It took me a beat to realize he was looking up in my direction.

Oh hell no.

Faster than the Flash, I let go of the blind and slapped a hand over my heart. I didn't know whether to be creeped out or excited beyond belief. I was going for the second option, since the butterflies were fluttering around in my stomach, seeming to travel south in droves. I squeezed my eyes closed for a breath to commit his bare chest to memory until a thought came out of nowhere.

He was just getting home and probably from a romp in the hay with Amanda. The need to scream was on the tip of my tongue.

Stella pushed her head against my leg and I jumped a mile. *Do I look again? Or do I go back to bed?* The answer to my second question was a flat no. I wouldn't be able to sleep even if someone paid me a million dollars. I also wasn't going to give Colton any ammunition to think I couldn't keep my nose out of his business.

Given that he lived next door and the walls were thin, it would be hard not to see or hear what our neighbors were up to. Only a strip of land about twenty-five feet wide separated his house from mine.

Stella mewled at my feet as if to tell me to go back to bed. Instead, I picked her up. I needed something to quench the thirst in my dry throat. "I'm going to get some water."

I carried her with me, passing my other window, which had a clear view of Mrs. Caldwell's office. I pulled back my curtain, then cracked open the blinds. Her room was dark. I didn't know what I was expecting, although Georgia's comment came to mind: *You could sneak into his room at night.*

I didn't know if Mrs. Caldwell had moved her office out to accommodate her son. I only knew the window I was looking at had been his bedroom before he'd left for the academy. One of the first weeks after I'd moved in, I'd forgotten to close my curtains, and I'd never been more horrified than when I caught Colton staring at me. It wouldn't have been embarrassing except I'd been completely naked.

I shook off the memory as I tiptoed out, careful

not to wake Nan, who was sleeping in the other bedroom on the second floor.

I set Stella down when I entered the kitchen. After getting a drink of water, I decided to check on Dad. I'd gotten into the habit of poking my head in when I couldn't sleep.

A light filtered out of Dad's room. Maybe he was awake. Or maybe Nan had forgotten to shut off the lights. Stella followed me in. Dad liked when she curled up with him. I did the same on occasion. His hospital bed wasn't that big, but I always found a small nook to snuggle next to him for a few minutes.

His computer screen was brightening the room, and I zeroed in on a picture of three older women smiling at the camera from a table in a restaurant. They appeared to be having a good time, drinks in hand.

Dad snored lightly as I studied the picture. All three women had varying shades of brown hair and brown eyes, and the one in the middle snagged my attention. She wore a cool, round, silver charm necklace that had some sort of inscription on it.

Dad stirred, yawning. He blinked a couple of

times, then gave me a faraway look as Stella nestled in-between his legs.

"Go back to sleep. I was just shutting off your computer." I rubbed his nose with mine. "I'll see you in the morning."

With all the strength he had, which was nil, he tensed and lowered his gaze to the slim spot next to him.

I wished upon a star every chance I had that he could talk, that I could hear his voice again, even if it was to say one word.

I crawled in as best I could and snuggled into him. "I love you, Dad." Tears burned as hot as a fireplace poker. "I really want to hear your voice again."

He moved so his cheek was on the top of my head, a gesture that said he wanted the same thing.

I swung my arm over his chest. I had so much I wanted to say, but couldn't without shedding an ocean of tears.

"Colton is going to fix the wheel on my skateboard. I need a new front axle assembly." Colton had called it a wheelbase, but I didn't correct him. I'd been so wrapped up in the close proximity of his body that I couldn't think. "I'm sorry I didn't tell you about him hitting me. I just don't want you to worry."

I was sure he had several things to say about my skateboard, about being careful, and so on.

"It won't happen again," I whispered. I did need to be more alert when riding in the streets or through parking lots.

We lay there as Stella snored.

Dad laughed weakly. Granted, he couldn't speak, but he did make grunting and laughing sounds.

"I should get back to my room," I said. I could have fallen asleep next to Dad, but I wasn't the best sleeping companion. I had a habit of taking over the whole bed, and I was a restless sleeper, which meant I would either end up on the floor or kicking Dad and hurting him. I hugged him as tightly as I could. "I'll see you in the morning."

He blinked in agreement.

Stella didn't move. I was about to grab her when Dad shook his head.

I kept the door ajar so Stella could get out. On my way upstairs, I wondered if Colton was still out-side. Probably not, but as always, my curiosity got the better of me, and I quietly padded over to the front window in the family room, my pulse soaring to new heights. Holding my breath, I gently moved the curtain out of the way with one finger and angled my head to get a view of his driveway, which was dark save for the landscape lights around a pear tree that stood between our property lines.

Exhaling, I let the curtain fall and quietly went to my room. I had to shut off my brain. I had to get at least a couple hours of sleep before school or I would be a zombie in every class.

I huffed as I flopped onto my mattress, my mind racing with thoughts of Dad, Colton, and homework. The only way to clear my head was to read. I got up and switched on the bedside lamp. As I hunted for that thriller novel I'd been reading, a soft glow lit up the space between Colton's house and mine.

Don't look, Skye.

But my legs had a mind of their own, and before I could think, I was standing in front of my window and looking directly into Colton's bedroom. The blood drained from my cheeks, and several expletives dropped from my lips in a whisper.

My belly did a thousand somersaults as I

watched Colton unbuttoning his jeans. As if he could sense me watching him, he lifted his head.

My stomach hollowed as horror careened through me and maybe awe too. I had a front-row seat to perfection. I licked my lips, but only because my mouth was dry. That ache in-between my legs was back with a vengeance.

Colton continued to remove his jeans while never taking his eyes off me. I couldn't look away. That pronounced V that disappeared below the waistband of his boxer briefs, the one Mia talked about on Grady, was ever-present on Colton.

He gave me a predatory grin that only served to make the sweat break out on the nape of my neck.

Go back to bed, Skyler.

Not a chance in hell. I couldn't move, and I didn't want to.

Colton stalked closer to his window.

I inched away from mine.

His grin grew wider, and if that wasn't the most belly-squeezing look I'd ever seen, I didn't know what was. I was a goner for sure. His pecs were toned to perfection. His biceps were lick-worthy, and if his Greek god upper torso wasn't enough to soak my panties, then what was growing in his boxer briefs was sending me over the edge.

He cocked his head as he watched me watch him, and when he slid his hand down to his crotch, my mouth fell open.

He grabbed his erection, never taking his eyes off me.

What in the world is happening? My heart rammed against my ribs like crazy. droplets of sweat trickled down my back, and that pulsing need between my legs was stronger than ever before.

I had to get out of there. If he whipped out his dick, I would probably faint or maybe run over to his house and attack him. While the latter was a great idea, I didn't have the courage to do that, and I wasn't that girl.

Why not? It's just sex. Mia does it all the time and she's happy. It's part of growing up too.

With my luck, I would look like a dimwit. Regardless of my inexperience, I didn't know if Colton was the kiss-and-tell type, and since he hung out with Grady, there was no way in hell was I making the first move.

If Grady got wind that I'd come on to Colton, he would spread horrible rumors about me being an easy lay or a tramp or something. I wouldn't be able to show my face in school anymore.

So I rolled my eyes at myself, and in clear Skyler stick-foot-in-mouth fashion, I flipped Colton off before storming out of my room with a throbbing ache in my body that was never going away. Ever!

11

The surf crashed along the shore, and music pumped out of the speakers, the party in full force behind Grady's sprawling beachside mansion. It seemed the entire high school was there. Some kids danced, some hovered around one of the two kegs, and others sat on blankets or in beach chairs, chatting around the bonfire.

Mia, Georgia, and I were somewhat away from the fire, but we were close to a group of cackling girls. One was gesturing with her hands while speaking.

I was glad the week was finally over, and I felt like the stress I'd been carrying was leaving me, thanks in part to the beer I was drinking.

"Our first week of senior year is behind us," Mia said from her chair across from me.

"Hallelujah," Georgia squeaked out beside me.

I raised my beer. "For sure." The first week had been epic. Colton returned home. I'd been hit by a car. My skateboard was still toast, and my aunt was due to arrive that night. Dad wanted me to hang at home, but Nan had come to my rescue.

"You probably should spend some time with your sister alone first," Nan had told him.

I'd almost hugged the crap out of her. If the circumstances with Dad changed prior to my eighteenth birthday, somehow or some way, I was not moving to California. North Carolina was my home, and it would stay that way even if I had to throw the biggest temper tantrum this side of the Mississippi.

Mia raised her perfectly manicured dark eyebrow. "Are you going to nurse that cup all night? Both of you. Loosen up. It's our senior year."

Georgia giggled, then gulped down a mouthful of her beer.

I brought the red cup to my lips. "I've been drinking it." Maybe not as fast as Mia. I'd been counting, and she'd been to the keg twice, while Georgia and I were on our first round.

Mia watched me intently. "Not fast enough."

I usually didn't give into peer pressure, but the alcohol was relaxing me, and it was a nice feeling to hang with my friends, enjoy a drink, listen to good music, inhale the salt air, and just let loose.

"It's called pacing," Georgia said. "We have hours to go." She swung out her arm and tapped my shoulder. "Drink."

I huffed. "Fine. But if I make a fool of myself, please come to my rescue."

"Always," Mia and Georgia said in unison.

I believed Georgia. Mia, not so much. I loved the girl to death, but her attention span when Grady was around was nil. I couldn't blame her. I might have been the same way if Colton and I were dating.

I took a big gulp, the skunk smell burning my nose hairs. "This shit is nasty."

My friends laughed as Mia hopped out of her chair. "I have something better. Be right back."

Georgia and I exchanged a wide-eyed look. "This isn't good."

Mia rubbed her big tits up against Grady, who was standing by the fire with a few of his cronies from the football team. The bright flames highlighted Grady's excited expression when he glanced down at Mia. If I wasn't mistaken, I thought I saw a hint of awe in the QB's eyes. The two were becoming quite the item.

"She really likes him." My pitch went up a notch. Mia deserved to be happy, and for as much as Grady could be an ass, he did too. I thought they made a great couple. Mia was the yin to his yang.

"She does," Georgia agreed. "I don't think Grady is interested in anyone else, either."

"I'm shocked. I mean, not that he likes Mia. She's beautiful. But I've only ever known Grady to play the field."

Georgia raised her knees so her feet were planted on the lounge chair. "I think she's taming him."

"I would like to see that. Maybe he'll stop talking shit about me to Colton."

Georgia rounded her green gaze to me. "What shit?"

I hadn't told Georgia or Mia everything that Colton had said to me in my garage or that I'd seen him in his boxer briefs. The less I talked about him, the better for my psyche. But if I didn't tell Georgia, she would be upset. I also didn't want to make a big deal about Grady's comment. I was trying not to let it bother me. But the liquor was toying with my emotions. "Grady thinks I look better with long hair."

She gasped. "Colton told you that?"

I shuddered. "I shouldn't have cut my hair."

She slapped my leg. "Nonsense. You're beautiful."

"Thank you, chica. I wasn't looking for a compliment." I searched the partygoers. "You think Colton will be here?"

Maybe he wasn't coming. When Georgia had picked me up, his truck had been in the driveway. I wondered if he'd gotten into a fight with his dad again. Or maybe he was grounded. Regardless, it was probably best I didn't see him. I still hadn't recovered from the other night.

Georgia nursed her beer. "He's probably running late."

Or getting pummeled by his dad. It was time to change the subject and get my mind off my crush. But it was hard to get the image of him in his boxer briefs out of my head.

"Are you still going to throw your party next weekend?" I asked Georgia.

"Of course. We need to live it up this year. Make memories and all that."

"If my dad gets his way, I might be leaving with my aunt." I was going out on a limb on that one—the alcohol was starting to screw with me. I didn't really think Dad would ship me off while he was still alive.

She jabbed a long blue nail into my bare leg. "You are not moving." Her tone was harder than the large rock next to my chair. "You're just going to have to show your aunt you are not a good girl. I doubt she would want to take on a teenage brat." She searched my face as she frowned. "I say this with heartfelt emotion. Your dad isn't gone yet, Skyler Lawson, and he wouldn't ship you off while he's still alive."

I sipped my beer. The more I drank, the less I noticed the skunk smell. "Let's not talk about that right now. We're supposed to have fun. Right?"

On my last word, I spotted Colton sauntering down the path from the house. Georgia and I had our backs to the ocean just so we could people watch better.

Georgia followed my line of sight, and that frown turned into an instant smile. "Yum to the nth degree. Now the party is heating up. You have got to lose your virginity to him. If you don't, I will."

It was my turn to poke her with my short nails. I didn't paint them like she and Mia did. I mainly chewed on them, a habit I'd developed since learning Dad had ALS. "Not on your life."

"Chill. I'm just kidding. Well, maybe not. That hair of his. I just want to run my fingers through it."

"I saw him in his boxer briefs the other night." I took another gulp of beer, suddenly regretting saying that, since I caught one of the girls on the blanket jerk her head in our direction.

Georgia screamed so loud it hurt my ears. Thankfully, the waves crashed at the perfect time to drown out the conversation.

She swung her legs over her chair and leaned into me. "How come you're just telling me this now?"

My face burned as images of the other night danced before me. "For this reason." I twirled a finger around her excited yet shocked expression. Might as well give her the biggest news of them all. "He's huge too."

"He had a boner?" Shock slammed into Georgia's sweet Southern voice before she raised her cup. "This calls for a drink."

Mia skipped back at that moment with a liter of marshmallow vodka—ew.

"Okay, ladies. Time to taste the good stuff." Mia sat on the edge of my chair, facing Georgia. She uncapped the bottle and drank like she was thirsty after a long cheer workout.

Georgia dumped her beer and grabbed the bottle.

My eyes bugged out.

Georgia shrugged. "What? You just told me you saw Colton's boner. I need to quiet my lady hormones."

Mia squealed. "Did you two fuck?"

It was my turn to drink.

Mia and Georgia waited for me to tell them more. There wasn't much to tell, and the less Mia knew, the better. She was too close to Grady. I didn't know why I was worried about her, though, since Colton probably told him that he teased me until my panties were soaked. He wouldn't have been wrong.

"I didn't exactly see him naked," I said.

Georgia shook her blond head of curls. "Doesn't matter. You will. And no, she hasn't fucked him. Again, she will."

I took another long swig of the marshmallow

vodka, which was rather tasty and went down easily. I tossed my beer, then poured vodka into my cup.

Both of my friends watched in quiet fascination. "You said to let loose. Well, when we start talking about Colton or his dick, I have to do something." The thought of having sex with him was making that spot between my legs throb endlessly.

The three of us fell into a fit of laughter.

"What's so funny?" a familiar but irritating voice asked as bitter laughter tumbled free. "I heard 'Colton's dick.'"

I snarled. The last person who needed to hear that was Amanda fucking Gelling.

"You did not screw him." Her glossy, ice-blue eyes were swimming in anger.

Mia popped up and pushed her chest into Amanda's. "What if she did?"

"I'm dating him," she said, not backing down.

"Did you screw him?" Georgia asked.

I didn't want to hear Amanda's answer. I would've bet my life she had.

"Five times this week," she said as sure as the moon was high in the night sky.

I cringed, gripping the hell out of my cup.

"So is he huge?" Mia asked as though she was talking about the damn weather.

Amanda got in Mia's face. "Bigger than Grady, and I should know. Stay away from Colton if you know what's good for you."

Mia flipped her dark hair over her shoulder, ready to brawl. "Oh, I will. And I doubt anyone has a larger cock than Grady."

I spit up my drink. Georgia snorted, doing the same.

Mia and Amanda were about to tear each other's hair out until Colton of all people walked up, towering over us.

I knocked back the half cup of vodka, afraid to look at him. Even at school, when I'd seen him at lunch, I turned away. I was relieved he hadn't shown up at my house with my skateboard yet.

Amanda hooked her arm around Colton's. "There you are. These ladies want to know how big your penis is."

I shrank in my seat. My cheeks felt like they were on fire.

Colton glowered, those brown peepers penetrating me like sharp daggers.

Great. Now he must think I'm a loser. I stood and the beach tilted.

Amanda laughed, a sound that grated on my last nerve. "Lawson, can't handle your liquor?"

The need to kill sat heavily inside me, and I started for her before listing to one side. Damn alcohol.

Georgia came to my rescue, almost falling in the process and laughing the entire way.

I held up one hand, holding my cup in the other. "I'm fine." I was buzzing for sure, but I wasn't so drunk that I didn't know what I was doing, at least not yet.

Colton watched me intently as Amanda pressed her tits against his arm.

It was time to get the hell out of Dodge. I didn't want to witness Amanda fawning over Colton like a horse in heat. Otherwise, the way I was feeling, powerful and free, my fist might land in her face. I wasn't ready to show Colton how jealous I was. I wasn't ready to make an ass out of myself, either. I was there to have a good time, not cause trouble.

I skirted my chair, digging my sandal-covered feet in the soft sand. I was about to breeze by Amanda when she stuck out her foot. My cup flew out of my hand as I landed face-first in the sand.

Laughter ensued from all around.

Georgia helped me up. "Don't engage."

I spit out sand as Georgia cleaned the rest off of me. When I finally managed to get most of the tiny pebbles out of my mouth, I spun around inelegantly. Once I had my bearings, I pushed Amanda, unleashing all my pent-up anger and jealousy on her.

She fell with an *oomph*, her face twisting with fury.

I flared my nostrils. "Try that again and I'll toss you in the ocean." So much for not causing trouble.

Before she climbed to her feet, Colton stepped in front of me, raising his hands and shaking his head.

I laughed at him before I sneered. "Get out of my way."

"Yeah," Georgia said.

Grady hurried over like security ready to break up the brawl—or maybe add fuel to the fire, given the grin he wore. "Lawson, what happened to you?" Then he busted out laughing. "There's a crab crawling in your hair."

I snapped at Grady like an alligator chomping on its victim. I could feel the critter tickling my head, but I wasn't afraid of a sand crab.

Mia plucked the energetic crustacean out of my hair. "There. All gone."

I craned my neck up at Colton. "Get out of my way." I wasn't sure if he was protecting Amanda or me. My guess was Amanda, and that only made my stomach churn.

Amanda poked her head around Colton. "You'll never get your hands on him."

"Good. I don't want him, anyway." *Liar. Liar. Liar.*

No fucking reaction from Colton. Not one ounce of emotion on his face.

It figured. I wanted to scream. He'd had that same look when I saw him leaning against his truck, staring up at my window. It was unnerving and downright irritating. At least with someone like Grady, I could see when I pissed him off and knew how to prepare.

Whatever. Carefully, I did another turn on my heel, hoping I didn't fall and make an ass out of myself. *That ship has sailed, girl.*

Georgia hooked her arm in mine before she tossed a look over her shoulder. "Colton is burning a hole in your back."

"Let him." For the moment, I didn't care. However, when Monday rolled around, I was sure I would be the brunt of the rumor mill at school, and Colton would look at me like a pathetic, foolish girl.

Mia came up to my other side, handing me the vodka. "Your performance deserves a toast."

I busted out laughing, taking the bottle from her. "Let's dance." I wanted to forget the incident, forget Colton, forget that Amanda was sleeping with Colton, and forget how jealous I was of her for that.

The three of us joined a group of girls who were dancing and letting loose.

"We Are Love" by Don Diablo belted out of the speakers.

As we passed around the vodka, my muscles began to loosen. I didn't know what the next day would bring, so it was time to enjoy myself.

12

I jolted upright, my head spinning like a merry-go-round on steroids. I grabbed my temples, wincing and moaning.

Where the heck am I? I blinked several times to orient myself. The opulent room with light-blue walls, expensive watercolor art, and luxurious furniture was definitely not my room.

I swished saliva around in my parched mouth. I felt as though I'd eaten a mouthful of sand. Maybe I had. I dipped into my memory bank as I slowly turned my head to the left, careful not to make my brain slosh around more than it already was.

When my gaze landed on the bare, muscled

back of the person beside me, I flew off the mattress. I didn't have to see his face to know Colton was sprawled out. His hair gave him away.

In true Skyler fashion, I tripped over a shoe and stumbled, catching myself before I face-planted into a very rich-looking fabric chair. My arms took the brunt of the impact, and I couldn't help but moan until something far worse than falling registered in my foggy mind.

I glanced down at my body and released a loud noise that was more like a grunt than a sigh. Thank heavens I was still wearing my clothes.

I straightened my spine as another horror froze me to the spot near the floor-to-ceiling shutters. I didn't have to check the time to know it was morning or maybe afternoon. Rays of light snuck through a few of the slats on the shutters, which weren't closed completely.

I was in huge trouble. Dad was probably freaking out.

I patted my pockets for my phone. No luck. I briefly closed my eyes.

Think, Skyler.

I retraced my steps. I'd had it when I'd gotten into the scuffle with Amanda. Maybe it had fallen out of my pocket when she tripped me. Or when I pushed her. Things had blurred when Colton blocked her from me as if protecting his true love.

I gritted my teeth as that irritating jealousy sloshed around in my stomach. I took another look at the guy who was making my knees weak. His hands were tucked neatly under the pillow, and his head was turned toward the door.

I started to hyperventilate. I still had my clothes on, unlike him. He was sprawled out in red boxer briefs and nothing else.

I wasn't complaining. I drank him in from head to toe, my gaze stopping to admire his toned butt and thick thighs.

Focus, girl. Find your phone, then get the hell out before he wakes up.

It was hard to get my legs into gear. My head was spinning and my stomach was ready to protest. Damn vodka.

I couldn't worry about that. I needed a bottle of mouthwash before walking into my house.

Maybe my phone had fallen out while I was sleeping. *Ha, sleeping? More like passed out cold.* I was usually a light sleeper.

I tiptoed over to my side of the bed and started to feel around, careful not to disturb the sleeping giant. I would lose the contents of my stomach if he woke up. I probably looked like death. On that thought, I swiped a finger underneath my eye to clear away the mascara that I was certain was smudged.

Georgia had made up my face before the party. I'd kept telling her I didn't want too much makeup on. Most of the time, I hardly wore any. But my BFF hadn't listened.

"I'm giving you the smoky look," she'd said. "Guys like that."

My breathing was somewhat labored as I checked under the pillow I'd been sleeping on.

Just as I felt around, Colton stirred, moaning.

I slapped a hand over my mouth.

He turned his head and the blood drained from me. Then his eyes opened lazily, his long lashes fluttering as he pinned me with a hooded but blank expression.

I held my breath, something I was doing quite a lot when I was around him.

He sized me up, licking his lips like he was hungry.

I gulped as my stomach twisted, setting me off balance and making me lightheaded. I lowered my hand, releasing the air in my lungs.

He watched as I searched for words. The

throbbing shifted from my head to that sweet spot in between my legs. "What are you doing here?" I managed to ask in a smooth voice.

He gave me an easy grin. "I was sleeping. What are you doing?"

I wagged a finger between us. "We didn't…" I couldn't even say what I was thinking, although the fact that I still had my clothes on was a good indication that we hadn't screwed each other's brains out. That thought only served to make the butterflies come alive again.

He studied me for the longest time with no indication of how he was feeling or if he was irritated, happy, annoyed, or whatever.

I stuck my hands on my hips. "Better yet, don't answer that. Have you seen my phone?" My voice was getting stronger.

"No." His freaking Southern drawl was even sexier in his sleepy voice.

Go, Skyler. Get out before you jump into bed with him.

We were in a stare-off, and the more he watched me, the more I was melting to the white carpeted floor.

I had so many questions, but I had to call Dad.

The thought of Dad fried the feelings thrumming through me. I became a madwoman, searching under the bed to find only dust bunnies. I spotted Colton's heap of clothes near the night-stand and picked through the pile. For all I knew, he could've taken my phone.

Colton didn't move anything but his head, watching me.

"You could get up and help me." Frustration and panic overtook me. That sour feeling was back.

"Don't think so," he said as though in pain.

My nostrils flared as I sneered, when all I wanted to do was lock lips with him. "For real?" I clenched my teeth. "Where's your phone?" It wasn't in his jeans or anywhere I could find.

He adjusted his big body before he propped his head up with a hand.

My panic over a damn piece of technology sub-sided for the moment as my gaze took a lazy hike down his body, stopping to admire the bulge in his boxer briefs. A very big bulge. I shouldn't have been staring, but he had an impressive dick. I'd never seen Grady's, and I didn't care to, but Amanda might have been right. Colton's mountain was huge—not that I was an expert in that depart-ment or could compare Colton's to another guy's.

I bit my bottom lip, hoping not to make a whimpering sound. I was sure my eyes were as big as basketballs.

Colton snapped his fingers. "Up here, Skyler." His tone was light and on the verge of laughing.

I clenched my jaw to prevent myself from saying something stupid. Still, my name coming from him fired heat south of my belly button. I needed water. I was beginning to understand the concept of cold showers.

I shuddered, blinking before I gave him my attention. And I shouldn't have.

He belonged on the cover of some magazine. His pose was definitely Hollywood-worthy as he grinned, his hair brushing his shoulder, his biceps taut, and his six-pack abs polished to perfection. But what had my thighs quivering wasn't any of his body parts, but the way he was looking at me, as though he was ready to pounce and pull me into bed with him.

The words "pretty please" screamed in my head.

A laugh tore free from my lips. I wouldn't have known what to do if he had. I needed to get out of there.

I cleared my throat, hoping my voice didn't fail

me. "I need to use your phone," I said, surprisingly calmly. My plan was to call mine. If it were in the room, I would find it that way. I also needed to call Nan to let her know I wasn't dead or hurt.

He swung his legs over the side of the bed before his hand disappeared under the pillow. With his phone in one hand, he rose and sauntered over to me, the fingers on the other hand dancing through his hair.

I stumbled backward as a gasp raked free. His arms snaked out like a whip, and before I knew what was happening, I was flush against a hard-as-stone body.

The room spun as I stiffened.

He smelled of the beach, a scent that was soothing to me. Or maybe his masculine cologne or soap was messing with my head.

His hand slipped under my tank top, landing on the small of my back. His clammy palm sent electricity vibrating through my limbs. My knees became weak. My breathing was shallow and my heart was thumping so hard against my ribs that I was sure he could feel it. Or maybe that was his heart.

My arms hung at my sides, resisting the urge to wrap them around him. My nose was aligned with his pecs, and I could feel his erection pressing into the waist of my shorts.

I should get away before my hand slides in between us, eager to feel his hardness, or before I lift up on my toes and devour his thick lips. The last thought made me crane my neck up.

Colton Caldwell grinned so darn easily as his gaze rounded on my lips, as though he was ready to take me to places I'd never been before.

The air flared with lust or maybe something more.

My tongue darted out as if to say, "Wait one minute, then attack."

He flinched.

"I..." *What was I going to say?* Words were becoming difficult to find in my mushy brain.

With the pad of his thumb, he traced the outline of my lips.

I whimpered as my body became limp in his embrace. "I really need to call my dad."

He studied my mouth as though it was the most fascinating thing to him. I could see the debate going on in his head: to kiss her or not to kiss her.

"Col—"

He placed his forefinger on my lips and shook his head.

Please don't do it. Sure, I wanted Colton as badly as I needed mouthwash. I also had to stink like alcohol and sweat and the ocean.

I flattened my hands on his bare chest. *Oh my!* Soft skin, hard abs. The perfect combo. "My dad. He's probably worried. He might think I drowned."

As if I dumped a bucket of ice over him, Colton let go of me faster than I could take the words back. He shoved his phone against my chest. "Call your old man." Then he dressed quickly.

I was such an idiot. "I'm... I'm sorry, Colton."

"For what?" He practically bared his perfect straight white teeth.

"I didn't mean—"

He got in my face. "You didn't mean what?"

Shut up, Skyler. Call your dad.

His nostrils flared. "What?" He spun on his bare feet, shoving both hands through his hair.

I felt like a total loser. I wanted to say something to console him, but I knew firsthand that words didn't mean much. Sure, the sentiment was nice when someone said how sorry she was for my loss, but it did nothing to erase the grief and sorrow I'd felt over my mom's death.

I set the phone on the bed and quietly started for the door.

"Don't you want to call your dad?" His tone was harsh, and he sounded hurt as well.

"I'll find Georgia." I hoped she was somewhere in the house.

Besides, in order to use his phone, I needed him to unlock it, and if I stayed in that room with him another second, I was seriously going to regret my actions.

"The last I saw her was in the sunroom downstairs. She was passed out," he said.

And on that note, I left Colton standing near the bed with hurt written all over his beautiful face.

As soon as I was out in the massive hall, I sighed, my body deflating as if Colton had just stuck a pin in me. I had no idea where I was going or how to get downstairs, but when I passed a room next door, I could hear moaning and heavy breathing.

"That's it," Mia said in a breathless tone. "I'm almost there. Harder."

I rolled my eyes and ran down the hall, passing

pics of Grady and his family. No way was I stopping to check out any. When the stairs came into view, I ran faster, my feet pounding on the dark hardwood floor. I took them two at a time, and when I reached the bottom, Georgia was sitting on a plush bench near the front door, looking like she'd had a wild night too.

Her blonde hair was matted to her head and sticking up in some places, and her eyes looked like a raccoon's with her smudged mascara. She yawned and popped to her feet when she saw me.

"Are you waiting for me?" I asked.

She yawned again. "I woke up a minute ago and was going to look for you, but my stomach protested. I had to sit."

"Let's get out of here." I rushed to the massive wooden door.

She hurried behind me with a groan.

Once outside, I squinted so hard, I lost my balance.

Georgia latched onto my arm. "We need coffee and food."

I blinked several times, the sunlight blinding. "For sure. But I have to call my dad."

Out of nowhere, she handed me my phone.

I raised an eyebrow. "You had it?"

"When we were dancing, it fell out of your pocket. I was going to give it back to you until you ran into the ocean."

I scrunched my nose. "I did what?"

Her green eyes glistened in the morning light. "Colton rescued you before you dove under." She delivered those words like it was no big deal.

My jaw hit the wood slats on the porch. "For real?"

She held her stomach, looking pale. "You passed out not long after that. But I texted Nan from your phone to let her know you were crashing at my place."

I didn't know whether to hug her or demand more answers—answers I was sure I didn't want. "He was in bed with me."

She gave me a smug grin. "I know. I stayed with you until he came in. Then he told me to go back to the party."

I clutched my neck, rubbing a knot I'd just realized was there. "And you listened to him?"

"Sorry, chica. But he was adamant about watching you. And Mia dragged me out. Honestly, I thought it was sweet that Colton wanted to be your bodyguard. I think he was afraid you would wake up and wander back in the ocean."

The haze was clearing from my brain. "Where was Amanda? You know, his girlfriend? The one he screwed five times last week."

"She didn't screw him."

My eyes bugged out. "How do you know that?" That, I had to hear.

She climbed down the porch steps. "Amanda's all talk. She was trying to get under your skin. But I'm not one-hundred-percent certain." She dug her car keys out of the pocket of her shorts. "I need coffee. We can chat more in the car, and you can tell me how you gave your virginity to Colton."

I laughed so hard I couldn't get air in my lungs. "I wish."

Once we were on the road with the top down and the morning breeze blowing in my face, I checked my text messages from Nan.

Text one: *Have a good time. I'll let your dad know you'll be home in the morning.*

Text two: *Oh, and your Aunt Clara didn't make it in. I'll explain when I see you.*

Maybe things were looking up.

13

I pushed food around on my plate as the hum of voices in the cafeteria droned.

Georgia tapped my tray with her fork. "You need to eat."

I wasn't hungry and hadn't been for the three weeks since I'd found myself in bed with Colton. Life had been up and down. I'd learned that my aunt couldn't commit to being my guardian. She'd recently been offered a higher position within her company, which would keep her on a plane five to six days a week. She'd canceled at the last minute because she had to go to Japan.

I was super stoked because that meant I wouldn't have to move to California. Dad, on the other hand, had been extremely quiet. In part, I suspected he was a little hurt that his sister had reneged.

Regardless, my future wasn't important at the moment. I was biting my nails because I was losing Dad faster than I wanted to. He wasn't able to lift a cup to drink anymore, he was sleeping a lot, and in just three weeks, he'd seemed to diminish greatly.

I cried most nights, and if someone looked at me the wrong way, I broke down.

Every night, I got up at the same time—three a.m.—and checked on him. Nan and I were taking turns, but Nan wanted me to get as much rest as possible because of school.

I didn't care about school.

A tear escaped as I lifted my gaze to my BFF.

She was at my side in less than a second, throwing her arm around me. "I'm here for you."

I couldn't cry in a room full of nosy students. It wasn't that I cared what they thought. I didn't want to fly off the handle. If one student mocked me, I would probably punch her lights out. And Amanda had been testing me for a few weeks.

Apparently, she blamed me for Colton wanting nothing to do with her anymore. I didn't know how that was my fault. Colton hadn't said a word to me since that morning in the bedroom at Grady's place. Well, that wasn't all true. I did ask him about my skateboard.

"Sorry. I've been busy," he'd responded in a terse tone, as though I'd been the one to ruin his relationship with Amanda. I suspected his irritation with me stemmed from that night in Grady's bedroom, when I made the comment about how my dad might've thought I'd drowned. I knew the word "drowned" had to have spurred memories of his brother's drowning.

In all fairness to me, he and his dad were arguing more and more as of late. It was hard not to hear them, or when Colton peeled out of his driveway like he was taking off in a drag race.

My bottom lip quivered. "I need to go to the skate park." I was itching to get back on my board and ride. The strands of my sanity were on the verge of snapping if I didn't.

"It's not fixed," she reminded me.

I scanned the room for Colton. "I know. I'm going to take it down to the skate shop." That would cost money, but I had a few dollars saved. First, I had to get it back from Colton.

My search for the hunk came up empty. He

was probably down on the field, making out with some girl, which was the rumor running around school. Apparently Amanda wasn't mad only at me, but also at a petite brunette who had been sticking her tongue down Colton's throat at lunch only days before. I couldn't say I blamed Amanda. If I'd seen the girl glued to Colton, I might have unleashed some of my jealousy too. On the other hand, I knew how rumors went. Some were true. Some weren't.

Mia bounced up, her dark hair braided, her hazel eyes sparkling, and her smile was as electric as if she'd just gotten laid in the janitor's closet, until she saw me. Then she frowned as she set down her leather bag and came over to my other side. She rubbed my arm. "What's wrong? Please tell me your dad is okay."

Lately, Mia and Georgia had been very attentive. They both knew Dad was getting worse, and they dropped what they were doing to console me.

I dashed away an errant tear. "Can you both sit down and look like nothing is happening, please?" I could feel eyes lasering on us.

My friends took their seats beside me like bodyguards.

"We should have that beach party," Mia said.

"You know, the one Georgia was supposed to have but didn't."

"After the drunk fest all of us had," Georgia piped in, "I figured it would be best to push the party out. How about a Halloween party? My parents are away at some medical conference that weekend."

"Ooh, costumes," Mia practically squealed. "I want to dress up as Snow White. One of you can go as Cinderella and the other as Princess Aurora." Mia had a fascination with Disney characters. "We can make it a Disney theme."

Georgia nudged me. "What do you think?"

I shrugged. I wasn't in the mood for a party. And after Grady's, I wasn't ready to make an ass out of myself again. Mia had filled me in on what she'd witnessed that night, which was exactly as Georgia had described it.

I'd been dancing and having a great time when I'd gotten the harebrained idea to go skinny-dipping. When I'd started to run toward the ocean's edge, trying to take off my top, Colton had bolted to my rescue. Over the last few weeks, I'd been remembering bits and pieces of my actions after the fight with Amanda.

I'd downed more marshmallow vodka while

dancing—the more I danced, the more I drank. The one thing I couldn't piece together was Colton carrying me up to the house. Then again, Georgia had said the minute I was in his arms, I mumbled something about his dick before passing out.

Heat gripped my cheeks. That was probably another reason he wouldn't look my way when I passed him in the halls. He probably thought I was just another chick hungry for his body. Well, that wasn't far-fetched. But I also wanted… I didn't know what I wanted from him.

As if Colton could hear my thoughts, he strutted into the cafeteria with a bad-boy swagger that most girls drooled over. He searched the room.

I guessed he was looking for Grady, who was at a table in the back somewhere.

Georgia squeezed my thigh.

Mia nudged me. "Grady tells me Colton has sworn off girls."

I wanted to remind her that the rumor mill said otherwise until Colton looked directly at me. I would like to have thought his eyes lit up, but that deadpan look he always sported was replaced with anger. He hated me. I could feel it in my bones. Or maybe the guilt was getting to me.

"Why does he always have a vacant look in his eyes?" Georgia asked. "He's a hard one to figure out."

"I think he wants to eat Skyler if you ask me," Mia added on a snort.

I choked on her comment just as Colton reached our table.

I cleared my throat. "Skateboard. I would like it back. I'll fix it myself."

He studied me for the longest beat, as if I was the most confusing person on the planet.

Mia snapped her fingers. "Did someone cut your tongue out, Colton?"

He ignored Mia, watching me. "Find me later." He lifted his arm, and his biceps bunched as he threaded his fingers through his hair and continued on his way.

I let out a huge breath.

Mia swiveled in her seat. "I think someone pissed in his Wheaties."

"That would be me." Before they could bombard me with questions, I told them my theory and what I'd said to him in the bedroom. "I said I was sorry."

"He'll come around," Georgia was quick to add.

Mia dipped into her purse and plucked out her lipstick. "Grady says Colton is butting heads with his dad."

"Their arguments are epic," I mumbled.

Mia dragged her lipstick over her lips. "That doesn't change the fact that Colton wants you badly." She tittered.

I snorted.

Georgia's pretty eyebrows knitted. "I did not get that he wants to eat Skyler."

I had to agree with my BFF. If anything, Colton wanted to tear me to pieces.

Mia leaned in and over me. "I know, guys. I see it on Colton. Grady had a similar look with me."

"Everyone knows what Grady thinks or is feeling," I said. "The guy wears his emotions on his sleeve."

Mia dumped her lipstick in her purse. "Maybe. But not the I-like-you-a-lot look. Grady comes off as a player, but deep down, the dude only has eyes for one chick." She sounded proud and in love.

Georgia leaned in. "Oh my God. You're in love with Grady Dyson."

"We might have dropped the L word to each other." Mia stuck out her chin, rubbing her lips together. "You have a problem with that?"

"I think it's great," I said. "He seems different this year. I had my doubts on the first day of school."

Mia rested her head on my shoulder briefly. "Thank you. And he knows if he so much as looks at another girl, or is an ass, he's toast."

Georgia and I busted out laughing. The act for me was exhilarating. I definitely needed to laugh more.

I grasped Mia's small hand. "I'm so happy for you." Grady might have been an asshat, but he was a handsome guy. And if anyone could tame the beast, Mia was the gal to do just that.

"Me too," Georgia piped in.

Mia perked up. "Now my mission is to get you both some boyfriends."

"Good luck with that," I muttered. I wasn't interested in anyone but Colton, and he didn't want a thing to do with me. Besides, he'd sworn off girls. So there was that.

Georgia sat back. "I think we can find our own. At least we know where to find one for Skyler." She giggled.

"You never talked about the night he slept next to you." Mia sounded eager for the details.

"I also never told you I heard you and Grady having sex either."

"What?" both girls asked in unison.

I laughed, and again, it felt liberating. "Harder," I said, trying to emulate the breathy tone Mia had used that morning.

Georgia keeled over, laughing.

"Hey, I like it that way." Mia's tone was so serious that she defied us to argue with her.

I raised my hands. "All I know is I hope one day I'm as free with sex as you. You're my hero."

"Are you mocking me, Skye?" Mia's tone had a hint of playfulness to it.

"Serious as I sit and breathe," I responded.

"If you ever want pointers, I'm your gal."

What I wanted first was for Colton to notice me without a blank look or an angry expression, to talk to me like I wasn't the one who'd crashed his world, and to stop ignoring me as if I had some sort of contagious disease.

14

———

After lunch, the rest of the school day had dragged by like a slow-moving train going nowhere. When the last bell rang, I tore out of the building, hungering for that fresh, cool Southern air that had a myriad of scents—ocean, newly cut grass, and fall flowers that provided a sweetness to the air.

Georgia wheeled into my driveway. "I'm sorry I can't go to the football game tonight. It's family time with Mom and Dad. It's their only day off together."

"No biggie. I want to hang out with Dad, anyway." I could have gone to sit in the stands and watch Colton play and Mia cheerlead, but Mia had told us right before we left school that Colton wasn't playing. He'd asked the coach for a night off. He probably had a thing with his parents, too, though I sort of found that hard to believe. His dad was a martyr.

Georgia flicked her chin at Colton's house. "Is that his dad? He looks just like Colton, only old and weathered."

I giggled at her reference. The man did look as though he'd gotten too much sun when he was younger. "Call me tomorrow. Oh, and say hi to your parents for me." I hopped out and waved as Georgia left.

Since I didn't have my skateboard, Georgia had been my chauffeur. Sure, I could have driven my own car to school, but spots were limited, and frankly, I wanted the company. It had been good to have someone to take my mind off my troubles, and Georgia was just the person to do that. She would ramble on about parties and college and boys, leaving me to daydream out the windshield.

I hesitated before going inside. Colton had said to find him later. I'd taken that to mean at home, but his truck wasn't in the driveway. Maybe he had gone out of town, hence why he wasn't playing football. Or maybe he just didn't come straight home from school.

"Skyler," Mr. Caldwell said. "How are you?"

I couldn't remember the last time Mr. Caldwell had said two words to me. "I'm good." I gripped the straps of my backpack as I crossed the yard in his direction. "Is Colton around? I mean, I don't see his truck, but are you expecting him soon?"

He regarded me with brown eyes I knew all too well as he toked on a cigar and rocked in his chair. "Don't know where my son is. How's your dad?" The cigar smoke billowed around him.

"Fine." That was the easy answer. I was tired of going into detail about Dad's decline. Sometimes I wanted to answer people with, "What do you think? The man is dying of ALS." But I wasn't rude to my elders. "I have to go."

"Skyler." Mr. Caldwell's deep tone scraped my skin, and not in a good way. "Do you know where my son goes at night? He hasn't been coming home until the wee hours of the morning."

I cocked my head so hard my neck kinked. "No, sir." *How would I know?* "Maybe he has a girl-friend." Okay, that shouldn't have come out of my mouth, but it could be the truth, even though Mia had told me he'd sworn off girls. "Or maybe he goes to his friend Grady's house."

"So he's not at your house or in your bed?" he asked.

The man was insane. I didn't know how to respond, and my face had to be contorted.

Thankfully, the screen door squeaked open and Bonnie came out, wiping her hands on her apron. "Arthur." Bonnie gave her husband the look of death. Then she turned to me with an apologetic expression in her soft dark eyes. "I'm sorry. My husband seems to have lost his mind."

My feet were moving way before my lips. "I have to run." And I did, like the freaking wind.

"Awkward" didn't begin to describe that interaction. *In my bed. Where in the fuck did that come from?* I wouldn't have minded if Colton *was* in my bed. But in no way on this planet would I share that with his dad, or even my own.

I flew into the house, huffing.

Nan rushed out of the kitchen. "What happened?" Her gold-rimmed glasses slid down her nose.

I shrugged my backpack off my shoulders, then dropped it on the kitchen floor near the pantry. "Just a weird talk with Mr. Caldwell."

"Is he drunk again?" she asked.

She knew him well too. She'd been up in the middle of the night with me to see him stumble out of his car more than once. I was shocked that the man drove himself home.

I went over to the island and snagged a piece of pork that Nan was getting ready to puree for Dad's dinner. "He seemed sober. He wanted to know if Colton was sleeping with me."

Her small nose wrinkled. "He asked you that?"

Nodding, I shoved another piece of pork into my mouth, savoring the juicy meat. Once I swallowed, I said, "I'm going to see Dad." I needed to shake the thoughts and the creepiness.

She tipped her head toward the sliding glass door. "He's on the deck."

I did a double take. "For real?" The fall weather was turning cooler, and Dad loved that time of year where he could sit outside without feeling like he was frying in the sun.

"He wanted to get some fresh air. He's all tucked into his wheelchair. Oh, and there's a present for you out there too."

"Present?" It wasn't my birthday, so I didn't know who was sending me gifts.

Nan shrugged knowingly.

I was all for presents, but I didn't get excited about them anymore. The only gift I wanted was to hear Dad's voice again, or a cure for ALS.

But the little kid in me ran out. Dad had his face tipped toward the waning, late-afternoon sun. He looked so content.

The present could wait. I circled the wheelchair to lean against the deck rail, facing him. "You look comfy. You need to get out more often."

He gave me a brilliant smile. Then he typed on his computer with his eyes. "It's nice out here. I've always loved the fall."

"You know what we should do is see if we can set up medical transportation to take you to the golf course. You can hang with your buddies."

We weren't fortunate enough to have a van fitted for Dad's wheelchair, but his insurance had given him just about everything else for his ALS.

"I wouldn't mind going to the cemetery to visit your mom's grave," he said.

The last time we'd done that was when he was using a walker. He'd wanted to see her one last time. He didn't know if he would ever get to again. "I would like that too." Dad and I had gone frequently until he was diagnosed with ALS, and neither of us had been since that last time.

"What else would you like to do?" I guessed I should've been asking him that more and more. *Argh!* I'd been so consumed with brooding and crying and freaking out.

"Right now," he typed, "I would like to have that tough conversation with you."

Now that I wasn't moving to California, I felt a little more in control, or at least open, and even excited that I wouldn't be moving away from my friends.

"First, though," he continued, "that came for you." He glanced out at the bench on the other side of the deck.

My skateboard was wrapped in a big green bow. My eyebrows came together as I pondered why Colton hadn't told me it was fixed earlier, but it didn't matter. I could cruise again. *Hallelujah!*

I ran over to it, my pulse soaring as I salivated to take it for a spin. "When did Colton drop this off?" Picking it up, I examined every inch of it. All four wheels appeared new. The red-and-green shark design I'd painted on the bottom seemed to be polished or touched up. I was about to flip it over to run my hand over the top when I spotted some lettering near the wheel that had been mangled: *Colton was here.*

Maybe he didn't hate me after all.

"About an hour ago," came the computer voice.

He must've left school early, or maybe he hadn't had a class last period. Colton and my questions dissipated as I practically hugged my board. I was eager to test it out. It seemed like it had been years since I'd ridden, and I was ready to feel the fall breeze in my face, music in my ears, and get back to catching some air.

As if Dad knew what I was thinking, he typed, "Go. Just be home before dark."

Normally, I would have rushed out without blinking an eye. "Didn't you want to talk?" I set my board down and returned to Dad before dragging a chair next to him.

I held his hand and read the words popping up on the screen as he typed with his eyes.

"I have a letter that I want you to read to me aloud," he said.

"Okay."

At first, I thought he was going to tell me to take his computer, but Nan must've been listening through the screen because she walked out with a piece of paper in her hands. I didn't know what to make of the pensive expression she wore.

I gently took the letter as though it held world-ending secrets.

She sat in one of the other chairs near the round table. "Your dad has asked me to be present when you read what he wrote."

I knitted my brows. She sounded like a lawyer all of a sudden, but I also caught a hint of sadness.

The paper seemed to burn a hole in my fingers, and I wasn't sure if I wanted to read what was on it.

The computer voice said, "It's okay, sweetheart. Nan will help answer some questions for me. She's been well-informed on the situation."

Situation? It didn't sound like she would be my guardian—or maybe she would, since Dad wanted her there.

I took in a breath and began.

15

"'Dear Skyler:

"'I will never forget the look on your mom's face when she laid eyes on you. It was pure perfection—love, adoration, and something far greater than I can articulate. That day was the happiest of our lives. We both cried tears of joy when we finally got to hold you.

"'I wish your mom was here to see how you're growing into a strong individual and a beautiful woman.'"

I stopped reading aloud as my tear ducts turned into Niagara Falls. Dad and Nan cried too. "I'm not sure I can go on," I said.

Nan tucked a stray brown hair behind her ear

and set her glasses higher up on her nose. "Try. It's important that you read the rest."

My vision was blurry, and I didn't see how I could. After one more intake of air, I picked up where I'd left off, when all I wanted to do was get on my skateboard.

"'I've struggled with the right words, on how to tell you. I never knew if there would be a right or wrong time. Your mom and I agreed we would wait until you were a teenager, but then the accident took her from us. After that, I couldn't bring myself to broach the subject, afraid that I would lose you too.

"'And whether this is the right time or not, you need to know. So please find it in your heart to forgive me.'"

Pausing, I rubbed the sharp pain spreading through my chest and checked on Dad. His eyes were closed. Nan, on the other hand, was staring at her lap, or maybe the deck. My gaze drifted past her to Colton's house. I wasn't sure why—maybe to let my brain relax for a second.

Swallowing, I pressed on. "'I will always and forever be your father, but I am not your biological father. Your mom and I adopted you when you were barely a month old.'" I read that last line to myself again, stopping on the word "adopted." I was adopted.

It felt like my jaw came unhinged as the thin piece of paper between my fingers began to shake. I didn't know how to process such shocking news. I read the first four words in the last line again. "Your mom and I." That meant neither Dad nor Mom were my bio parents. In turn, it meant I had another mom and a dad somewhere in the world.

My vision blurred, but not from crying. I was seeing stars. I whipped my head at Dad as a ton of questions hit me all at once. *Who are my mom and dad? Where are they? Why did they give me up?*

He was staring at me, tears flowing freely, with so much sorrow written on his handsome face. Nan seemed to be holding her breath.

I tried to speak, but my tongue wouldn't work. My mom wasn't my mom. My dad wasn't my dad. The two people who had loved and cherished me, who had given me everything I could possibly want, weren't my biological parents. Confusion spiked through me, wound its way into my brain, and stopped on a flashing neon question: *Why didn't my real parents want me?* I didn't know whether to be sad or angry.

Suddenly, I felt numb from head to toe. If someone stuck a knife in me, I wouldn't feel it.

"I'm adopted." It wasn't a question, but a statement to get my mind to unwind the meaning of that word.

Part of me understood why Dad was telling me now. Part of me didn't. Anger simmered deep in my gut about why he hadn't told me years ago. *Then what would you have done?* Whether now or before, nothing would have changed. *You don't know that.*

What I knew was that I loved the man sitting beside me. I loved Mom, God bless her soul. They had both given me a life that was filled with love and devotion. They had given me everything I could have possibly wanted.

They are your real parents.

Yet I was curious about the two people who didn't want me.

Nan cleared her throat. "Skyler, I can see the war going on in your head. Keep reading."

Dad typed on his computer. "If you need a break, I understand. But please know I love you." Then he sobbed, the sound of his crying echoing in the backyard.

My heart broke into a million pieces. I would never doubt his love for me.

I squeezed my eyes shut, my heart racing so hard I swore I was about to pass out. But I had to be strong for him. I could see how hard it was for him to tell me the mind-blowing news.

I stood and wrapped an arm around him as I pressed my cheek to his. "Dad, you'll always be the dad I love. You'll always be my hero. And if I could trade places with you, I would."

Nan broke into a sob. Dad cried even harder.

I was serious. Sure, my mind was blown, but my feelings for him would never change. He was and always would be my superhero, the man who had taught me how to swing a baseball bat, throw a ball, ride a bike... the list went on.

Nan came over, extending her hand. "Why don't I read the rest?"

I shuddered, handing her the letter without any protest since I was having a hard time seeing through my tears.

I sat back down as Nan brought her chair closer to Dad and me.

She swallowed before she began reading. "'Your mom couldn't have kids, and we tried like heck. But after several miscarriages, we finally decided to call it quits and try the adoption route. The process we went through was a closed adoption, so the records were sealed. The only thing we knew at the time was the girl was young when she'd gotten pregnant.

"'When I found out I had ALS,'" Nan continued reading, "'I contacted my lawyer, Mr. Wilson. He'd explained that he could probably get the adoption case reopened since I had a dire medical reason, but that it could take quite a long time. I told him to start the process. If I weren't here then, he knew to contact you. Recently, he was able to get a judge to grant access to your adoption records. I always planned to tell you, sweetheart. And I've been doing some heavy thinking in the last few weeks. I've been so distraught over who would take care of you. I want you to be happy. I want you to make the decision about who you would like to be your guardian in the event I pass before you're eighteen. You mentioned Nan and Georgia's parents, and now you have the option of your birth mom.'"

"Do you know who my birth mom is? Or where she is?"

Mom and Dad had relocated south from New England eighteen years before. Dad had told me his company had relocated him, but I was curious if they chose to move here because of my birth mother. My pulse sped at the thought that she could be living right under my nose. I mean, the town we lived in wasn't that big.

Dad glanced at Nan.

"Mr. Wilson hasn't located her yet. However, if or when you decide you want to learn more, we can contact Mr. Wilson," Nan said.

Dad typed, "Skyler, I love you so darn much, and your happiness means everything to me. No matter what you decide, I will always be your dad. I've loved you from the moment I saw you, and I will go to my grave with all that love in my heart."

I popped out of my chair and threw myself at the man who had given me everything. "I love you so, so much. I have no idea how I'll survive without you. But I know one day I'll see you and Mom again when the three of us are flying with the angels." The words tumbled free as if I were saying my last words to him. I knew it killed him not to have told me before now, and I couldn't let him think I would just drop him without a thought because he didn't father me.

Dad's shoulders shook as he cried. My heart

splintered into a trillion little pieces, and I couldn't help but sob.

Nan came over and held Dad's hand. "Randall, rest assured, I will be here for Skyler no matter what she decides."

I flung myself at Nan, "Thank you."

"You're special, Skyler. You're like a daughter to me."

Dad and I had been lucky in finding Nan. I hugged her as tightly as I could. "I love you." If not for her, Dad would probably be in a nursing home, and I would probably be living with my aunt or in foster care. He'd come close to making the decision of a nursing facility. He'd had three caregivers prior to Nan, but they hadn't been committed to living with us.

She kissed me on the temple. "Right back at you."

A cool breeze blew, picking up dead leaves from the pear tree that hung over the fence from Colton's yard.

Nan let go of me. "We should probably get your dad inside. It's dinner time, and there's a chill in the air."

He typed, "One more thing, Skyler. I would like you to make a decision on your guardian soon.

I need to take Aunt Clara out of the trust. Mr. Wilson wants to make sure we have the paperwork in order before I go. Otherwise, my sister might be forced to take care of you, and with her new job, I would rather not put her or you in a tough spot."

Nan handed me the letter. "So don't take too long."

I heaved a sigh as I neatly folded Dad's written words. I had two choices—Nan or Georgia's parents. I wasn't about to live with a woman I didn't know, blood or not. *So what if she gave birth to me? She didn't want me seventeen years ago. Why would she now?*

Nan engaged the attendant control wheel on the back of Dad's wheelchair.

"I don't have to think," I blurted out. "I want Nan to be my guardian."

Nan's expression was a mixture of happiness and hesitation. "Are you sure? You don't want to reach out to your birth mother?"

Dad studied me, eagerly waiting for me to answer.

I tucked the letter in the front pocket of my shorts. "Doesn't matter if I do or don't. You're more family to me than she is." The woman who'd carried me for nine months was a stranger. "This house is mine when Dad goes. And I want to stay in it. I want you to stay here too." Nan wasn't married. She didn't have a boyfriend. Her only family was her mom, who lived in Arizona. Her dad had died of cancer many years before—that was how she'd become a caregiver. She'd taken care of her father alongside her mom, and she'd "gotten the bug," as she told Dad and me.

"Let's just sleep on it," Dad said. "See how you feel in the morning."

I didn't think I would change my mind, but I nodded. It wouldn't hurt to see how I felt in the morning.

I thought to ask about my bio father, but I didn't want Dad to feel awkward or make him feel even worse than he already did.

Nan drove Dad up the ramp and into the house.

I collected my skateboard, feeling somewhat lighter now that a major decision had been made. But with one problem gone, I had another one to noodle on.

16

Oranges and reds blazed through the sky. The cemetery glowed like something out of a watercolor painting. Sweet-scented flowers graced carved headstones far and wide as the fragrance floated on a light breeze.

Sometimes, sitting in front of Mom's grave took me to another place—peaceful, tranquil, no worries, no problems, and just a wonderful sense of belonging.

I wiped off the ledge of her headstone before placing a single yellow rose I'd cut from our yard on top. I tried not to visit without one. Roses and maple trees had been her favorites, and Dad had picked out her plot specifically because of the maple swaying nearby.

"Mom," I said out loud, "I miss you so much. I wish you were here to guide me through what I'm about to face. To help me navigate this crazy time with Dad and the shocking news that I was adopted."

The leaves swished together, and I took it as a wishful sign that maybe she was with me. If she was, she would have said, "Skyler, you're tough. You're brave, and you can get through anything."

I didn't have her confidence. I didn't consider myself the least bit strong. I'd barely handled her death. She'd been taken from us in a blink of an eye, and now I was watching my other parent wither away, limb by limb and muscle by muscle.

At least I was getting the time to say goodbye to Dad. I'd never had that chance with Mom. That fateful morning, she'd left work before I'd even gotten out of bed.

I didn't know what was worse, watching Dad erode or enduring Mom's instant death. I swore, with each day that passed, it felt like someone was plucking my heart out, one tiny piece at a time, and I was dying with him.

I closed my eyes, clasped my hands in front of

me, and prayed. I mainly prayed for Dad, that he didn't suffer or experience pain. I prayed he would be around another couple of years or three or five, although he didn't have much of a life. I knew he was fighting as hard as he could for me. But I didn't want to let him go. I didn't want to think of a future without him.

"God, if you're listening, please take care of my dad, and make sure he goes peacefully. While you're at it, can you also find a cure for ALS? I know my dad won't see a cure, but for all those people who will come after him."

I blinked away tear after tear as I glanced up at the beautiful painted sky, looking for some sort of sign that God had heard me. All I got was a rush of air from a hard wind that blew out of nowhere.

I ran my fingertips over Mom's name. Candace Lawson: mother, wife, and a woman who had put her heart and soul before anyone else's.

Her name began to blur as my thoughts took a sudden shift to Dad's letter. *"I will always and forever be your father, but I am not your biological father. Your mom and I adopted you when you were just a newborn."*

I wasn't ready to know my birth mother or even

my biological father. Heck, I wasn't even ready to deal with the fact that I was adopted. Yet I had so many damn questions. *Why did she give me up? What does she look like? Where is my father? Are they married? Do they have other kids? Does she think about me?*

My stomach twisted at the notion that my own birth mother had carried me for nine months, then given me away.

A salty tear slid into my mouth as I replayed the scene on the deck with Dad and Nan. I knew it had been difficult for him to break the news to me, and I believed he'd died a little more inside.

My gut was telling me he was getting close to joining Mom. Frankly, I believed he was still here because he had unfinished business to take care of, and as soon as those things were in order, he would finally give in to his fate.

My phone chirped in the peaceful air, making me flinch. I plucked the annoying thing out of my back pocket, and when I did, Dad's letter fell to the ground. I went to grab it when a hard wind blew, taking the letter with it.

Fuck! I flew to my feet as if an invisible being had picked me up. I chased the letter as though it would save my life.

But the wind held the letter in its grasp, blowing it across the cemetery.

I dodged stone angels and other religious figures, more gravestones, a dying wreath, and several trees. I couldn't lose that letter. I ran like a gazelle, darting in one direction then the other as the wind seemed to be playing with me, a game of tag like the ones I'd played at recess in elementary school.

The wind died, and the letter floated to the ground. I reached out to grab it when the universe said, "No, Skyler, you can't have it just yet." I was again chasing Dad's heartfelt words, attempting not to kill myself by face-planting on concrete or falling into the empty grave that loomed ahead.

I looked down for a split second and plowed into what felt like stone but was really a solid wall of muscle. I stumbled back and glanced up at the most beautiful creature, who had graced my dreams and psyche for the last month.

Colton bent down and plucked the letter from under his Nike. He examined the piece of paper. "This must contain secrets for you to almost kill yourself." His raspy Southern drawl wrapped me in gooey warmth.

He had no idea. I huffed and puffed to regulate

my breathing as I snatched the letter from him before he thought to open it. "Thank you."

I pinched the letter in my grasp so tightly that someone would need a chisel to pry it out of my hands. I was afraid even to shove it in my pocket, in case I lost it for good if the wind wanted to mess with me again.

Colton studied my hand, his expression loaded with questions.

I had a few of my own. I opened my mouth to ask, and then noticed the name Caldwell on the gravestone to my right. A twisted part of me was hoping he'd been following me, just not in a creepy way.

Two beats passed as our gazes tangled, knotted, and molded. He was sucking me into his brown depths, and I felt like I was falling into a vat of chocolate—warm, sweet, and delicious.

Shivers trailed down my spine, and air seemed to be nonexistent. He had a way of making me feel things I'd never felt before. He also had a way of making me a pile of mush.

I watched him watch me, my heart beating a staccato rhythm that I was afraid he could hear, since we were almost toe-to-toe. Dead foliage kicked up around us, as did his scent—a concoction of rich earth whipped together with floral accents and topped with a spoonful of sugar that seeped into every vein, relaxing me, exciting me.

"What are you doing here?" he asked, breaking the trance he had me in.

"I could ask you the same thing." As the drunken haze Colton had put me into wore off, I noticed the whites of his eyes were red. Maybe it was the glow of dusk that streaked the horizon.

His chin ticked up, setting his jaw in place as though he was ready to do battle. "I'm not stalking you. I was here first."

At least I could get a glimpse of his emotions rather than his usual blank mask, and his tone screamed annoyance.

I laughed for no other reason than to quiet my pulse. The guy was imposing, intimidating, and downright gorgeous. His biceps peeked through his Deer Run Academy T-shirt, the sleeves frayed on the edges. His hair was seemingly damp, either from sweat or a recent shower, and his ripped jeans hung low on his hips. His square belt buckle glistened in the waning daylight.

He folded his arms over his impressive chest. "What's so funny?"

Me. My thoughts. My crazy idea that we're alone

in a cemetery with no one else around but the dead.
Wouldn't it be odd, cool, nuts, to make out among the
dead? Okay, I'm losing my mind.

Images of him pressing me up against the tree
behind him, trailing his lush lips down my neck,
and feeling his body against mine played out in
my head. I puffed out my cheeks, not knowing
what to say next until my gaze wandered to the
headstone. That time, I zeroed in on the full name
—Josh Caldwell.

He followed my line of sight, his body going
ramrod straight as though I'd invaded a private
moment.

I guessed I had, but not intentionally. "I'm
sorry for your loss."

A muscle ticked in his jaw.

My heart severed in half, but that time for
him and not for my own depressing life. "I'm
also sorry for being insensitive at Grady's
house the other day. I chose the wrong word."
As in drowning. I didn't want to say that word
again.

His shoulders rose to his earlobes.

"I also wanted to thank you."

His head turned, but he kept his focus on the
ground.

"Georgia told me you rescued me before I dove into the ocean that night."

That muscle in his jaw was still jumping. I had no doubt he was thinking of his brother. And while I knew little about his brother's death except that he'd drowned, my gut was telling me Colton had been there when the ocean swallowed up Josh.

We stood together in the quiet of the landscape with only the sound of the restless trees.

My hand was on the move before my brain thought about what to say next. When my small palm was in his larger one, he squeezed with all he had.

Pain zipped up my arm, but I wasn't about to complain. He needed a friend, and I was more than happy to help, to allow him to shed some grief. In a weird sort of way, I believed our souls were tangled together, maybe because we were the only ones standing among the dead. I mean, the wind blew that letter out of my hands for a reason—to help Colton.

The longer we were tethered together, the more my pulse sprinted like a runner who was primed to win an Olympic gold medal.

"My mom died in a car accident," I whispered.

I'd told him I'd lost my mom, but I didn't remember if I'd mentioned how she died.

His grip grew tighter, if that was possible. Still, I didn't flinch or make a sound. Instead, my heart bloomed with warmth.

"I shouldn't have come home," he said so quietly that I wasn't sure I'd heard him. "I should've stayed away." That time, his voice was a rumble louder, the circulation in my hand nonexistent.

I winced, letting out a weak grunt.

He dropped my hand quicker than I could track. Then he roughed his fingers through his wavy locks, something he did when his emotions were tearing him apart. "Stay away from me, Skyler. I'm not a good person."

I barely shook off the proverbial bucket of cold water that had been dumped on my head when he pivoted on his heels and stormed away.

I wanted to tell him he was a great guy. I wanted to tell him that things would get better, that his loss would not hurt as much in time. But that would've been a lie. Mom's death still gutted me as strongly as when she'd died three years ago. "Colton."

He stopped next to a black marble headstone

half his size, his shoulders rising so high they almost reached above his ears.

"What if I don't want to stay away from you?" The words tumbled free, and I felt a little lighter for finally speaking my mind.

"You have no choice," he tossed out. "I'm not interested in you."

His words punched me in the stomach, knocking out whatever air I had remaining in my lungs. "I meant as a friend." *Liar.*

"I don't need a friend." He marched off, leaving me with my mouth hanging open and my ego black and blue.

My phone beeped, reminding me that someone had called me earlier. I imagined it was Georgia, or maybe Nan. Then the thought that something had happened to Dad briefly cleared any remnants of Colton.

I fumbled to answer it, careful not to let the letter fly off again. "Nan, is Dad okay?" He'd been fine when I left, but that didn't mean a thing.

"Calm down. He's watching TV," she said. "But he's asking when you'll be home. I'm sure he wants to see if you're okay too. What he told you is a lot to take in."

The breath that escaped was one of complete

relief. "I'm good." In part I was, except Colton was occupying my thoughts again. "I'm headed home now."

I followed Colton's path, but by the time I reached the road where my car was parked, he was nowhere in sight. Probably for the best, even though my body was protesting along with my hurt ego.

17

———————

I couldn't sleep. Thrashing around and kicking the covers off me as my mind spun out of control was becoming a habit.

I hadn't had a chance to dwell on my birth parents. Sure, the whole idea of being adopted wasn't going away, but no matter how I picked apart the questions I had, I wouldn't get any answers unless I contacted my birth mom. Even then, I had no guarantees that she would want to talk to me. Besides, Mr. Wilson, Dad's lawyer, hadn't located her yet.

I had plenty to ponder as I lay in bed, staring at the time on my ceiling and trying to make sense of the boy next door who had hijacked my brain for most of the night. He had a way of pushing all my other problems aside and saying, "Here I am."

At three in the morning, I was analyzing our conversation in the cemetery.

"I don't need friends. I'm not interested in you."

The latter stuck like superglue, and I wondered what was wrong with me. I considered myself to be in great shape. Nice chest—not huge, but the right size for my body. He probably agreed with Grady that I looked like a boy.

Maybe Mia was onto something when she'd said I should dress in a sexy outfit. Maybe then Colton would do a double take.

Guy problems. Argh.

I wondered if sex was the key, the lure, the magic potion to get a guy to like me. It had worked for Mia. My belly flipped at the idea of having sex with Colton.

How would it feel to have his muscled body on top of me? To have his lips all over me, everywhere? To run my hands through his hair? To feel the dips and valleys of his abs, wrap my hand around his erection or even...

I pushed out an exasperated sigh as that throbbing ache in between my legs roared awake. Closing my eyes, I dipped my fingers into my panties before finding that swollen sweet spot, and as soon as my finger grazed over it, my hips shot upward as I moaned.

Stella jumped off the bed.

Suddenly, I felt like I was doing something wrong. But sex wasn't wrong. It was a basic human need. I circled my nub, chills skating down my legs, my belly beginning to tighten in a sensuous knot. I pictured Colton naked as my limbs relaxed and the sensation built, growing stronger the more I continued to play with myself.

But my ecstasy was short-lived when a loud boom pierced the night.

I jolted upright, listening intently as I sought the baseball bat I kept in the corner behind the door.

A breath of silence fell until glass shattered.

I shot off the bed and over to the front window in my room. Maybe Mr. Caldwell had dropped a bottle as he got out of his car.

Stella meowed from somewhere nearby.

No sign of movement outside.

Another loud noise made me jump. I ran over to get the bat but stopped short when the light in Colton's room caught my eye. I blinked once, then twice to make sure I wasn't seeing things. Then my hand flew to my mouth just as he drove his fist into his wall.

A second later, Mr. Caldwell stormed in like a category-five hurricane, his hand primed to wield it at his son, and he did just that.

Colton stood there and took blow after blow from his father as if more than happy to be a human punching bag.

I felt like I had toothpicks holding my eyelids open. I really should have looked away, gone back to bed, or done anything other than watch a father beat his son.

Why isn't Colton fighting back? What is wrong with his dad? He was evil.

The man took another crack at his son's jaw, and again Colton endured the wrath until his dad went to deliver yet another blow. Colton stopped him as shouting ensued. It was so loud, I felt like I was in the room with them. Then again, his window had a hole in it. I guessed that was the glass-breaking sound I'd heard.

"That's the last time you'll ever hit me," Colton said.

It was either rage or drunkenness or both, but Colton's statement fell on deaf ears as his dad punched him again.

Colton ducked that time.

Blue lights cut through the swath of darkness between our houses.

I zipped over to my other window just as Nan appeared in the doorway.

"Skyler, what's going on?" Her voice was sleepy.

I pointed to the window closest to her. "A family feud. I think the cops are here."

Wisps of her brown hair fell out of her hairband as she looked over at the Caldwell house. "Oh my. I should check on your dad." She hurried out.

I was sure Dad was awake but fine. His room was on the same side as mine, so he probably heard too. It was impossible not to.

A cop car pulled into the Caldwells' driveway. Either Bonnie had called them, or a neighbor had. Two men in blue got out, one tall, the other short. Both scanned the area as they disappeared from view.

I leaned against my wall and waited, biting my nails as I did.

Stella slinked over and rubbed against my bare leg.

"I know, girl. Crazy night."

After ten quiet minutes, the cops got back into the cruiser sans Mr. Caldwell or Colton.

I tiptoed over to the other window facing Colton's room, my nerves on edge, hoping and praying that he was all right. As if he knew I was watching, his head swiveled in my direction.

I waved like an idiot, not sure if he could see me.

For the longest beat, he just stood there, blood under his nose, hair disheveled, jaw hard, and his eyes were riveted to me until something made him flinch. Then he started piling clothes into a bag. His movements were violent, rushed, and frantic.

He'd said he wasn't a good person, but I didn't believe that. He could've hit his father, but he didn't. Instead, he took each blow stoically and without flinching. I wasn't saying that made him a good person, but in my mind, he had a heart.

He gave his room a once-over before hiking his bag over his shoulder. *Oh my God.* He was leaving. Surely, his parents wouldn't throw him out in the middle of the night.

For whatever reason, my birth mother popped into my brain. I knew giving me up for adoption wasn't the same as Colton's predicament. Yet I was beginning to understand the feeling of not being wanted.

I watched the guy who had wriggled his way into my heart and psyche walk out his door.

I sprinted down the stairs as if on a mission to stop a bomb from detonating. A door slammed, shaking the walls of our house. I raced out my front door and onto the porch just as Colton stalked toward his truck.

His mom chased him. "Son, please don't go. Let's talk," she cried.

"Mom." Colton's tone was caustic. "I need some space, and so does he." He stuck a finger at his house. "The cops should've taken his drunk ass to jail."

I wondered for a second why they hadn't. Colton was a minor as far as I knew, or maybe he was eighteen. I honestly didn't know, and it didn't matter.

"Where will you go?" She hugged her herself as she wavered on the top step of her porch.

I slinked into the shadows and out of the rays of the porch light.

"Grady's," he said as the *beep, beep, beep* of his truck unlocking blared in the quietness of the humid night air.

Bonnie wiped her face with a tissue as she returned inside, seemingly giving up on her son.

I knew I shouldn't be sticking my nose where it didn't belong, but he didn't need to go to Grady's.

I was walking down the steps before I could think. "Colton." My voice was barely audible.

He whirled my way.

I waved as I stood rooted to the bottom step, afraid that if I moved, he might blow me over with one stern look or that annoying blank expression.

He threw his bag inside his truck, and for a mere second, I thought he was about to get in until he came toward me with his fists at his sides, hair wild around his face, bloody nose, and probably a bruised jaw.

His sense of purpose was both unnerving and exciting, and his body language was screaming that he could kill or devour all that pent-up rage he'd bottled up.

I held my breath, searching for words that I was sure wouldn't come, and if they did, they wouldn't make sense.

He towered over me like an ethereal gorgeous creature, and *poof*, I forgot the reason I was even outside in the dead of night.

My witless brain decided to take a nap. My

body, though, was a completely different story. Every vein in me was burning with a pulsing need for him to do things I had yet to do in my teenage years. My fingers twitched to run through his hair or feel how soft his lips might be.

His gaze took a long, slow, and sensual hike up and down my body.

My nipples hardened instantly, poking against the thin fabric of my tank top. Suddenly, my heart kicked into an all-out sprint. I wasn't wearing a bra, and I was standing outside in only a pair of short shorts beneath my top.

I should have covered myself, but when his eyes landed on my chest, I became an ice sculpture. My breathing increased. My lower region ached, and out of nowhere, a dose of bravery hit me, and my hands were on his chest, sliding up, up, and up.

For a moment, he didn't react in any way. Not until my fingers touched his lips did his hands shoot out and grip my hips.

A strong electrical charge blasted through me and straight to the spot that I'd been playing with earlier. If sex was what he needed to forget his troubles, I wouldn't protest. *I mean, isn't that what friends did for each other?*

He doesn't want to be friends.

He lifted me up, and I squealed, my eyes colliding with his. That blank mask he'd always worn came down, and behind it was something I wasn't prepared for—hunger.

My legs wound around his waist as though they had a mind of their own.

He moaned or growled. I honestly couldn't tell because my pulse was pounding so loudly in my ears that I couldn't hear much else.

He carried me to my doorstep, searching my face, seemingly snapping picture after picture.

Call me crazy, but his dick was stone beneath me. I tightened my hold around him, hoping he got the message not to let me go. I wasn't sure I could stand, anyway. With my luck, my legs would give out the moment my feet were on the ground.

Then his lips grazed my ear. "You need to stop getting under my skin, Skyler. I have a lot of control, but every time I look at you, I want to lose that control."

I gasped, clinging to him like he was my lifeline. I wasn't sure how to respond. He was right— he had self-restraint. He'd let his dad beat him and hadn't reacted. But the way he was suddenly nibbling on my ear told me that control of his was something far different than unleashing any anger.

"Stay here tonight," I whispered in a breathy tone.

He tensed, his lips on my ear. "In your bed?"

God, yes. "You can sleep on the couch."

"I don't think that's a good idea," he whispered. "My control is ready to snap."

"Then let it snap, Colton."

He dragged his scruffy jaw along mine, his lips never touching my face. I was tempted to turn so our mouths would meet, but maybe he was right. Nan was probably wondering where I was or watching, although her view was probably obscured since Colton and I were against the front door.

"I'm going to put you down now," he said reluctantly. "Then I'm going to get in my truck."

I pouted but said nothing as I slid down every inch of his hard body. He groaned when my stomach grazed his erection.

I closed my eyes for a second, absorbing all of him, and when I was on two feet and shaky legs, I flattened my palm on his jaw. "You're a good person, Colton Caldwell." I had other words on my brain, but they escaped me.

He leaned into my touch. "No, I'm not." He took one step back, his gaze never wavering from mine. He was allowing me to see so much emotion —restraint, desire, anger, and sadness. Then he blinked, breaking our connection, and just like that, he was walking away.

I gnawed on my lip, my legs trembling, my body screaming for him to come back. He didn't have to worry about his control. I was sure I would lose mine too.

As his engine faded, I snuck into the house and ran right into Nan.

She stood with her arms crossed, looking out the window in the family room. "Is Colton okay?"

I lifted a shoulder, my body singing and heated. "I don't know." He was a dichotomy between his words and his actions.

"He likes you, you know."

I snorted. "He says he's not interested."

She half grinned. "I'm sure that isn't true. I saw how he was looking at you when you were on the steps."

I hoped she was right, but for the time being, my body was on fire, and there was only one way to douse the flames. So I ran up to my room to finish what I'd started earlier.

18

———————

The sweltering late Saturday morning sun mingled with a few wispy clouds. The September weather felt like the middle of July—hot and humid. The only difference was that the beach wasn't as crowded. Tourists had packed up and gone home not long after Labor Day.

Sinking my feet into the sand, I scanned the immediate vicinity. The tide was low, and the waves slid along the sandy shore like a conductor leading an orchestra through Beethoven's Symphony No. 2. Mom came to mind as I searched for Georgia among the handful of beachgoers who lounged on blankets and in chairs.

Mom had loved classical music, and I'd often

found her listening to a symphony while she sketched on the back porch, absorbed in her craft as a way to unwind and relax.

I did one last pass, not seeing Georgia. Her text that morning had said to meet at the beach. Maybe I'd read it wrong. Hiking my bag higher on my shoulder, I opened the text app on my phone.

Georgia: *Beach. Noon. Be there.*

I didn't misinterpret her message. "Beach" meant our usual spot. It always had. I checked the time. I was five minutes early. Maybe she was running late.

I was primed to text Georgia when a little boy squealed. "Mom, look at my sandcastle. Isn't it awesome?"

With the nod, the mom acknowledged the blond-haired tyke before she resumed reading.

I couldn't help but remember when Dad and I would build sandcastles.

Don't you dare cry, Skyler Lawson.

My phone rang, distracting me from the emotions that wanted to break free.

"Where are you?" Georgia shouted in my ear.

I scratched my neck. "What? I'm at our usual spot."

"Yikes. Didn't I text you to meet on the beach in front of Grady's?"

"Um, that's a fat no. Why Grady's?" Colton was there, and I wasn't ready to see him, but the butterflies in my stomach said otherwise. Truth be told, I was anxious to see how we would react to each other after our intimate and intense encounter on my porch. I was curious if he would blow me off as if nothing had happened or if he would act awkward. I knew I would do just that.

"Shit. Sorry. My mom and I got into it about something stupid, and I spaced. Just get your cute butt down here. Mia and I are hanging."

"Is anyone else with you?" I couldn't see Colton lounging on the beach with Mia and Georgia unless Grady was with him. Even then, Colton didn't strike me as the type to lie on the beach.

She snorted. "If you're asking about Colton, then yes. He's here, but he and Grady are playing pool in the game room."

"Maybe I should bag out today." As soon as the words dribbled from my mouth, I knew I was in trouble.

In true Georgia fashion, her voice sounded like a bomb going off in my ear. "Like hell you will. If I have to come get you and drag you by the arm, I will. And you'll want to hear what I learned, anyway. Before you ask, it does involve you. So chop chop." Then the line went dead.

I couldn't even begin to think of what she'd heard. So much had happened in the last eighteen hours. I'd found out I was adopted. I'd witnessed a father beating his son. And above all else, I'd had not one, but two moments with Colton.

Georgia and Mia were about to get an earful, unless Colton had overheard that I was adopted. After all, I'd been on our deck when I read the letter. But if he had, and he'd told Georgia, she would've been at my house the second she found out.

Ten minutes later, I was dropping my mesh bag, which had my towel and wallet inside, on Georgia's sun-kissed stomach.

She sat up. "What the..." She removed her sunglasses, squinting up at me, ready to break my nose. "You're lucky this isn't heavy." She tossed my bag on the sand.

"That's for sending me to the wrong location." Playfulness weaved through my words.

She rolled her big green eyes as she rested back on her elbows. "You love me."

No question about that.

Mia popped up from her spot next to Georgia and adjusted a strap on her white bikini top, which was blinding against her tanned skin. "Took you long enough."

I threw both of them the finger.

A laugh bounced around as the three of us giggled. I snagged the striped towel big enough to be a blanket from my bag and spread it next to Georgia. Then I shimmied out of my frayed denim shorts and my black tank top.

Mia tried to whistle. "Girl, Colton is going to drool over those sculpted abs."

A blush stained my cheeks as I stole a look at the whitewashed mansion behind us. Colton had seen me in my tiny top and sleep shorts with no bra, so I guessed a bikini wasn't any different.

"She's right," Georgia said. "Colton will not be able to take his eyes off you." She sighed. "I wish I could find someone who made me all wet and gooey."

I sat cross-legged on my towel, facing both of them.

Mia tilted her head at Georgia, and when she did, thick strands of her brown hair fell from her hair clip. "I could arrange something for you."

Georgia straightened and picked up the bottle of sunscreen next to her. "Thanks, but no thanks." She proceeded to lather the lotion on her shoulders and chest, careful not to get any on her red swim top. "I'll pick my own." Her voice was a tad sad.

I knew she was thinking of Kyle, a guy with hair as dark as night and eyes the color of the shores off Bora Bora. Sadly for Georgia, Kyle had only been a fleeting crush. He was a tourist who had spent the summer in one of the rental homes in town. They really hadn't done much beyond groping, but he'd stolen her heart much like Colton had mine.

I reached out and touched her thigh. "You should text him."

She capped the top of the sunscreen. "Nope." Her resolve was strong. "Kyle is dead to me."

Mia and I swapped a pained look for our dear friend.

"Skye, care to dish about why Colton is talking to Grady about you?" Mia changed the subject quite quickly.

I could feel my eyebrows dipping down. "He told Grady about last night?"

Georgia's somber expression disappeared into

the salt air as she reared back, her smile galvanizing. "You had sex with Colton?"

Mia whipped off her sunglasses. "'Bout time. How was it?"

With my hands, I gave them a coach's time-out signal. "Slow your roll, you two." I quickly glanced at Grady's house just to be sure Colton wasn't lurking—or Grady, for that matter. We were far enough away that they couldn't hear our conversation even if they were outside. "I wish. But we did have a moment. A very sexy one." I had a permanent blush, which wasn't going away as long as we kept talking about Colton.

Georgia adjusted her bikini top around her breasts, checking to make sure her ladies weren't falling out. She had Mia and me beat in the chest department. "Start from the beginning."

Automatically, I, too, checked my swim top. I was a bit self-conscious ever since they'd fallen out one summer at the water park.

Georgia tapped my leg. "Details."

"Wait," I said. "What did you learn that involved me?" Obviously, it wasn't about my sexy moment with Colton. *So what did he tell Grady?*

Georgia exchanged a somber look with Mia.

My nerves perked up. Maybe he'd told Grady

he'd gotten laid. Friends did tell friends that, and in some cases, they lied about it.

"Don't deflect," Georgia said so seriously. "Spill your guts about that sexy man."

Mia and Georgia leaned in, salivating for all the juicy details.

"I'm adopted." I wanted to start there rather than give them a play-by-play of Colton and me. I would tell them eventually, but right now, I had to get the adoption news off my chest.

Shock slammed into Georgia's expression, then volleyed to Mia, whose chin hit her bright orange towel.

Georgia's wide eyes were glued to me. "What the fuck? For real?"

I picked sand off my ankle. "It's true. My dad told me yesterday."

"You don't seem freaked out," Mia said.

I hiked one shoulder up to my ear. "I'm still processing." I didn't know how to unpack my feelings on the topic.

Georgia rubbed her lips together. "I have no words."

My eyebrows climbed to my hairline. "Now that is a shocker." A light, playful tease colored my tone. Usually my BFF always had something to say, even if she was caught off guard.

"I don't know whether to say sorry or... I don't know. That had to be extremely hard for your dad to tell you," Georgia said.

My head started bobbing like an idle boat riding the waves. "He was gutted. It broke my heart. One of the reasons I'm not ready to deal with the whole adoption thing. I feel if I do, I'm hurting him. He deserves to be as happy as he can be with the time he has left. The good news is that Nan is going to be my guardian."

Georgia clapped and squealed. "That's great news. That means you don't have to move."

"Exactly," I said as movement caught my eye on Grady's deck.

Georgia and Mia both looked behind them.

Colton sauntered down shirtless, wearing royal-blue swim trunks low on his hips. I wished I'd worn sunglasses so he couldn't see me drooling —that prominent V disappearing into his swim trunks was making me squeeze my thighs together.

Grady stopped him, and they chatted.

Mia pressed her lips into a thin line. "Colton's father is a monster."

I bobbed my head. With Colton in close proximity, I didn't want to give them all the details. Colton's nose had been bloody, but I was curious if he had black eyes. "I couldn't agree with you more."

"Aside from his split lip and bruised jaw, Colton seems different," Georgia said.

"No black eyes?" I asked.

"None." Mia sighed as though she was relieved for Colton. "And he's different because of our pretty friend here." She smiled at me.

My stomach hollowed. "What?"

Georgia leaned into me. "That's what we want to tell you. Mia overheard Colton talking to Grady this morning. Your name came up."

Oh, this I had to hear. My gaze burned a hole into Mia.

She scooted closer and whispered, "Colton said that if it weren't for you, he might have driven into a tree last night."

I scrunched my nose. "Come again?"

"Apparently, after his fight with his dad, he was so mad he couldn't see straight. He told Grady you were the one who brought him down off the ledge," Mia said.

"Huh." I had no other words, but my stomach

churned like a storm in rough seas, my pulse unsteady. If I hadn't run out of the house to stop him from leaving... *holy shit! What if I'd woken up that day and Colton was gone?* Surely he hadn't been thinking of harming or killing himself. *No. No. No.*

Georgia's gaze latched onto mine. "Don't go there."

"How can I not?" My hands trembled.

"Skye," Mia said softly. "He's here. And he has Grady and us."

She rubbed my leg. "Mia's right. He's got us and you. What did you say to him?"

I eyed Colton, who was still chatting with Grady. They seemed to be in a serious convo. Maybe Grady was knocking some sense into him. "I asked him to stay at my house, and before I knew what was happening, I was in his arms. Then he said some things about his control being ready to snap around me."

Mia's expression lightened as she gave me a cheeky grin. "You need to make the first move. Sometimes guys don't know how to."

"Says my sex therapist." I laughed, but it was laden with nerves.

Georgia giggled, followed by Mia, and just like that, the tension and despair snapped.

"She's right," Georgia said. "And sounds to me like he wants you badly."

If he did, he had an odd way of showing it. In one breath, he'd told me to stay away from him. In another, he was ready to eat me whole.

Grady's voice cut through my Colton problem as he and Colton finally drew near.

"We'll talk later," I said. My pulse was on a fast-moving train whenever Colton approached.

19

Bending over, Grady kissed Mia on the head, then whispered something in her ear that made her cheeks flush. I was speechless. I had never seen Grady so loving before.

In contrast, Colton tucked his hands into the pockets of his swim trunks and stared out at the Atlantic, not looking at me or anyone. He seemed as though someone had shocked him into silence, and I was silently pointing the finger at myself. Nevertheless, his bottom lip was swollen, and he did have a bruised jaw. The area around his eyes was pinched, but I didn't see any discoloring.

The tension skyrocketed into the clear blue sky. Good thing we were out in the open air, where oxygen was in great supply. Otherwise, if we were in a closed room with no windows or a way out, I would've been laboring for breath.

Grady got comfortable behind Mia, kicking out his strong legs and big feet. The dude was a giant. "Lawson, where's your skateboard?" His tone was nice and even and didn't hold the animosity it usually did when he spoke to me.

If I hadn't been with Georgia and Mia, I would have thought I was in some alternate universe. Or maybe Mia had trained him well.

I narrowed my eyes at the blond QB. "Not here." My tone held a smidge of sarcasm. It was hard to shuck the snarky attitude with Grady. It didn't help that I was on edge.

Grady glared daggers at me with those blue eyes of his. He went to open his mouth, but Mia clutched his thigh as though she could sense him about to spew a retort.

It didn't matter if he did. I was ready to spar if Grady wanted to. Maybe that would jar Colton from his frozen state for good. He snuck a look at me for a split second before he resumed his soldier position, as though he was guarding Buckingham Palace.

My stomach twisted and twined in an overpowering need to shout at Colton, to fracture that wall he'd built around him. To hell with swapping words with Grady. Colton needed a jolt of something. Sadly, I didn't have the nerve to be the one to shake him back to reality.

I couldn't believe how he'd changed since the first day of school, when he'd been kind and nice. *He hit you with his truck. He had to be nice.* I knew the fights with his dad were one cause of his darkness, but I also believed I'd played a part in his crankiness.

After all, he'd said, "You need to stop getting under my skin, Skyler. I have a lot of control, but every time I look at you, I want to lose that control."

It was clear by the tension in his shoulders that he was hanging on by a thread, and amid the host of emotions thrumming through me, pity stood out. But I didn't want to feel sorry for him because I didn't like when others did that to me. Mia and Georgia had been great in taking my mind off Dad and showing me how much they loved me. Colton needed someone who could do the same. I would gladly step up, and I'd tried, but he didn't want a friend, and he wasn't interested in me. His words, not mine. I took comfort in knowing he had Grady.

Georgia's gaze darted to the ocean, then back to me as if she was trying to save me from a downward spiral. My BFF knew me so freaking well. It was time to let the cold water from the Atlantic jar me out of my Colton haze and kick-start my heart.

I stood slowly, just in case the trembling in my legs got worse and made me collapse. Hell, I would probably fall just from the warm breeze blowing.

Grady was saying something in Mia's ear again, and given how she leaned back into him with the shyest of looks, I suspected it was both mushy and rated R.

Yeah, I was not ready to watch the show Mia and Grady were about to put on. Once on my feet, I adjusted my bikini bottom so my ass cheeks weren't hanging out.

I was waiting for a jab or snark from Grady, but nothing came. Maybe he was changing.

Georgia hopped up. "I'll come with."

As we headed down to the shore, Georgia glanced behind her. "Colton is watching you or checking you out."

A slight shiver blanketed me, and I was afraid to look. "Is he still in soldier form?"

"He's sitting on the sand."

"I hope he's okay," I said as the waves broke over our feet. The cold water was a welcome relief to both my skin and my torn emotions.

Georgia walked into the water until she was waist deep. "He will be. Grady talked to him in depth, according to Mia."

I followed her through the surf. "I hate to say this, but maybe Grady is good for Colton."

She dragged her fingers through the water and giggled. "I agree." Then she dove under.

Again, I followed suit. I needed a distraction. I needed to put out the inferno blazing through me. I swam out just as Georgia surfaced.

"God, I needed that," she said. "The tension was too much back there."

I needed more than an ocean of cold water, but I had to agree on both counts. We swam around before floating, letting our bodies go with the current and the ebb and flow of the waves. For the briefest of moments, I cleared my mind, staring up at the wispy clouds. After a minute, I sighed, feeling like my world wasn't in a state of unrest, as if my heart wasn't racing because of the guy who was a blend of confusion and chaos.

Georgia tapped on my leg. "Colton is watching."

And just like that, I was back to the present. "So?"

"Maybe you should rescue him. He needs to be rescued."

I giggled as I flipped over, ducked under, and resurfaced, combing my fingers through my hair. "He isn't a stray dog."

She splashed water at me. "You know what I mean."

Grady and Mia were making out. "Ugh. How can he stomach those two?"

"He's got willpower. For sure."

"No shit. He told me that very thing last night."

She grinned. "Ooo. Tell me more. I've been dying to hear the play-by-play."

I treaded water. "Best damn moment ever. I'm not going to last one second around him, not after he held me in his arms." I quivered at the memory, almost feeling like I was back in his arms.

"He so likes you."

"He has a funny way of showing it."

Treading water with me, she said, "Look, Skye. Mia is right, in a way. Make the first move, but don't throw yourself at him. Go sit next to him. Let the silence direct you. Let the space between you and him speak louder than words ever could. He needs a friend. He said you were the one that talked him down last night. Whatever you said, say it again."

I watched Colton pick at the sand. It was clear he wanted to be anywhere but where he was. "I told him he was a good person. That's all. And he doesn't want a friend. His words, not mine."

She playfully pushed me. "One, when do you listen? Two, since when do you give up? That's not who you are. And three, he does need someone other than Grady. While Grady might be good for him, he's probably telling him to find a random chick and get laid."

I mumbled a swear word at her last sentence, but she was right. I didn't give up easily. I was a fighter. I had to be careful, though, of where the line ended as a fighter and began as a whiner or beggar. If Colton didn't want anything to do with me, I had to come to terms with that.

"The minute I go up to him, he'll run," I said. "He did that at the cemetery yesterday."

"Maybe. Maybe not. Just try again. I want to

see you and Colton together. You deserve to be happy."

I flung myself at her, or at least tried to. The ocean had other plans for us, and a wave threw us in.

We both laughed.

"I appreciate the advice, Ms. Love Therapist. And I love you."

"I know," Georgia said. "Let's go. The tide is coming in."

The wind was picking up and the water was getting a bit choppy.

Georgia swam ahead of me. I wasn't in a rush. I needed as much time as possible to find the courage I'd had last night, the thing that had made me run out of my house in the middle of the night.

Georgia was just getting out of the water as I dove under to gain some ground, and when I surfaced, I broke into the breaststroke. My parents had sent me to swim classes when I was a toddler, and Dad had taught me as well. Living around the ocean, he thought it was imperative to know how to swim, to know the good, bad, and ugly of what could happen in the ocean. He'd always said, "Swimmers are at the mercy of water that can be powerful and commanding. In a blink of an eye, anything can happen."

I thought about Colton's brother as I swam, wondering about the details behind his drowning.

I was getting closer to shore when the sea sucked me out, erasing the distance I'd made. I let myself go with it. *No matter how strong you are, the ocean is so much stronger.*

I looked back, unprepared for the wave careening toward me. I would never make it to shore before it crested. So I dove under, giving in to mother ocean, a move I'd done many times. Before long, the force of the water would push me in. I swam as long as I could underwater then surfaced. When I did, I'd gotten nowhere. The current was too strong.

Don't panic. Then a wave took me under and tossed me around like a rag doll. I tried to resurface, breathing in, and I gulped down a mouthful of saltwater.

I gagged and fumbled for air while the ocean kept pushing me around. I tried again to cough out the water, but the wave just pulled me under once again.

Panic gripped me.

Then a strong arm wrapped around my waist,

and suddenly I was on the surface, gagging for air in Colton's arms.

He swam toward shore until he was able to stand. Then he set me on two feet. "Are you okay?" He flattened his big palms on my face, his voice in freak-out mode, which matched his expression.

I coughed a few times, nodding. "I'm good."

He hugged me tightly, his body trembling. I swore I could feel his heart punching his ribs, or maybe that was mine.

Either way, I said, "I'm okay, Colton."

He lightly dug his chin on my head as we stood in the surf, the water spreading out like tentacles, claiming the dry sand as the tide roared in. "I'm not."

"Well, we better get out before another wave decides to fling me around." I giggled nervously, when all I wanted to do was stay in his arms.

Softly, he tipped up my chin until I met his gaze. "Don't do that again." His tone cracked on the last word.

I might if you rescue me, I wanted to say, but I didn't. I knew the ocean had a way of screwing with his emotions. I knew he would never be the same around the sea. Then something hit me like a hard wind on a stormy day. He didn't like the beach. He didn't like the ocean. The way he'd been staring at it earlier suddenly made sense to me. I'd been stupid to think it was all about me, when in fact, he was probably thinking of his brother. He probably had PTSD.

I grabbed his hand. "Let's go." He seemed to be the one who needed saving.

He pressed his hand to the small of my back and molded his body to mine. "Not yet."

I gripped his taut triceps as I sought out Georgia. She, Grady, and Mia were standing on the shore, watching us. I was sure Georgia was freaking out as much as Colton was.

"You could've drowned," he said with so much pain.

I felt like a royal ass. "I know. I'm sorry." The last thing I wanted to do was scare the crap out of him.

He shivered as we stood in knee-deep water, and the longer he held me, the more an impressive bulge was growing and poking me in my stomach.

He leaned down, his lips on my ear. "Feel what you do to me?" His fingers danced up my back until they were in my hair, then he searched my face. "You're so fucking beautiful."

I didn't have words, and if I did, they floated

away when he lifted me, hooking one arm under my knees, and the other around my back.

"I can walk." My protest was weak at best.

"Maybe, but I need to do something to get rid of my boner," he said with a grin and a little pain.

"Really, carrying me will take it away?" That didn't make sense.

Not much did with Colton, except how hard and fast I was falling. Or maybe I'd fallen on the first day of school. It didn't matter. I was in his arms. He thought I was beautiful. And for that, life just got a hundred times better.

20

———

When we reached our friends, he set me down. I had to hold onto him for a minute to steady myself, and not because a wave had thrown me around like a volleyball in a tense match. My jitters were due to the brown-eyed guy who was looking at me as though I had saved him.

"About fucking time, man," Grady said to Colton. "I thought you wouldn't go through with it."

Mia, Georgia, and I exchanged a perplexed look. *Did Grady mean save me or something else?* I didn't want to ask, but Colton's don't-you-dare expression made me go with something else. Maybe he liked me but had been afraid to make the first move, although saving me wasn't what I'd had in mind.

Georgia and Mia snapped into action, asking me if I was okay.

"I'm fine," I told my friends.

Mia narrowed her eyes. "Don't scare us like that again."

I didn't plan to. It was a freak accident, and if I hadn't gulped down the saltwater, I might've been able to swim in.

Georgia hugged me briefly. "Let's not go swimming for a while. Now that you're good, I have to run. Mom is taking me to dinner for our monthly mom-and-daughter time."

Normally, depression set in any time Georgia and her mom did the whole bonding thing. I often thought of my mom. If she'd been alive, we would have many similar nights. But with Colton near me, I couldn't think straight, let alone drop into a deep depression.

"What?" Mia squealed. "I thought we would grab a bite. You know, all five of us."

I couldn't eat. My stomach was in a knot the size of Earth, a love knot or a lust knot or both. But if going out to eat meant sitting next to Colton, I was all for it. I wasn't sure about hanging with

Grady. He brought out the feisty side of me, and I didn't want to ruin the high I was on.

Grady cocooned Mia in his arms from behind, nuzzling her neck. "You're my dinner, baby."

I refrained from rolling my eyes as Mia giggled.

"We have the house all to ourselves. My dad is gone until tomorrow," Grady said, looking at Colton as though he dared him to agree to dinner.

Colton waved him off. "It's time I head home and face the music."

I let out a quiet sigh. I didn't want to watch Grady and Mia suck face all night. On the other hand, anxiety settled in my bones, hoping Colton didn't take another beating from his dad. Maybe he didn't have to go home just yet.

"Want to have dinner at my house?" I asked Colton. "Afterwards, you can change the oil in my car like you promised."

He gave me the sweetest look. "Sounds like a plan."

A swarm of butterflies went wild in my stomach. I wanted to say really or seriously or something shockingly idiotic, but I kept my lips glued together, feeling like I'd just won the boyfriend lottery.

Georgia's eyes got bigger the longer she stood

there. "Well, my work is done. Now I can enjoy my night with my mom."

Colton actually laughed, a sound that sent yummy shivers tiptoeing down my spine.

Mia, Georgia, and I collected our things while Colton and Grady chatted about something I couldn't hear. Grady was probably thanking him for getting the quiet message about not agreeing to dinner.

I slipped on my shorts, checked to make sure I had my phone, and swung my bag onto my shoulder.

I was ready to slip my sandals on when Colton grabbed my hand. "Wait for a minute."

Georgia and Mia waggled their brows as they said their goodbyes.

Grady said to Colton, "Good luck, man. If you need anything, call."

Colton nodded at his friend. "I'll be in to get my stuff in a few." Then he flicked his thumb toward the ocean. "Want to take a walk?"

I stuffed my sandals in my bag. "Sure." *I will go anywhere with you.*

We headed down the beach, silence following us except for the sound of the waves crashing along the shore and the seagulls cawing above. Yet the farther we walked, the more the silence ate at me. I stole a look at him, and he was chewing on the inside of his cheek as if trying to find something to say.

Maybe he wanted to take back what he'd said about me being beautiful. Maybe he wanted to let me down easy.

Shut up, Skyler. Stop psychoanalyzing everything.

A giggle escaped my lips.

Colton whipped his dreamy gaze at me. "What's so funny?"

To tell the truth or not? I went with the truth. "Did you mean what you said about me being beautiful?"

His lips curved upward slightly on the edges. "You are the prettiest girl I've ever met."

I reared back. "Not Amanda Gelling?" For real, she was beautiful.

"Not Amanda Gelling," he parroted. "Skyler, beauty is the whole package, not just looks. Besides, I find short hair sexy as hell. My friends at the academy always ribbed me when I dated a girl with hair shorter than mine."

Warmth radiated throughout my body as desire pooled between my thighs. Colton did like me. He found me sexy. *Best day ever.*

"I'm sorry you had to witness the fight with my old man last night."

It seemed so long ago. "No need for an apology. Families fight." Although I'd never seen a parent flat out punch his kid like Mr. Caldwell had.

Before my brain caught up with my actions, I grabbed Colton's hand, praying he didn't pull away or run like he had at the cemetery.

One or five minutes passed, I didn't know for sure, but when we reached a barrier of rocks, indicating the end of the line, Colton's hand was still tethered to mine.

He guided us up along the rocks toward the last house standing. It appeared empty with a "for rent" sign tacked to the deck.

Before my thoughts could take a trip down memory lane, Colton stopped and gave me the most loving look.

I swallowed one gasp, and then another when he grabbed my chin gently and tenderly, eyeing my mouth as though it was the most interesting thing he'd ever seen.

Whoa! If he kissed me, I was sure to self-combust.

The more he studied me, the more the air around us seemed to flare as though we were in our own little bubble. That blank mask he'd always worn was nonexistent. In its place were emotions galore, but one that stood out like a shining beacon on a dark night was lust.

His big brown orbs darted back and forth, and the longer we stood alone at the end of where the sand met rock, where my heart was blasting off into outer space, and where my legs were becoming weaker by the second, the more this guy was stealing a part of my soul.

I flattened my hands on his chest to stabilize myself in the event my knees gave out.

When I did, he briefly closed his eyes and shivered. "I can't do this anymore, Skyler." His words were a whisper on the wind.

I licked my dry lips. "Do what?"

It was crystal clear we were attracted to each other, that he was straining against his resolve not to take me right there.

He leaned down, snaked his arm around my waist, holding me like I was his lifeline, and pressed his forehead to mine. "I'm a fucking mess."

"We all are." Because as humans, we were. Not all the time, but we each had struggles and problems and regrets.

"Not like me," he said.

My chest rose as high as the swell of a large wave. Words were on the tip of my tongue, but I was afraid to say something stupid.

He traced circles on my bare lower back. I'd left my tank top off like I usually did when leaving the beach. "I want to kiss you. I want to do things to you and with you that I've been dreaming about ever since I saw you at the Latte House."

A heady feeling coursed through me, giving me the courage to say, "Then what are you waiting for? Kiss me like you mean it. Lose that control you said you had."

He moved away, shoving both hands through his wet hair.

My stomach clenched, my eyes wide, and my ego black and blue. Nausea was on the precipice of crawling up my throat. If these were the feelings I had to endure to like a guy, I wasn't ready to take the plunge.

He paced in short, violent strides, his bare feet pounding into the sand.

I took one faltering step toward him, then another until my trembling hand latched onto his steely forearm.

He flinched as though he'd made a mistake in telling me how he felt. As much as his actions were gutting me and injuring my heart and ego, he needed a friend.

Then I remembered what Georgia had said: *He said you were the one that talked him down last night. Whatever you said, say it again.*

"You're a good person, Colton Caldwell."

He jerked up his head, his expression soaked in turmoil.

"You are." I put more emphasis behind that statement.

He shrugged out of my hold, padded over to the cluster of rocks, and sat.

I dropped my bag. "Colton, what is it?" He needed to let go of whatever demon had its claws into him. I'd learned that from my therapist after Mom died.

I knelt in front of him, my knees digging into sharp pebbles, but I didn't care. "Your dad?"

He leaned his elbows on his thighs, his hair cocooning his face. "I can't talk about it."

"You can tell me, Colton," I said softly. "Get it off your chest. I promise what you say stays between us." Maybe he was worried I would tell Georgia and Mia. I tucked his hair behind his ear. "Colton." I tapped on his chin. "Look at me, please."

When he did, I wasn't prepared to see tears in his eyes. My heart bloomed and hurt at the same time. I felt honored that he was comfortable enough to show me his true feelings and also gutted that whatever was plaguing him was tearing him apart.

Georgia's advice was a soft cadence in my head. *"Let the silence direct you. Let the space between you and him speak louder than words ever could. He needs a friend."*

I climbed to my feet and sat next to him, hooking my arm in his. When he was ready, he would tell me, or maybe he wouldn't. Either way, I was showing him I was there for him no matter what, and regardless of how I felt for him, first and foremost, I wanted to be his friend.

His shoulders shook, and I rubbed his back up, then down in what I hoped was a soothing kind of way.

He sighed, the frustration coming out in a long, audible sound. "I killed my brother, Skyler."

21

My hand stopped midway up his back. I was afraid to ask him to repeat those words, yet not sure I really heard him.

"I killed my brother." That time, he spoke louder.

"No, you didn't." I didn't believe it for a minute. The sea was unpredictable.

He cried a little harder. "I did. I sure as fuck did."

I resumed rubbing his back, and that time, the motion of my hand was more for me than for him as my brain scrambled to find the right words to say. I was going out on a limb. "Your dad blames you." It wasn't a question but a revelation for me.

The reason why his dad beat him. The reason why his dad drank. Maybe even the reason why his parents had shipped him off to private school.

His head moved up and down.

"Tell me about Josh," I said quietly.

He pushed off the rocks, gripping the back of his opposite arm, looking at the water. "He was the best brother I could have. He loved surfing, skateboarding, sports in general."

"He was younger than you, right?" I remembered the dates on his headstone.

Colton dropped down on the sand and hugged his knees to his chest. "Yeah, by two years, yet he thought he was the older brother."

I snuggled up next to him. "He liked skateboarding, huh? Sounds like my kind of guy."

His gaze drifted out to sea, grinning, no doubt thinking of Josh. "I hate the water now. I haven't surfed since that fatal day. I replay the scene over and over and over. I haven't been able to sleep through the night since his death. I live his death every goddamned day. And now that I'm home, I'm reminded of how much of a fuck-up I really am."

I slid my hand under his arm to rest on his inner thigh. "It wasn't your fault."

His biceps bunched. "It was, Skyler. I was supposed to watch him. I was supposed to make sure he was safe. What did I do? I fell asleep on the fucking blanket while my brother was drowning."

I swallowed thickly, tears ready to spill.

Growing up in a beach town, I knew locals didn't surf where the public did, and that meant no lifeguards.

As if Colton knew what I was thinking, he continued. "We were down three miles that way." He pointed to another private beach area where another row of mansions resided. "The waves were better, bigger. Josh wanted to surf so bad that day. I didn't. I'd been tired from a week of hell at football practice. My mom begged me to take him. So I did. I surfed with him for a bit. Then my legs were burning, and I was spent." He paused, tears pooling in his eyes. Then he licked his lips. "We both came in, although he protested. At thirteen, he had more energy than the Energizer Bunny. We ate sandwiches Mom had packed for us that day. Then I laid on my towel. Told Josh to stay put. Since we had just eaten, we both needed to rest before going back in." A lone tear cascaded down his cheek. "I don't know what made me wake up. I think it was the thunder rolling in. But when I did, the sky was dark, the waves were higher than normal, and I couldn't find Josh anywhere. He was a pretty good surfer and knew how to swim, of course, but no amount of expertise can save you from the power of the ocean. Funny how Mother Nature takes a turn on a dime and life changes instantly."

I blinked away my own tears.

He sucked his lips in. "I dove in the water, not even thinking straight. I swam and swam and swam. But it got me nowhere with the way the ocean was tossing and turning. I almost drowned, myself."

I swallowed a bucket of emotions, trying not to cry my eyes out. As he was telling me the story, I could picture the ocean, the waves, the storm clouds. I'd seen many days like that while sitting on the beach, and I knew how quickly the weather could change.

"Anyway," he said, "it's a day I want to take back. I want to try again." His body trembled. "I'll never get that chance." He turned so fast, I didn't have time to track him. "Please, Skyler, don't ever drink and walk into the ocean. When you did that night at Grady's party, I lost my shit. Then today. I hadn't been that frightened since Josh's death."

I gasped. "I'm sorry, Colton." I threw myself at him. "I'm so sorry, for Josh, for you, for causing you to relive a terrible incident." Nausea settled in my throat.

He opened his arms, his legs, and when I was holding him as tightly as I could, I cried for him, for me, for my stupidity, for Josh, for Mom, and even for Dad. No amount of words could heal, but as Dad always said, "Hugs are the medicine everyone needs."

So with all my strength, I locked my arms around him, and I wasn't letting go.

"Skyler." Colton's sexy drawl tickled my ear as he rubbed my back.

Funny how the roles had reversed, and I was the one who was emotional and shedding tear after tear.

Sniffling, I adjusted myself so I was sitting cross-legged between his legs.

He swiped fingers over one side of my face, taking with it a lone tear. "I'm leaving town, Skyler."

My eyebrows drew down, the air leaving my lungs on a gush. "Why?" He couldn't leave. "Are your parents sending you back to the academy?" *Oh God. Please say no. Please don't leave.*

"No, but I'm going to stay with a friend from the academy who lives in Virginia."

Panic clutched me like a vise, a crushing force that was stealing more and more air, making it harder to breathe. It was none of my business. *But does he mean girlfriend? Is that the reason he won't kiss me? Is that the reason he couldn't lose control with me?*

"What about school?" An earthquake rocked through the question.

He entwined his hand with mine like he knew I needed comfort. "I can get my GED online."

"Football?" My voice began to wobble. I needed to come up with something, anything, to convince him to stay. I was beginning to realize I needed him. He was the one who kept my mind from wandering down a dark lane with no future. He was the one who had a way of massaging my heart when it was about to break over Dad.

"I'm only playing to fill my time, and to do anything other than be home."

"Stay at my house." That came out desperate. We didn't have an extra bedroom, but we had a couch, and he could even share my bed. Dad would have a cow. Nan probably wouldn't allow it, but I didn't care. "Seriously. You can't leave,

Colton." *You can't leave me. We are just getting to know one another.* I scooted as close to him as I could, inhaling the salt and sweat that intoxicated me because it was pure Colton. "Please consider my offer." I wasn't above begging.

The corners of his mouth tipped up as he leaned in, his lips an inch from mine. "Where would I sleep?" His eyes darkened.

Worrying my bottom lip, I looked down, and when I did, I gulped. The bulge in his swim trunks was a sight to behold. I blinked just to make sure I wasn't imagining things. *Nope, not at all.*

A fire burned low in my belly, sparking flames to my core. At that moment, I wanted nothing more than to lose my virginity. No one was around. The home behind Colton was empty.

We didn't say anything for long seconds, minutes, or maybe hours. I lost track of time, lost track of reality.

"Make the first move," Mia or Georgia had said. I couldn't even think straight. Regardless, I had to take a chance. If he was leaving town, who knew when he would return. I might never get another chance to be with Colton Caldwell.

My fingertips glided up his bare chest, tracing every dip and valley along the way. When I finally reached the base of his neck, his Adam's apple bobbed. I stole a look upward to his lush, thick lips, then farther until our gazes collided, and I sucked in salt air.

His brown eyes were darker than a storm cloud. His chest rose and fell.

The saying "go big or go home" was a faint whisper in the back of my head.

So I went big and crashed my mouth to his.

He stilled, not moving, not reacting, not opening his mouth for me.

I pushed down the hurt and was about to get up until he grasped my hips, and one second later I was straddling him.

He studied me, one beat passing, then five or maybe ten. So I tried again, only this time, I gently pressed my lips to his, silently pleading that he wanted me as much as I wanted him. In a flash, his tongue dove into my mouth, aggressive, possessive, and wild with need.

I squealed and moaned, tasting salt and him.

I was floating, soaring, flying like I'd been set free from the cage I'd been in for so long.

Mom had told me once that Dad had been the love of her life. She said I would know mine when he made my stomach flutter, made my spirit tingle, and when he gave me that feeling that he was the only one for me.

I believed Colton was that person. I believed that he was the one I wanted to be with forever.

My hands clutched his shoulders as my tongue knotted with his.

He groaned, a sound drenched in a torrent of emotions, making me lightheaded.

With one flexed move, I was lying on my back, and he was on top, hovering over me, hands buried on either side of my head.

I whimpered at the loss of his mouth on mine.

His hair tumbled forward, creating our own private hideaway. "You're beautiful, Skyler. So fucking beautiful."

I latched onto his biceps and my belly pitched and rolled from his words and the emotions dripping from them. "Don't leave," I begged, sticking out my bottom lip.

He kissed my nose, my eyes, my forehead. "I have to." His voice sounded sad. "I need to breathe. I can't do that living at home."

I nibbled on his bottom lip. "Shh." Then my hands were on the move until I grazed the backs of my fingers over his erection.

He growled, his eyes rolling back in his head.

I started to untie his swim trunks.

He let out an exaggerated sigh. "We can't," he said painfully.

I couldn't take no for an answer. It might be my only shot with him. "I want to." I had to sate the intense ache I had, which was becoming more than I could handle. I needed relief. I needed to explode. I needed him so fucking bad.

My pulse pounded in my ears as an obvious war raged in his head, his breathing still labored, his eyes darting back and forth over my face.

I held his gaze, managing to untie his swim trunks, but then I stilled. We couldn't have sex. I didn't have a condom. I was ninety-nine percent sure he didn't, either, and I wasn't on the pill. As much as my body was steering the ship, I had to be responsible.

He saw my resignation and crawled off me, roughing his fingers through his hair. I couldn't tell if he was relieved or disappointed.

I went with the former and sat up, brushing sand off me.

"We should go," he said. "I have to get my bag from Grady's."

"Colton," I said softly. "Will you come back? I mean, are you leaving for good?"

"I don't know. If my old man continues to be a dick, then I will probably stay away for a while."

"Have you talked to him?"

"He's always got a drink in his hand. Besides, what's the point? He'll never forgive me. I'm not sure I can forgive myself."

"At least your dad isn't dying." I swallowed air and held my breath. *Where did that come from?* "I'm sorry. I didn't mean to sound like a bitch."

His grin was galvanizing. "You could never be a bitch."

I half-smiled. "Have you seen Grady and me spar? For real. I have claws."

He laughed. "He tells me you and he butt heads a lot. But he thinks you're cool."

I choked. "No way. Was he drunk? Did he tell you why we hate each other?"

"Some kiss in elementary school. He said you started the rumors that made him hide in corners."

I laughed so hard I had tears in my eyes. I was blown away that Grady would even tell anyone about that. Grady was too proud to show his embarrassment.

"He's a good guy," Colton added. "I see how he can be an ass, but he has a big heart."

I was slowly coming around to see a different, good side to Grady. But if he hurt Mia in any way, I would definitely break his QB arm.

Colton pushed to his feet and extended his hand. "Come on, baby doll. I need to change your oil."

I accepted his hand, blushing at his pet name for me. "Among other things." I wagged my eyebrows, hoping he caught the underlying message as I collected my bag.

He nodded my way, giving me the most brilliant smile I had yet to see on him. "For sure."

Another blush washed over me, and I swore I didn't need to have sex with him. The way he looked at me with so much want in his eyes, I could have an orgasm right there.

Out of nowhere, he plastered on a serious expression. "I want you to know something. I don't sleep around, Skyler. And while I'm dying to feel what it's like to be inside you, I'm not ready. My head isn't ready."

My jaw plummeted to my feet at the honesty in his voice and at the sheer strength he had to exert when his erection, which hadn't gone down, was still so glaringly evident.

He stood toe-to-toe with me. "You deserve someone who is all in."

I shuddered from equal parts disappointment and excitement. In one breath, I wanted to cry. I wanted to beg him for so much. But I understood he had to sort out the mess at home. In the next, he wasn't telling me he didn't want me, and that meant there was hope for us. I clung to that hope, and the idea that one day our paths would meet again.

Then something hit me. "Amanda Gelling," I said. She'd bragged that she'd screwed Colton five times.

"I'm not interested in her, Skyler, and no, I didn't sleep with her. I know she told you we did, but she was just getting under your skin. We did kiss, and she didn't do it for me." His tone was resolute.

I believed him. He wasn't trying to get in my pants, and he didn't seem like a person who lied, either. "When are you leaving, Colton?"

He looked out to sea, seemingly reflecting on the past or maybe the future. "Next weekend."

Pouting, I followed his line of sight, zeroing in on the whitecaps that crested over the tops of waves. "A storm is coming in," I said mostly to myself, hoping to quell the sadness that was seeping in.

He reached out and took my hand. "Thank you, Skyler, for listening. For being there for me." He sounded like it was the last time I would see him.

I staved off tears and squeezed his hand. I wasn't going to cry. I wasn't going to break down. Not yet, anyway. I had a week to try to convince him to stay.

I prayed that I could.

22

———

The next morning, tears slid down Georgia's face as she hugged Dad. "You're a great man, Mr. Lawson, and so undeserving of this. Please know I love you with all my heart."

I held back tears as I stood at the end of Dad's bed. I loved my BFF more in that moment than ever before. She was more than a friend. She was the sister I'd never had.

Georgia sniffled as heels clicked on the hardwood, the sound echoing in the hall before Nan waltzed in.

Dad's face lit up as if Nan had come to save him. But I knew Dad adored her. In another life, I had no doubt Dad would've asked her out. She wasn't Mom, but she was just as pretty. Her dark hair was coiled in a sleek bun, her crisp white blouse hung over her blue pencil skirt, and her tan-and-blue heels made her legs look longer than her five-foot-three-inch height.

With a smile all for my dad, she said, "Morning. How is everyone?"

Georgia dabbed the underside of her eyes, careful not to ruin her mascara. "You look fantastic, Nan. I'm used to seeing you in your scrubs."

Nan blushed. "Why thank you, Georgia."

"How was Sunday mass?" I asked Nan. She didn't take much time off, except for church and a few hours here and there to run errands. On those days, I stayed with Dad.

"The priest gave a great sermon this morning," she said. "You two"—she wagged a finger at Georgia and me—"should accompany me one Sunday. Well, one of you, anyway. The other would have to stay with your father."

Georgia raised her hand. "Take Skyler. I'll stay with Dad."

I wasn't opposed to going with her. My parents believed in God, as did I, but they hardly went to church. I could only remember a few times when we'd gone to Sunday mass, and that was when I'd been in elementary school.

"What was the sermon about?" I asked. Maybe the priest had talked about teenagers, given how adamant she was that Georgia and I attend church with her.

Nan's face brightened, eager to share. "Salvation." She pinned me with a pointed look, as though I needed salvation. I was sure I would need a lifeline when Dad finally passed.

Georgia eyed me for some odd reason. "Everyone needs saving. Right, Skye?"

I could feel a deep crease forming in between my eyebrows until I got her silent message— Colton. Or maybe she meant me.

Dad and Nan exchanged a surprised look.

"Are you talking about Colton?" I asked Georgia.

"Maybe," Georgia said.

Nan went over to Dad and fluffed his pillows. "What's going on with Colton other than family troubles?"

Georgia sidled up to me and hooked her arm in mine. "Yeah, Skye. Want to dish?"

Nan laughed. "We know Skye likes Colton."

Dad grinned.

What they didn't know wasn't my story to tell, though, and I would never betray Colton's trust. It was time to change the subject.

Nan beat me to it, as though she knew I needed help. "I bought some cinnamon rolls from the bake sale at church. They're homemade."

My stomach growled as if on cue. I was famished. I hadn't eaten anything since the morning before. I had planned to eat dinner with Colton that day, but after he'd finally changed the oil in my car, I hadn't seen or heard from him. The Caldwell house had been quiet all night. Even Colton's room had been dark like he wasn't even there. But I knew he had been—his truck had been in the driveway. I suspected after that tense night with his dad, he and his parents were probably working things out. Or at least I hoped they were.

I gave Dad a quick peck on the cheek. "I'll see you later. Maybe we can watch a movie?"

He blinked once, telling me yes, he would like that.

Nan rolled his table away from the bed. "Skye, I know it's only been a couple of days, but have you thought any more about your birth mother?"

My mind wasn't on her, and I felt weird talking

about the woman who'd birthed me with Dad present.

"I'll be in the kitchen," Georgia said, then bounced out.

I gnawed on my bottom lip. "Not really. But I haven't changed my mind about Nan being my guardian." I looked at Dad when I spoke. "Honestly, I have too much going on right now to process and dissect the whole adoption thing."

Dad raised an eyebrow, wanting me to explain.

"School, for one. And I'm not ready." I didn't want to tell him that Colton had taken possession of my thoughts just about every minute of the day. Or that I felt like I would be betraying Dad if I learned more about my biological mom.

"When you're ready," Nan said.

Dad blinked in agreement.

I gave him a hug, then met Georgia in the kitchen. "What in the world are you doing?"

She was up on her toes, her face practically plastered to the kitchen window. "Shh. Colton is outside with his dad."

I yanked on her pretty silk top. "Get back. They'll see you."

She stepped away. "Oh, come on," she whined.

"I can make out words here and there. Colton called his father a dick."

I glanced quickly. Colton sat tensely in a chair, clearly ready to jump up. The good news was that a table separated him from his dad, and they seemed calm, not throwing punches. Mr. Caldwell's features said otherwise, though. He was definitely angry.

"Do they normally air their differences outside?" Georgia asked. "It's kind of odd."

I guided her away from the window and up to our small square island. "Maybe his mom is vacuuming and it was too noisy. I don't know." I wasn't about to try and understand why people did what they did. I had enough of my own problems.

She backtracked to look at them again, but I blocked her. "I don't want his dad to see us eavesdropping." Once again, I ushered her to the island. "If his dad sees us, he's likely to storm over here. It's bad enough that I had a weird encounter with him the other day."

She commandeered a barstool. "Weird encounter? Please tell me he's not a dirty old man."

I shuddered. "Ew. But he did ask if Colton was sleeping in my bed."

Her pretty blonde brows lifted. "OMG! What did you tell him?"

I grabbed the milk out of the fridge. "Nothing. Mrs. Caldwell interrupted us."

She dove into the homemade cinnamon rolls. "So I'm dying to hear what happened with Colton after I left the beach yesterday. And don't leave out a drop of detail."

I poured two glasses of milk, giggling. "I'm surprised that wasn't the first thing you asked me when you walked in this morning."

"I would've, but you were with your dad."

"When has that stopped you?" I teased.

She bit into the cinnamon roll while I set the glasses of milk on the island. "Mmm. These rolls are heaven."

I sank my teeth into one, and the cinnamon exploded on my tongue. "Yum."

As we ate, I kept looking at the kitchen window, but I couldn't see much from where I sat.

Georgia inhaled her roll, watching me as she chewed. "Well, talk."

"How can I?" I asked between bites. "This is too good." I pointed to the roll in my mouth.

"Okay, I'll talk. I sent Kyle a text last night, but he hasn't responded."

I twirled an imaginary circle around her mouth. "Then why the frown?"

"He read it, but nothing."

I hated when someone read a text and didn't respond. "I'm sorry. Maybe he was in a place where he couldn't."

She wrapped her fingers around a glass of milk. "I should just stick to guys around here. Those out-of-towners only break your heart."

I sagged in my seat. "Colton is leaving town next weekend."

She almost spit out her milk. "What the... seriously? He's going back to the academy?"

"Not really. He needs space. He's going to stay with a friend."

"Girl or guy friend?"

I took a drink of milk. "Don't know. I don't want to, either." The less I knew, the better my mind would be. It was none of my business, anyway.

"Is Colton okay?" she asked. "You know, he would've run into a tree Friday night if not for you."

"I didn't bring that up. He didn't seem as agitated yesterday. I think Grady helped too. Plus, he didn't tell you or Mia. Remember, Mia overhead him tell Grady. Anyway, I couldn't blurt out, 'Hey, were you really going to run into a tree?' I figure when and if he's ready, he'll tell me." He'd shared one of his demons with me, and that was a step in the right direction for him to heal.

"Fair enough. What else happened?" She checked the archway. "Please tell me you lost your virginity." Her voice was low.

"No. Although I tried."

"Shut the front door. You came on to Colton? I think you're my new hero."

I snorted. "I'm sure Mia has that trophy. She's the one having sex." It was my turn to check if the coast was clear. While I wouldn't care so much if Nan heard, I wasn't ready to cross that bridge if she decided to play mom. Satisfied she wasn't anywhere nearby, I said, "But we had an extremely passionate kiss. And yes, if you must know, it was the best ever." I touched my lips, almost feeling his on mine.

"You're toast, girl. We need a plan to make sure he doesn't leave."

"For sure." I was praying he was working out his differences with his dad. Maybe he wouldn't leave after all.

"Back up," Georgia said. "You tried to get him naked and he said no?"

"I was wondering when you would catch on to that. He isn't ready."

She choked. "What dude in their right mind says he isn't ready?"

"In all fairness to him, I guess I wasn't either. I'm not on the pill, and he didn't have a condom, anyway."

A shudder wracked my body as I reminisced about our intimate interlude.

"But he slept with Amanda."

"He didn't."

She straightened her spine. "Mmm." Her tone was skeptical. "She is all talk, though."

It didn't matter if she believed that statement or not. I did, and no amount of skepticism on her part would change my mind. *Then why do I suddenly feel nauseous?*

23

I cruised around the track that circled the football field, feeling free and energized. The last time I'd been on my skateboard was the day Colton had run over it with his truck, which seemed like eons ago, when only a month had passed.

With the balmy wind in my face, I scoured the field for Colton. It had been four long days since our time on the beach, and I hadn't seen him at all, not even at lunch, when he usually sat with the football team. When I left school each morning, his truck was gone.

Mia had mentioned that Colton was staying with Grady for a few days. That told me the conversation he'd had with his dad hadn't gone well. Still, he wasn't in school, and he hadn't left town because Mia would've told me... unless she didn't want to hurt my feelings.

I kept scanning the field as my stomach wound into a ball of knots. I homed in on Grady, who was getting ready to throw. I coasted along, watching as the football left his hand and soared through the air until it landed in the hands of a beefy guy who wasn't wearing red cleats. Colton was the only one on the team who wore red cleats.

So I inspected each player, coming up empty each time. I hoped I hadn't missed the chance to say goodbye to him, or a last-ditch effort to convince him to stay.

I hopped off my board, ready to scream. I'd never obsessed over a guy like that. I needed to skate to clear my mind—and not around the track, but at the skate park. I needed to catch air, concentrate on jumps, and feel like I hadn't lost who I was.

Georgia was going to be furious with me. We'd agreed to meet at her house after school, but for my mental health, I had to do something to tame the thoughts running rampant in my head. Maybe

Colton had left. He didn't say goodbye. He was going to stay with a girl.

Then my worry over Dad wormed its way in. The night before, Dad had had a near-death choking episode at dinner. I'd never seen Nan so scared. Dad's face had turned a thousand shades of blue, and I'd held my breath, praying he wouldn't die right in front of us.

I silently scolded myself. I was worrying about a guy, and my dad was on the fast track to live with the angels. It was time to get my head on straight and focus on the most important person in my life.

I patted my ass where my phone should have been, but it wasn't in my pocket—then I remembered I'd forgotten it at home that morning. I was surprised my head was still attached to my body. Even in class, I hadn't paid an ounce of attention to any of the teachers or their lectures.

Georgia had chided me. "Who forgets their phone? You'll die without it."

By the time I'd met her and Mia at the Latte House before school, it had been too late to go home. And that morning, I hadn't been in the mood to rush home, then explain to the vice principal why I was late. We couldn't use our phones in class, anyway, which would've been his retort.

I clenched my teeth, walking over to Mia. She and her cheer squad were in the middle of a routine, their collective voices loud as they shouted one of their cheers. The upcoming home game that week was a huge deal. We were playing one of our biggest rivals.

I waved at Mia, hoping to get her attention, but three girls who had just climbed down from the bleachers garnered mine.

The blonde in the group said, "I saw Colton at Amanda's last night."

I swore the sky darkened as my blood gelled. Sure, they could've been talking about some other Colton and Amanda, but the odds were nil that another couple in our small school had the same names.

"I thought Colton didn't want anything to do with Amanda?" the petite brunette of the three asked.

I wondered briefly if the brunette was the same one who'd had her tongue down Colton's throat the week before.

The blonde shrugged. "I guess that was just a rumor."

Rage seized my muscles. I gulped down a growl. *What the fuck?* So many things ricocheted off the inside of my skull, faster than a rocket shooting into outer space.

Mia jogged up to me, out of breath. "Girl, what's wrong?"

I lifted my chin. "Can you tell Georgia I'll call her later? I have something to do."

I set my skateboard down, ready to ride like the freaking wind, when Mia's nails dug into my arm. "Wait. What's going on?" Her hazel eyes were filled with fear. "Is it your dad?"

Air punched from my lungs. "God, no." The minute the words came out of my mouth, I felt the need to lose my lunch. Since school was out for the day, I didn't have any way for Nan to get ahold of me. "I need to go."

She wiped her sweaty brow with the back of her hand. "I'm almost done here. I can give you a ride."

"I want to skate." As I hopped on my board, tears stung my eyes.

"Skye!" Mia shouted.

I waved her off. "I'm fine." That was the biggest lie I'd ever told. I was far from fine. I was about to break down. I was about to have the worst crying session yet.

Hearing that Colton was at Amanda's felt like

someone was carving out a hole in my chest. I skated past the three girls until they climbed the grassy knoll up to the parking lot. When I reached the cement stairs, I had no choice but to get off my board.

I took the steps two at a time, grinding my molars down to nothing and shaking my head like I had some sort of nervous tic. Once on the parking lot pavement, I got on my board, ready to blow that popsicle stand, when I spied a certain guy with shoulder-length hair. I wavered, practically falling off my board.

Great. Way to make an idiot out of myself.

Colton rushed over like a Greek god ready to save the woman he loved.

A maniacal laugh barreled out of me like an F-5 tornado as I managed to stay on two feet. My skateboard, though, decided it'd had enough of me and traveled toward Colton's truck like the stupid piece of wood missed him.

Thank God his truck was parked. I would seriously deconstruct into a blubbering mess if the one thing in my life that kept me sane busted once again.

Colton's strong hand latched onto my arm. "Are you okay? Is it your dad?"

Words were on the tip of my tongue, but when I opened my mouth, nothing came out, which was a good thing. I would have stuck my foot in my mouth and said something brilliantly stupid, such as "How's Amanda? Did you screw her again?"

He prodded me with those brown eyes, drinking me in and revving my pulse.

We stared at one another until a car drove up, breaking our connection.

I pushed out the breath I'd been holding until I saw the driver. Then I laughed again. Amanda fucking Gelling was behind the wheel of her convertible, looking beautiful with her auburn hair tied up on her head, diamond-stud earrings sparkling, and an off-the-shoulder blouse that gave her a seductive vibe.

The need to scream was strong, but I straightened my spine and plastered on a fake smile. I wasn't about to show my jealousy. Dad had taught me to be the bigger person. *Don't ever let them see you sweat.*

It was probably too late for that. I was sweating like a pig. Dad had meant it metaphorically.

"Amanda." My tone was as sweet as I could make it. "Did your mom sell that house on Pony Circle in Crane Plantation?"

She looked at me like I had five heads. "Why would you want to know that?"

Colton tucked his hands into the pockets of his black jeans, which were hugging his body nicely, and inclined his head.

No harm in telling them the truth. "My mom designed that house. I lived there until she passed away." I wouldn't expect her to know any of that. We'd never been close friends.

"That's a badass house," Colton said.

I could feel my lips forming into a smile that would brighten a dark room. "My mom was a great architect."

"I don't keep up with my mom's business." Amanda's tone was curt. Then she regarded Colton. "I just wanted to say thanks for last night."

My eyebrows disappeared into my hairline. I was such a fool for believing he liked me. *You were just his means to salvation. He saved you to forgive himself.*

Swallowing, I willed my legs to move. To get the hell away from him. To find a dark hole to curl up in and cry.

24

I ran to get my skateboard, which was lodged under the back tire of Colton's truck. My hands shook as I pushed the tears away. I wasn't going to cry. No way in hell. Dad had said to "live and learn" many times when I made a mistake as a kid, but I didn't like learning when my heart was on the line.

As soon as I retrieved my board, the darn thing fell to the ground. That time, my board rolled over to Colton's feet. I was beginning to believe he'd put a curse on it when he'd fixed it.

I debated whether to interrupt their conversation, since Amanda was blushing at something Colton was saying. *Unbelievable.* I fisted my hands at my sides, and when she laughed, I walked in the opposite direction. To hell with my skateboard. My heart was more important than a piece of wood with wheels.

I'd barely made it ten feet when Colton called my name. Goosebumps immediately pebbled my skin at his Southern drawl.

Damn him. Damn my body.

"Wait!" he shouted.

My legs stopped, against my better judgment.

Amanda sped by, honking her horn.

I was ready to throw her the finger until Colton's breath tickled my ear. "Don't forget this."

I pivoted on my heel, and I shouldn't have. A tear ran down my cheek.

"Hey, what's wrong?" His tone was gentle, soft, and soothing. "Seriously, is your dad okay?"

I took my board from him. "My dad is fine. It's nothing that concerns you." I was lying through my teeth. "Why are you here, Colton? Shouldn't you be on the football field?"

"I quit football."

I shouldn't have been surprised. He'd said he was only playing so he wouldn't be home as much. Yet my body felt chilled. "You're leaving earlier than you planned?"

The sadness in his eyes said it all. "I am. I came to say goodbye."

I was grateful that he was showing some emotion rather than a deadpan expression. In fact, upon further scrutiny, he seemed as though the weight of the world he'd been carrying had fallen away. The pain in his eyes, so evident on Saturday, was no longer swimming in his depths.

Another tear escaped. "To me or to Grady?"

"I didn't want to leave without seeing you first. Mia told me earlier you would be here. She also gave me your number, but I got your voicemail."

"I forgot my phone at home."

Colton closed the tiny distance between us. "Skye, thank you for Saturday and for listening, and thank you for the mind-blowing kiss. That, I'll never forget."

I had so much to say, but jealousy took possession of my tongue. "I'm sure you told Amanda that too."

He answered by growling before his mouth landed on mine, his tongue trying to break the barrier that I had sealed up tightly. He tugged me to him. "Open." His tone was possessive, demanding, and downright painful, as if he would die if I didn't do as he ordered.

The sound of my skateboard hitting the ground boomed, or maybe it was my heart ramming against my ribs.

I shook my head. "No. I don't move in on other girls' boyfriends."

"Damn it, Skye. I told you, I'm not into Amanda."

"Then why were you at her house last night?"

He stiffened before he let go of me. "Did you follow me?" He grabbed the back of his neck, guilt written all over his handsome face.

"I might be a lot of things, Colton, but I'm not a stalker." Or maybe there was some truth to that. I was always looking out my window since he'd returned from private school. "I heard some girls talking today."

As if he knew who the girls were, the skin around his eyes relaxed. "I needed to apologize to Amanda. I've been an ass to her, and I realized after talking with my parents yesterday that I had to stop making everyone's life around me miserable. I led Amanda on, and that isn't me."

Admirable. "Are you leading me on?" I had to ask even though a large part of me knew he wasn't, or I wanted to believe he wasn't, toying with my emotions.

He grasped my arms. "Never. I like you. I can't get you out of my head. Please understand that I need time." His voice was gentle, his plea desperate.

My chest pitched and rolled. I didn't know how to respond.

He rubbed his nose against mine. "Please understand."

My pulse was racing like a horse at the Kentucky Derby. Maybe hope existed for him and me. Hope that he would return. Hope that I would see him again. I frowned as we stood in the quiet parking lot overlooking the football field below.

"Awkward" came to mind. I should have walked away, but I couldn't bring myself to say goodbye.

"You're cute when you pout," he finally said. "And you're making it extremely hard for me to leave."

I did an imaginary fist pump. "Did you think I would make it easy?"

He nibbled on my lip. "I guess not. Kiss me?"

"On one condition," I said through a giggle.

He wrapped his big, muscled arm around my waist. "Anything."

"Text or call me every day." That was the only way I wouldn't go out of my mind.

He stole my breath when he mashed his mouth to mine. His answer was steeped in so much emotion, I was certain I would falter.

I should go ran through my brain. *It will be fifty times harder to say goodbye.* But I didn't care. He needed to know how I felt. So I gave him everything I had, practically climbing his body. If anyone were watching us, they had front-row seats to a steamy show.

I didn't know how long we locked lips, but when he broke away, I whimpered, and when he marched over to his truck, the little air remaining in my lungs dissipated.

Then something dawned on me. "Your control. It's about to snap?"

He barely nodded as he opened the door to his truck. "I'll give you a ride."

As much as I wanted to get in that truck with him, I couldn't. We were only putting off the inevitable. And once I got in, it would take the jaws of life to pull me out.

So I collected my skateboard. "It's best if we say goodbye now."

He briefly closed his eyes, struggling with the gravity of what was happening. I was too.

On shaky legs, I walked up to him. A rush of emotions blazed through me as he drank me in. I couldn't shake the feeling that I was falling hard and fast. Maybe I'd already fallen for him. I didn't know what love felt like. All I knew was I couldn't get him out of my head. Every waking minute since he'd returned, I thought about him, and he was taking my heart with him as he left.

He didn't say a word and didn't have to. The look in his eyes said it all. He didn't want to leave. I sure as hell didn't want him to, either.

"Stay." I had to try one last time.

His grin was crestfallen. "I would, baby, if my old man agreed to get help for his drinking, or even stopped blaming me for Josh's death. I have to find a way to get past my guilt and the pain crushing me. I can't do that if my old man continually reminds me how it was my fault Josh drowned."

I seriously disliked his father. "What about school?" We had laws about how many days a student could miss without any ramifications.

"I dropped out today. I turned eighteen last week."

I rubbed his chest, the act keeping my tears at bay. "Happy belated birthday." I was surprised Grady hadn't thrown a party for him. But Colton probably hadn't mentioned his birthday to anyone. "Remember, call or text me. If not, I might have to hunt you down." I lifted onto my toes and gave him a chaste peck on the lips.

Then I pivoted on my heel. I was a nanosecond away from flipping on the waterworks. I hated goodbyes, though it seemed the norm for me.

He grabbed me, spun me around, and crashed his mouth to mine.

I gave in, allowing him to take what he needed, my body trembling, tears spilling, and heart breaking.

When we came up for air, his soft lips glided along my jaw until he was nibbling on my ear. "I like you a lot, Skyler. Don't ever forget that."

I stiffened. Not because of his admission, but he sounded as if I would never see him again, and suddenly my mouth was ten miles ahead of my brain. "I think I'm in love with you."

He tensed.

Oh my God! I just messed up.

His breathing grew heavy. "I need to get on the road."

And I needed to bury my head in the sand. I eased out of his embrace.

He stared at me like he didn't know me all of a sudden.

I wasn't sure I knew myself, either.

However, it was clear by his shock that he wasn't ready to hear how I felt. I wasn't sure I was, either.

I stabbed a thumb behind me. "I better go."

He opened his mouth to speak, but I raised my hand. "Don't." I didn't want an excuse or a cold response, and if he did feel the same way, I didn't want to hear it when he was driving out of town.

I jumped on my skateboard and rode hard and fast out of the school lot.

25

I coasted around the cemetery, the only place where I could think clearly. I scolded myself the entire way there for opening my big mouth and telling Colton how I felt.

I screamed at the top of my lungs. Good thing no one was around, which was the reason I chose that place.

A strong scent of freshly cut grass wafted on the late-afternoon air. The sky was drenched in orange and red as the sun slid down on the horizon in the distance. I was headed toward Mom's grave when I passed Josh's headstone.

I backtracked and jumped off my board, leaving it on the pavement. I wanted to say a quick prayer, something I hadn't had a chance to do when Colton and I were there the other day.

As my Vans dug into the soft earth, a sudden wave of dizziness washed over me. I wavered for a second as I held my stomach. *Whoa!* I was ready to puke.

I lowered myself to my knees, closing my eyes and willing the queasiness to go away. I inhaled and exhaled, realizing I hadn't eaten anything that day. I kept rocking back and forth, tamping down the nausea that was ready to rush out when the whir of an engine tickled my eardrums.

The sound grew louder as the nausea increased. Any second, I was about to puke. Then the engine died, and someone called my name.

For a beat, the nausea settled. *What is Colton doing here? He must've followed me.*

He called my name more loudly. "Skyler!" Concern—like, a ton of it—dripped in his tone.

My mind scrambled to process why he would be so upset or worried. Surely, the word "love" hadn't made him agitated enough to hunt me down... unless he wanted to tell me he felt the same way. If that were the case, I would expect a different emotion. Maybe happiness.

I blew out a breath as I wobbled upright, dizziness washing over me. Maybe it was Colton's presence. He stood inches from me, looking like something that authors described in romance novels. A Greek god. Lips that tempted women into sin. Muscles that bulged with strength and purpose, and eyes that rendered me tongue-tied. He drilled his smooth gaze into me as though he wanted to taste me, tempt me, and devour me.

He caught me before I had a chance to fall. My knight in shining armor. He was always saving me.

He searched my face. "You look pale."

I was sure I was, given how sick my stomach felt and not the fact I was swooning over a guy I was hopelessly in love with.

I gripped his belt in an attempt to keep myself from passing out. The combo of his presence and my sour stomach were becoming too much for me to stay on my feet. "I'm feeling a little sick. I haven't eaten today." I craned my neck upward. That small act clouded my vision. "What are you doing here? You followed me?"

One of his shoulders lifted. "I kind of did, then lost you until I spotted you turning on Taylor Road. I've got protein bars in the truck. Come on. We need to get moving. My mom called when I was trying to catch up to you. It's your dad."

If I was pale before, I turned white as a ghost, afraid to ask the tough question, afraid that if he said my dad was dead, I would bury myself in that cemetery right then with Mom.

"We need to get to the hospital."

No. No. No. My entire body trembled like a ten on the Richter scale. "Please tell me he's okay." I clutched my chest. A stabbing pain so severe was cutting off my circulation and my ability to breathe.

His tender touch on my cheek said it all as he gave a pitiful look. "I don't know, baby doll. Can you walk okay?"

I didn't know if it was "baby doll" or "walk," but a sudden adrenaline boost kicked my legs into gear. Within a second, I was running like a wild horse through the cemetery.

Colton's heavy footsteps pounded behind me. He threw my board into the back of his truck, the sound exploding like a flash bang. After we were strapped in, he peeled out and sped through town as if rushing to a crime scene.

Please, please, let Dad be alive. I repeated that mantra over and over as buildings, store fronts, and homes blipped in my peripheral vision.

He handed me a protein bar, but I refused. Any

ounce of food would come back up. I bounced my knee to keep me from jumping out and running faster than Colton was driving. Red lights stopped us at every corner, and slow cars in front of us were making me want to yell at them to get out of the way.

Finally, after what seemed like eons, Colton screeched to a halt outside the emergency room entrance. I darted out and into the hospital like a crazy woman on steroids.

I sprinted up to the information desk manned by a gray-haired woman. "Randall Lawson. I'm his daughter."

Colton came up behind me, grabbing my hand. "He was brought in about an hour ago." Colton's placid tone did nothing to soothe the nerves that were making me chew one nail after the other.

The woman typed as she concentrated on her computer screen. Time stood still. My heart was ready to stop at a moment's notice. I'd known this day would come. I was hoping it wouldn't be so soon, though.

"Yes," the gray-haired lady said, shattering the cloud hanging over me. "You'll have to wait for a nurse to escort you."

I dashed over to the double doors and pulled on the handle, only to find them locked. I banged on the door, tears spilling faster than I could wipe them. Dad couldn't die yet. I had to say goodbye. I had to look into his eyes and tell him I loved him and not to worry about me. I had to tell him I was in love with Colton, and I needed to thank Dad for being the best father on the planet.

A waterfall of tears poured out like a hard rain.

Colton wrapped his arms around me from behind, and he nuzzled my neck. "I'm here for you. Lean on me."

I wanted to ask him what about leaving town, but I was selfish and wanted him to stay. No, I needed him to stay. I needed him like I'd never needed anyone before. I was afraid that if he let go, I would disintegrate.

I spun around and buried my face in his chest. "He can't die, Colton. He just can't."

He smoothed a hand over my hair. "What's Nan's number? I'll call her. She can come out to get you."

"I don't know. It's programmed in my phone." Which I didn't have. I silently kicked myself. I could've been there before now.

Colton managed to return to the gray-haired

woman without letting go of me. "Can you page Nan..." He glanced down at me. "Last name?"

"Winston," I said. "Nan Winston."

While the woman paged Nan, Colton guided me to a chair that faced the emergency room doors.

I bounced one knee, then the other, gnawing on nail after nail.

A middle-aged woman in a wheelchair rolled by. A child cried somewhere behind me. A drone of hushed voices peppered the room.

Colton pried my fingers from my mouth and held my hand in his lap. "I want to say he'll be okay," he started. "I want to say so many things. But I know it's not the time. Just know I'm not leaving until I know you're okay."

Sadly, I didn't think I would ever be okay if Nan had bad news. Sure, I knew the outlook of Dad's plight. But that didn't make me feel better or make things easier.

I leaned my head on his shoulder as I fixated on the doors, impatiently waiting for a nurse or even Nan to emerge, trying not to think the worst, but I couldn't stop. Dad had ALS. From the day he'd told me he'd been diagnosed with the disease, I'd been wishing and praying for a miracle.

Hell, I still was. To distract myself, I asked, "Why did you follow me?"

"I felt we didn't quite finish our goodbye."

I cried softly, holding him like he was my lifeline. He was. He had to be. I had no one else who would comfort me like he could. I felt safe in his arms, and he'd been through the death of his brother, so he knew what it felt like to lose someone.

I was sure Georgia would be there for me, but it wasn't the same as someone who had experienced the grief and suffering I was about to go through.

Nan ran out, looking wrecked. Her hair was disheveled, her eyes were red, and her skin was ashen.

I couldn't move. I couldn't breathe. Dad had died. I was sure of it.

Nan held out her arms as I shook my head furiously, refusing to move, to believe Dad was gone. I hadn't said a proper goodbye.

Colton helped me to stand. "I got you, baby doll."

My head never stopped moving back and forth as Nan drew close, lowering her arms. Tears dropped down her cheeks, and with each one, I cried harder. "Please tell me he's alive." I could barely hear myself talk.

Her bottom lip wobbled. "He is, but things don't look so good. Your dad has a high fever, and he's in and out of consciousness. They're pumping fluids and meds into him now."

I sagged against Colton, who squeezed me to him. "Dad's alive." For a mere second, hope bloomed like a spring flower.

Colton traded places with Nan. "We'll get through this. Let's go see him."

A male nurse opened the doors as we approached.

"Can I have a second?" I asked Nan. Without waiting for her response, I ran to Colton and hugged him. "Thank you. Thank you for following me. Thank you for being here. You always seem to be saving me in some way or another."

He held me tightly to him. "I didn't save you. You've saved me, Skyler Lawson."

Tilting my head up, I scrunched my face. "How?" A one-word question that would probably take longer than a second to answer. Still, I had to know.

"We'll talk when you have more time. Go see your dad." He flicked his chin at Nan.

"Aren't you leaving?" I asked Colton.

"Skyler." Nan's tone was urgent.

Colton pecked me on the lips. "I'll call you." Then he gave me a little shove. "Your dad needs you."

I couldn't protest. Dad was the most important person in my life, but Colton was becoming a close second. "You promise you'll call?"

His head dipped once as he gave me a blinding grin.

My stomach did a few flips, but quickly soured when I entered the hub of the emergency room.

26

———

The fluorescent lighting overhead blinded me as I approached Dad's glass-walled room. My pulse thundered in my ears as I chewed on my nails. Before long, I would start on my fingers. Nan was right beside me as Isaac, a nurse who had kind brown eyes and a warm smile, walked in.

An astringent odor tickled my nostrils, and that sour stomach I'd had at the cemetery had only intensified.

Nan cupped my elbow. "I'm right here."

I glanced into Dad's room, and the tears were endless. My heart literally hurt. I shook my head. "I can't."

Nan's arm came around my neck. "Come here."

I turned and sobbed into her chest.

She rubbed my back. "He needs us, Skye. And Dr. Branson will take care of him."

I blinked several times to clear my vision. "Georgia's dad is working today?" I pushed out a relieved breath, as though Georgia's dad had a miracle up his sleeve. He didn't, but he knew my dad and what he was going through, and that comforted me.

Nan gave me a sad smile. The whites around her brown eyes were red. "Let's go in." She sounded hesitant.

Isaac was fiddling with Dad's IV when Nan and I entered. As Dad lay unconscious, I couldn't help but think he was in peace for the first time in over a year.

"His fever has dropped slightly. So that's a good sign," Isaac said.

I wasn't sure if I agreed, but I would take anything I could get and celebrate the small wins, the small moments, even if the outcome was still the same.

The room didn't have much except the essentials, such as boxes of gloves in holders on one wall, a monitor above Dad's bed that read his vital signs, and a rolling cart with a keyboard and computer. Underneath that were syringes and other medical supplies needed for the doctors and nurses to do their jobs.

I shuffled up to Dad's bedside on shaky legs, with Nan right on my heels.

"The tests aren't back yet, but Dr. Branson is ninety-nine percent sure it's pneumonia," Nan said.

"He should be in shortly," Isaac said as he finished adjusting the drip on Dad's IV.

I found Dad's clammy hand and held it, careful not to touch the pulse oximeter on his finger. "Is the pneumonia from him choking last night?"

"I couldn't say," Isaac said. "Aspiration pneumonia does come on rather rapidly, though, and is common in ALS patients."

He wasn't telling me anything I didn't already know. I'd remembered Dad's neurologist saying that very thing, which was why I always freaked out when Dad choked.

I stared at him through a cloud of tears, trying not to think the worst. "Can I be alone with him?"

I loved Nan to death, but I wanted time alone with my dad. Even if he wasn't lucid, maybe he could hear me.

Nan patted my arm. "Take your time. I'm going

to get coffee, and I need to call the hospice people back."

My heart rate sped. Hospice was coming, so he probably only had a few months left.

Nan brushed a stray hair out of my eye. "It doesn't mean he's going to die in the next month. But we need to prepare, and a nurse will come in once or twice a week to monitor your dad's progress and keep him comfortable."

Even though I knew she was right, it seemed that we were hammering the final nail into Dad's coffin. "I know." I worried my trembling bottom lip. I wanted my dad around longer.

She pinned me with a motherly look, lifting her chin. "He needs us to be strong."

I wasn't sure if I could be. But she was right. If Dad—no, scratch that. *When* Dad woke up, I wanted him to see us happy.

Once Nan was gone and Isaac was no longer in the room, I mindlessly stared out the glass doors, digging deep for strength and courage. A group of nurses laughed at something Isaac was saying at their circular station, which seemed to be where the party was. Envy washed over me. I wanted to laugh as though I didn't have a care in the world.

A tall man ambled toward the group, and it

took me a second to realize it was Dr. Branson. He said something to the nurses before they broke up, scurrying to get back to work. Dr. Branson spoke with Isaac before he flicked his blond head of hair toward me.

Isaac's lips moved as he responded to Dr. Branson. Georgia's dad didn't look pleased as the features around his green eyes wrinkled. Then he nodded to Isaac as he strutted my way.

I prepared for the bad news I was sure Dr. Branson would deliver. He entered with his hands tucked into his white coat pockets, stoic and professional instead of the casual and relaxed vibe he usually wore when I was at Georgia's house.

Before he said anything, I was in his arms as though he could save Dad and me. "Please tell me he'll come out of this."

He grasped the sides of my arms, his expression soft. "I can't, honey."

I knew he couldn't, but I wanted hope. I needed hope. I needed something to take away the grief burning a hole in my chest.

"Skyler, we'll do everything we can."

I could hear the "but" in his voice, and he didn't have to say anything else.

"Can Georgia see my dad?" The hospital rules

said only close family was allowed in, but Georgia was family. Besides, if anyone could break the rules, it was Dr. Branson. He was head of the ER.

"Tell you what," he said. "Let's see how your dad responds to meds. And we're about to run some scans on his lungs. Until then, no other visitors."

"She doesn't know about Dad," I said. "I don't have my phone, either."

"I'll tell her. I'll be back after I have the results of the scan."

The minute he was gone, I cried hard. The heaviness on my heart was too much. As I had a ton of times before, I checked his chest to make sure he was still breathing, although the monitor behind his bed said he was.

Holding Dad's hand, I bowed my head. "God, if you're listening, could you give my dad a little more time with me? And Dad, please pull through. I want a chance to tell you more about Colton. I want to tell you that I love you more than you know. I want to see you smile, to see your blue eyes light up when we reminisce about Mom." I sighed, trying so hard not to collapse with grief, which was an impossible feat.

Whatever happened next was in God's hands.

27

————————

Nine solid days of hell had passed since Dad had been rushed to the hospital. I'd barely eaten or slept, and I definitely hadn't gone to school. I wasn't leaving Dad's side even if truant officers tried to pry me away.

Nan had insisted I go home, have a shower, and get a good night's sleep. I almost laughed in her face. Home was the last place I wanted to be. Too many memories, and Dad wasn't there.

I couldn't leave the hospital. I had to be close and able to react at a moment's notice, especially since Dad had slipped into a coma. He'd had several ups and downs with his fever spiking, then dropping. The scan of his lungs showed pneumonia, which wasn't surprising. What was, though, was the fact that meds weren't working to clear it up.

A pine scent mixed with some other type of cleaning solution burned my nostrils as I passed an open door to a restroom on the first floor. The smell seemed to jar my brain and open my eyes just before I bumped into a person in a wheelchair.

I skirted around the old man. "I'm so sorry."

The gray-haired man gave me an easygoing grin as though people ran into him all the time. I was sure they did. When Dad had gone out in public in his wheelchair, people didn't pay an ounce of attention to where they were going and often stumbled or fell into him.

I continued down the hall, passing medical personnel. I was on my way to meet Georgia. I hadn't seen her since the day Dad had been rushed in, and with him in ICU, there were definitely no visitors other than Nan and me. No matter how much pull Dr. Branson had in the ER, he didn't have a say in the ICU.

I rounded the corner and found Georgia. It was easy, considering that the lobby was empty, save for Georgia and a man in a business suit who was pacing near the entrance with his phone to his ear.

She pushed off the wall, and even though sadness was stamped on her pretty face, I was stoked to see her.

We met in the middle and embraced like lovers who hadn't seen each other in years.

She cried. I cried.

After a long minute, she guided me to a bank of empty chairs along the wall.

"You look great," I said.

She was dressed in black skinny jeans, ankle boots, and a knit top that hugged her curves.

She tucked a blond curl behind her ear. "Given what you're going through, you look good too."

I smiled weakly. I didn't think I did. But Nan had brought clean clothes. I'd been able to freshen up in one of the restrooms up on the ICU floor. That day, I was wearing an old pair of yoga pants and an oversized sweatshirt. They kept the ICU rather cold for some reason.

"I begged my dad to let me see your dad," she said. "He told me this morning he would get me up to ICU."

"Really? Dad isn't awake, but he might be able to hear your voice." I believed he could hear mine.

Anytime I talked to him, I swore the corners of his mouth turned up a tick. Deep down, I knew I was imagining that, but I had to believe he was listening.

She frowned. "Everyone at school is asking about you. Mia wanted to come, but she has a game tonight, and I told her she couldn't see your dad even if she did."

I picked at a finger. My nails were gone. I'd bitten each one down to the nub. "Do you know if Colton is still in town?" I swallowed before holding my breath.

I hadn't heard from him since he'd brought me to the hospital. I had, however, thought about him a lot and about what he'd said: *I want to say so many things. But I know it's not the time. Just know I'm not leaving until I know you're okay.*

His last line had found a home in the forefront of my mind as I wondered if he had left after all. Nan had told me the Caldwell house seemed quiet and dark, which she'd found odd. I did too. Colton had planned to stay with a friend in Virginia, but maybe he and his parents had decided to get away as a family. For Colton's sake, I hoped he could work out his differences with his dad. He didn't need to shoulder the blame for his brother's death.

Regardless, as much as I would have loved to see Colton, Dad came first.

Georgia placed her hand on my thigh. "Grady tried calling him several times with no luck."

I jerked my head up. "You don't think anything happened to him?" Oh God. I couldn't lose another person I loved.

"I don't think so. I went by his house before I came here. No answer. There were no cars in the driveway, either. I peeked in the windows of their garage, too, and it was empty. If you ask me, I think they left town."

Relief coursed through me, warming my veins. "I told him I loved him."

She gasped. "For real? And?"

I licked my chapped lips. "Not sure. He told me we would talk when I have more time. I haven't been home. So I don't know."

She puckered her mouth like she was about to whistle. "Wow. I mean, I know he's your crush, but to tell him... Now, it's real."

I giggled. "For sure."

"He'll surface," she said with confidence.

Whether he did or not, I couldn't worry about him.

My phone pinged. I fumbled to get it out of the tight pocket of my yoga pants.

A text from Nan: *Please come up now!*

I vaulted off the chair as the blood drained from me.

"What is it?" Georgia's eyes nearly popped out of their sockets.

"It's Dad. I've got to go."

"I'm coming with, whether or not I'm allowed."

I wasn't going to stop her. I could use her support. Even though she was as emotional as I was, she had a way of steadying me.

Once at the elevator, Georgia stabbed the up button hard and several times. It felt like centuries passed before the door opened, and even longer when we were inside and the car seemed to move at a snail's pace.

I leaned against the wall. "Dad's gone," I muttered more to myself. I could almost feel it in my bones. I might be crazy, but that sense of loss was all-consuming.

"You don't know that," Georgia fired back. "Maybe he woke up."

A small part of me rejoiced at that thought, praying she was right. I'd told Dad everything I could possibly think of over the last nine days, not certain he'd heard me. So getting that one last chance to see his blue eyes and tell him I loved him would give me a sense of closure. Despite the time I'd had to prepare for this moment, I wasn't ready.

Maybe he woke up. That was my mantra, and the only thing I focused on as Georgia and I finally exited the elevator.

She grasped my hand as we entered ICU. "Think positively."

Easier said than done, but I took her advice just the same. I lifted my chin and rolled back my shoulders. "I'm glad you're here with me."

The room tilted on its axis when I spotted Nan crying outside Dad's room. Normally that wouldn't freak me out, since she and I had been shedding enough tears to fill several oceans since Dad had been admitted. But she squatted down with her face in her hands, and I knew instantly that he was gone.

Surprisingly, I didn't cry, not even when I saw how peaceful he looked, as though he'd found freedom from that stupid disease. I made it to his bedside without collapsing and kissed him on the cheek. "I love you, Daddy. I hope heaven is everything you dreamed it to be and that you see Mom.

I hope you can walk and talk again and tell all your friends in heaven jokes until they're laughing so hard they're crying. Embrace peace. Hug Mom for me and know I will be fine. I'll be thinking of you every day for the rest of my life."

Georgia sobbed, the sound tearing out my soul. "I'm sorry." She stood on the other side of the bed. "I love you, Mr. Lawson. You were always like a second dad to me."

Nan cried in the background.

I went over to console Nan—or maybe it was my way of consoling myself. Either way, we needed each other.

Georgia joined us, and the three of us formed a group hug.

Nan said a prayer. Then I gave Dad one last glance and blew him a kiss.

I wasn't sure if I was prepared for tomorrow or the next day or even the next hour. I wasn't even sure I could walk into my house without Dad being there. But I had to believe I would get through it. I had to believe that everything in life happened for a reason—a good reason.

For the time being, I had to hold on to that thought because if I didn't, I wouldn't make it through the night.

28

I hated to leave the hospital. I felt as though I was leaving my entire world behind. I was a zombie as Nan drove through the town I'd grown up in, one that appeared foreign to me. Memories of Mom, Dad, and me eating at many of the restaurants we passed pricked my psyche. A smile broke out as one memory in particular bombarded me.

We'd been eating at my favorite Chinese restaurant, and Dad decided to tell one of many jokes he had in his arsenal. It wasn't so much the joke I remembered as how animated he'd been when he told it and how he'd laughed harder at his jokes than Mom and me.

Reality sped by outside as people went about their days as if they didn't have a care in the world. I wanted to experience that again, the freedom I'd had when Mom and Dad were alive. I was desperate to wake up the next day and feel happy, as though everything had been just a nightmare. I wanted to run downstairs and watch Dad make his famous blueberry pancakes or talk to him about baseball or football or whatever the sport was for that season.

Stop torturing yourself, Skyler.

I leaned my head against the passenger window. "Mom's death hit me hard," I muttered. "But why do I feel like Dad's is worse?"

Nan patted my leg, keeping her attention on the streets ahead. "Oh, sweetie. You've lost two parents. No child should lose both at such a young age. I love you, Skye. We'll get through this."

I sure hoped she was right because at the moment, I felt like it would take years before I would feel joy in my soul. "I love you too. I'm glad you're here with me and for me." I loved Georgia, but I wasn't sure I wanted to live with her.

The bright lights of town dissolved into a dimly lit street as Nan navigated through our neighborhood.

"Can you keep driving?" I asked.

She slowed about three houses from ours. "I could, but you need rest."

"I can't sleep. I can't go into the house, either." I rubbed my chest, hoping the fire burning a hole in my lungs would simmer.

"You need to try, Skyler. Also, we need to talk."

I was certain she wanted to talk about Dad's funeral, but the topic became a blip on my radar screen when I saw who was sitting on our porch.

Nan jerked her head toward me. "Does he know?"

"Not sure." Georgia had told me before we left the hospital that she would let Mia know, which meant Mia would tell Grady. Maybe Grady had finally been able to connect with Colton.

"He looks like he needs a shoulder to cry on," Nan said as a matter of fact.

Our porch light cast a glow, highlighting Colton's forlorn expression. If my heart wasn't broken, it would've cracked in several places for him. I wondered what had changed so drastically since he'd taken me to the hospital. He'd been so relaxed that day in the school's parking lot.

The car came to a stop in our driveway, and Nan left the engine running. "I just remembered we don't have anything to eat in the house. Why don't I run and get some Chinese?"

I didn't know if she was trying to give me some time alone with Colton or not. It didn't matter. What mattered was the sudden dark thought that had gripped my brain. "Did something happen to his parents? You said you hadn't seen them all week." She'd been home a few times while I'd stayed at the hospital.

"I don't know."

Given that Colton's dad drank or was drunk more times than not, I wondered if something had happened to his dad.

My hand was primed to open the car door, but my limbs were locked. I couldn't take any more bad news. I couldn't bear to see Colton looking like he'd lost his best friend.

"Skyler," Nan said. "My mom once told me that emotional pain can heal faster when you help another who is suffering." She glanced out her window, then back to me. "That boy, he's about to explode. So find a way to channel your pain to help him. Maybe in the end, you two will help each other."

I believed Colton had helped me by occupying every waking thought I'd had since he returned home from the academy. I believed he was the reason I hadn't stressed over Dad as much as I had before school started.

I got out on shaky legs and waited until Nan backed out before I started toward Colton. When I did, my legs quivered, feeling heavy with each step I took. My stomach fisted into a knot that grew tighter the closer I got to him. I wondered if he remembered that I'd told him I loved him. But that wasn't the topic I wanted to start with.

I waved tentatively as I settled on the bottom step.

Seconds, minutes, hours seemed to tick by. Then ever so slowly, he unfolded his muscular frame and climbed down the steps until we were barely an inch apart.

I sucked in the warm night air along with his clean, soapy scent, and I almost whimpered.

"Hi." His Southern drawl caused my skin to tingle. "Grady told me about your dad. I'm sorry for your loss."

My bottom lip started to wobble. Instead of saying thank you, I wrapped my arms around his waist and pressed my ear against his chest. It didn't matter that I hadn't heard from him in a week. It didn't matter that he'd made himself a ghost.

What mattered was that he was with me then, and he'd come at the perfect time. I wouldn't have paid much attention to Colton with Dad in a coma, anyway.

He held me to him as though he needed me as much as I needed him. I couldn't help but think of what Nan had just told me about channeling my pain.

He rested his chin on top of my head as he rubbed my back. "I wanted to be there with you this week, but I had to take care of my parents."

I stiffened.

"My mom checked my old man into a rehab center in South Carolina this week. I was just getting back into town when Grady sent me the text."

I craned my neck up at him. "Where's your mom?"

"She's staying with a friend in Charleston, not far from the rehab center, for a few days."

My shoulders sagged, relieved that his parents were okay. "Why do you look like you lost your best friend?"

"I'm just tired, Skyler. And I'm kicking myself for not being here for you. I told you I wouldn't leave until you were okay."

Oh my word. He blamed himself for his brother's death and endured punch after punch from his father, yet he was worried about me. "Hey, stop that. Your parents come first. It's great your dad is getting help. And your mom needed you. Plus I'm a tiny bit better now that you're here."

His lips split into a thigh-squeezing grin. "Just a tiny bit?"

I batted my lashes, ropes of pleasure spiraling downward. "Maybe a lot."

He chuckled, a sound that was glorious and only heightened my desire to give him my most precious virtue.

"You should laugh more, Colton."

His lips feathered over mine. "I plan to, and only if you're with me."

I was definitely not going anywhere. "Wait, aren't you staying with your friend in Virginia?"

"Not anymore. My mom is giving me some space this week, and she's convinced me to finish school here."

Maybe I had an angel watching over me. Maybe that angel was Dad. "That's great news."

"Yeah?" he asked, fixated on my lips.

"You can kiss me." *If he doesn't, I might combust.*

"Not yet, Skyler."

My forehead creased. I knew he wanted me

and wondered what had changed. "I don't care about your control."

"It's not about that."

"Are you afraid, then?" That didn't make sense, either. Colton didn't strike me as the type of guy who was afraid of anything.

He backed far away. "Not afraid in the least, but you need to process your dad's death. I'm not about to take advantage of your emotions."

As sweet and considerate as he was, I needed something or someone to take my mind away from Dad, to take away the pain and numbness, to hold me and tell me everything would be okay.

But Colton wasn't a distraction. He was the love of my life. "I'm in love with you, Colton." Life was too short to mince words. The two people I loved the most were gone. I wasn't about to lose him too.

I could see his mind working hard, as if trying to find the next thing to say.

"You could never take advantage of me or my emotions. Not when I want you," I added.

He rushed toward me, captured my face in his hands, and kissed me like I was the only one who could give him his next breath.

The ground seemed to shake beneath me as

his tongue dove into my mouth, insistently and possessively. I gripped his arms, hoping I didn't pass out from the sheer passion that was pouring out of him. If I'd been unsure of how he felt before, I wasn't anymore.

"Fuck, Skyler." He toyed with my bottom lip. "I have to stop. If I don't, we won't come up for air."

"Who needs air?" He was the conduit to breathing life back into me, the person who I had no doubt could dim the anguish and suffering gripping me.

Our gazes tangled for a split second before I jumped into his arms.

He caught me, grabbing my butt as I locked my fingers around his neck. Then it was my turn to show him how much I wanted him.

"I'm crazy for you, Skyler." The husky timbre of his voice slid over me like silk.

"Then let go. I'm yours, Colton Caldwell."

He growled as our mouths collided—hungry, frantic, rough, soft, hard, sloppy—and I loved every minute of what he was doing to my heart, body, and soul.

I didn't know how long we were glued to each other, but I pouted when Nan drove up.

"I should go. I have a meeting with the football

coach to see if I can get back on the team. I'll see you tomorrow?" He nodded at Nan, who was carrying a bag of Chinese food.

"You can stay for dinner," Nan said to Colton.

I didn't want him to leave, but considering how intense that kiss was, we needed a break. Otherwise, Nan might find us in a compromising position in my bedroom after dinner, and that wasn't the way I wanted to start my new relationship with her.

The deck lights lined the perimeter around the railings, providing a soft glow to an otherwise eerie night. A drizzle fell as I stared out the sliding glass door in the kitchen. Sleep had escaped me, but I wasn't surprised. My mind was more awake than ever. Dad had only been gone for seven hours, and the weight of his passing felt like a boulder on my chest. If Dad wasn't in my thoughts, then Colton was. I believed Colton was the reason my soul was still intact.

The creak of the stairs made me flinch. Nan probably couldn't sleep, either.

I hugged myself as I watched the branches sway in the distance.

She sidled up to me, gently touched my arm, and let out a soft sigh. "A storm is coming."

As if she'd willed the gods, the wind lifted the leaves and errant pinecones off the deck and tossed them around.

"I can't stay here," I mumbled. I felt like a storm was brewing inside me, turbulent, wild, and destructive. "It's too painful."

I wished Colton was with me. When I'd been securely cocooned in his arms, the pain had dulled. But I didn't expect him to be at my side in the middle of the night. He wasn't home yet, anyway. He was probably hanging with Grady after the meeting with the football coach. I imagined they were playing pool or kicking back. If Colton had been next door, I would've been nestled in his arms.

Nan tucked her hands into the pockets of her robe. "Maybe you should spend the weekend at Georgia's. I'm sure she needs you as much as you need her. It will take your mind off things."

Georgia had texted when she'd gotten home from the hospital. I knew she was worried about me. "I don't want to leave you." Nan was mourning too.

She snagged me into her side. "I'll be okay."

I lay my head on her shoulder, watching the wind wreak havoc on the trees outside.

"Try to enjoy the weekend with your bestie. When Monday rolls around, we'll talk about school."

It sounded odd to hear the word "school." I hadn't thought about classes or teachers or grades. Since Dad had been admitted, everything had become one big blur. "Don't we have to talk about the funeral?"

"We have plenty of time for that next week. Right now, we both need some time to mourn."

After Mom had passed, Dad and I had taken a road trip to clear our heads. We'd talked endlessly about Mom and celebrated her life. The time away had helped to ease our suffering, so I wasn't about to argue. I knew Georgia would keep my mind occupied. She had a way of knowing how to make me laugh, even if I really wanted to hang out with Colton. He could definitely relate to what I was going through.

A car door slammed, making me pull away from Nan. Colton was home. I'd peeked out the window a few times since I'd been up to see if he'd gotten home.

As if Nan knew I was thinking about him, she said, "You love Colton. Don't you?"

"It's that obvious, huh?" No sense in denying how I felt. After all, she'd witnessed us with our tongues down each other's throats when she'd returned with dinner.

The light from the hood over the stove cast a glow around the kitchen, highlighting her tired and red-rimmed eyes. "First love is always intense. Do me a favor? Please make sure you practice safe sex."

A flush of heat crawled up my neck. It wasn't so much the topic that was making me burn from the inside out, but the thought of sex with Colton. Aside from the play-by-play Mia had given Georgia and me from time to time, I didn't know much.

A knowing smile played across her lips. "I was a teenager once. No need to be mortified."

"I guess it's more of the fact I'm still a virgin."

She slumped as though relieved. "Maybe we should put you on the pill."

I imagined a similar convo if Mom had been there. No way could I have spoken to Dad about the birds and the bees. "You would be okay with that?"

She smoothed a hand over my hair. "I'm here to guide and help you, not lay down strict rules to keep you from growing into a young woman. I know you have a good head on your shoulders. But do me a favor?"

"Anything." I wanted to make her proud of me, as if she were my mom.

"Anytime you feel like you can't make it through the day, I want you to talk to me or Colton or Georgia. Please don't suppress your feelings."

I hugged her with all I had. She was the best gift God could've given Dad and me. "Thank you."

"Aw, sweetie. I love you."

I couldn't keep the tears at bay anymore. "I love you too."

"We should try to get some sleep."

Rain began to fall, battering against the sliding glass door. Then thunder boomed.

Nan and I turned our attention outside as a flash of lightning brightened the yard.

"I love the rain." Nan yawned. "I'm going to bed. Maybe the rain will help me sleep. The sound is soothing. I'll see you in the morning." She left just as Stella came into the kitchen, purring.

I wasn't ready to put my head on a pillow or lie in bed and watch my ceiling fan turn endlessly.

I picked up my Maine Coon and stroked her ears. "Hey, girl. You can't sleep, either?" I imagined she might have been wandering around, looking for Dad.

She jumped down just as the front door opened.

"What are you doing out there?" Nan asked. "It's pouring. Come inside."

I ran into the family room and stopped short.

Colton flicked his worried gaze in my direction.

I shuddered, hoping nothing had happened.

"Colton, it's two in the morning. Is everything okay?" Nan asked in a concerned tone.

I was beginning to think the worst. Maybe something had happened to Grady, or even to Colton's dad.

"Yes, ma'am," he said, not breaking our connection. "I saw Skyler's light on in her bedroom. I wanted to check on her."

A rush of air escaped me.

Nan folded her arms over her chest, regarding me.

I sent her a silent plea with my eyes, hoping she would get the message and not tell him to leave. If there was one thing that could help me relax, it was Colton holding me.

"Well, don't stay too long," Nan said to Colton. "Skyler needs rest."

Not true. I needed Colton.

Nan climbed the steps with Stella taking off ahead of her. Colton and I didn't move until Nan's bedroom door clicked shut.

Then Colton crossed the room in three long strides, hauled me to him, hoisted me in his arms, and pressed his lips to mine as though we'd been apart for years. My mind cleared, and I was transported to a sea of calm waters and warm sunshine.

"I missed you," I said, licking my lips as he nuzzled his nose against my neck.

"I've been thinking about you all night. You okay?"

My fingers danced through his damp hair. "I am now. It's been hard to sleep."

He carried me over to our leather couch and sat down with me straddling him. "Want me to stay until you fall asleep?" His voice was rough yet smooth.

Nan might not like that, but I couldn't imagine her wigging out too much if we stayed on the couch.

"I would like that. But first I need to do something."

He arched a brow. "So do I."

His tongue was in my mouth again, teasing and taking in frenzied strokes.

Lust curled its way through my body until I was grinding into his growing erection.

His hands were everywhere yet nowhere. His tongue was doing things to my mouth that I envisioned him doing in other regions of my body.

I rocked into him, needing friction, needing to sate the hunger that had overpowered my senses.

The sound of rain was our music. The beat of my heart kept time with it. I was ready to tear off my clothes when I heard a bang. Colton stiffened. I glanced up, opening my ears.

"It was probably something outside," Colton said. "The wind is brutal."

I crawled off him and snuggled at his side. He cocooned me in with his big, strong arm. It was best we didn't take our lust any further. With my luck, Nan couldn't sleep.

I rubbed his chiseled abs as I stared at the fireplace. "Did you get back on the team?"

"I did. Coach understood."

The sharp burst of lightning followed by the

rumble of thunder made me nestle deeper into him.

He chuckled. "Do you not like thunderstorms?"

"I don't mind them. I guess I'm just on edge. Please stay until I fall asleep." If I even could.

"I'm not going anywhere." His tone sounded like a lullaby as I closed my eyes, trying not to think of Dad, but it was hard. I couldn't shake the images of him in his hospital bed, not breathing. Suddenly, one tear, then another, fell, and before I could stop, I was sobbing.

He dragged his fingers lightly over my arm. "Let it out, baby doll." He kissed the top of my head. "I know the feeling like it was yesterday." His voice cracked.

I buried my face in his chest. "I miss him so much already."

He squeezed me tightly to him, pressing his cheek to my head. At that moment, I cried harder. Dad had always done that very thing.

Several minutes passed as we sat in the dark, quiet room, the ping of the rain dripping off the roof of the porch.

I sniffled as my tears began to lessen. "Colton, is your dad going to be okay?"

"I hope so." He sounded sad.

"Are you?"

He lightly tickled my arm in an up-and-down movement. "With you, Skyler, my darkness isn't so dark anymore. You saved me."

I recalled him telling me that at the hospital, but I hadn't had a chance to ask him. "How?"

His chest heaved. "Do you remember saying, 'At least you have a father'?"

"That was rude of me."

I could feel his grin on my head. "No, it wasn't. It was the truth. Anyway, when I saw the sheer pain you were going through at the hospital, I realized what I had to do for me to get past the years of grief that has eaten away at me for so long." His heart pounded like the little drummer boy. "I had to tell my old man that I loved him despite how he treated me. I hadn't uttered that to him since before Josh's death. My guilt blinded me so much, I couldn't see how my parents were suffering too. I will always feel responsible for what happened to my brother, but you made me see that sometimes we're given a raw deal in life, and we need to find a way to look forward, not backward."

"I did all that?"

"You're strong, baby. You're so emotionally strong that I'm in awe."

"I don't think so. The only reason I haven't broken down is you. Since you returned home, you've been the star of my dreams, and that has helped me to focus on something other than despair."

"Star of your dreams, huh?"

"Number one." I giggled.

Silence dangled, the fridge compressor and the rain pelting the house the only sounds.

"Grady told me you just found out you're adopted."

Thanks to Mia. I couldn't be mad at her, though. It wasn't a secret. "I am." I wasn't sure I had the energy to go any further than that. I yawned. "Can we talk about something else?"

"Try to sleep," he whispered.

I yawned and took in a deep breath. Then my body gave in to sleep.

30

———

The fire crackled while the hum of the surf broke along the shore. Unlike the stormy night before, stars twinkled, the moon shone like a beacon in the dead of night, and the sea was serene. Georgia, Grady, Mia, Colton, and I sat on the beach outside Grady's mansion. The mood was somber and chill. My friends were mourning with me. The plan had been to hang at Georgia's for the weekend, but Mia had called and told us to get our asses over to Grady's.

"Skye needs to take her mind off of things," she had said.

I agreed. Otherwise, my eyes would have been swollen shut from bawling, which I'd done since the minute I'd woken up that morning. The house felt empty, cold, and depressing. I understood why Dad moved us to a new house after Mom died—the memories were painful. I'd cried for an hour before I even got out of bed, then tried to go into his room but couldn't.

"It's too soon," Nan had said. "Go to Georgia's and try to unwind."

So I'd showered, dressed, and packed a bag before heading to my BFF's.

"Baby doll, are you okay?" Colton said in my ear.

His gravelly voice shattered the depressing haze I was in. "I am." I loved being out on the beach and listening to the waves. I especially loved being in his arms. The grief that was settling in had become stronger that morning, but his presence dulled the pain.

"I feel like the lone wolf." Georgia giggled as she stared at the flames.

I guess I would have, too, if I was alone with two couples. Mia was cozied up to Grady, and Colton had his arms around me while I sat between his legs with my back to his front.

"You could always join us," Grady announced as he waggled his eyebrows.

Mia pinched Grady's leg. "Grady." Her tone was lethal.

"What?" he asked innocently, though all of us knew otherwise. "Come on, babe. You know you want to have a threesome."

Colton cleared his throat. "So, man, is your dad at another timeshare convention this weekend?"

Grady's expression went from playful to perplexed, or maybe he wanted to deck Colton for changing the subject. "Something like that."

Grady's dad owned several resorts from Florida to the Bahamas, which kept him busy with traveling just about every weekend. Apparently, weekends were the busiest times for selling timeshares. In addition, since Grady's parents had divorced a few years ago, his dad worked constantly.

"You know what we need to help Skyler," Grady said.

I glared at him. If he so much as said "threesome," I would throw him in the ocean.

Mia perked up. "Party, music, dancing."

I wasn't sure I was up for a party. I would prefer to spend time alone with Colton. But I knew my friends were trying to help.

"Babe," Grady said to Mia. "You read my mind."

They were definitely a match made in heaven.

Georgia was on her feet in seconds, grinning from ear to ear. "I'll send some texts."

Before long, Mia and Grady were both on their phones.

"Want to take a walk?" Colton asked as he brushed his lips over my ear.

"Instead of a walk, can we do something else?" I asked.

"Mmm. I have an idea." He peppered kisses along my neck.

I leaned into him, relaxing even more. I wanted nothing more than to let him do whatever he wanted to me. But I needed to expend some energy. Sure, sex could probably have done just that, but I had the sudden urge to get on my skateboard. There was something about the feeling of catching air or just cruising that gave me the sense that Dad was with me. Maybe because he'd given me my board.

I popped up and held out my hand. "Come on." I tipped my head toward Grady's house.

His brown eyes darkened as he plastered on the most belly-tingling grin I had yet to see on him. He was upright in one second flat.

I hated to disappoint him, but I tugged him as we bypassed Grady's house.

"Where are we going?" he asked. "The door into the house is that way?" He stabbed a finger behind him.

"Skate park." I stuck out my bottom lip.

Confusion lined his forehead. "You want to skate?"

I pouted more. "Please. Afterwards, I'll do whatever you want."

He lit up like a Christmas tree. "Whatever I want?"

I captured my bottom lip between my teeth and nodded.

"Deal," he said too quickly.

I giggled, knowing he had something intimate in mind for later, but I was cool with that.

Fifteen minutes later, Colton and I were at the skate park.

"I hope you don't want me to get on that board." He pointed to my baby in my hand as we walked up to the bowl.

"Why not? Don't you surf?"

"I haven't since Josh died. But surfing and skateboarding are not the same."

I rolled my eyes. "Kind of similar."

"Yeah, but if I fall on my face in there"—he stabbed a finger to the brightly lit bowl where four boys were flying high and doing verticals —"I'm toast. At least in the water, I might be bruised, but my bones won't be connecting with cement. Coach might kill me if I break a bone."

"How about you watch while I do my thing?"

"I'll watch you do anything." He wiggled his eyebrows. "Remember, when we're done here, it's my turn. You'll do what I want. Right?"

I rolled my eyes and shrugged as I headed in.

"Skyler," Colton called. Then he swaggered up to me, his hair loose around his shoulders, his jaw full of scruff, his red T-shirt stretched across his broad chest, and his jeans encasing his thick thighs and narrow hips.

My lady parts throbbed at how gorgeous he really was, and the closer he got, the need to skate died a quick death.

He sized me up with a hooded expression. I shivered where I stood, with my skateboard in one hand as the other landed on his waist for nothing more than to steady myself.

He gripped my neck with his big palm as his forehead touched mine. "You're all mine after this." The huskiness of his voice threatened pleasure and passion.

I swallowed the dryness in my throat. "Promise."

He leaned down, captured my lips, and bit lightly. "Good. Now, let's see what you can do on that board."

I had a feeling I wouldn't be able to do a damn thing, not after that pulse-racing moment.

31

A couple of hours later, Colton carried me into Grady's house. Bass pounded from the speakers in the ceiling as kids drank, mingled, and danced in all corners of the open floor plan.

"I can walk. It's only a scrape." Apparently I was rusty, and I'd skated like it had been my first time.

"Move," Colton snapped at a group of girls who looked as if they'd seen a ghost. I did have blood running down my leg.

As I bounced in his arms, I spotted Georgia talking to a guy with curly red hair. I'd never seen him before. They seemed to be into each other, and Georgia waved her hands in the air as she often did when she talked excitedly.

I locked my hands around Colton's neck. "Seriously, I can walk."

He grunted. "You're not."

"I'm fine," I assured him. I really was. I'd fallen many times on my skateboard, and I'd relayed that to him when he sped through the streets to get to Grady's. At first, he'd wanted to take me to the emergency room. He'd thought I'd broken some bones.

"I'm not," he said, a little breathily. After his brother's fatal drowning accident, I imagined Colton would always be on edge with people he cared for.

I rubbed his neck while kids opened a swath to let us by. Colton didn't even stop to say anything to Grady, who was playing beer pong at the long kitchen island. All he did was shake his head at Grady, who seemed to get the silent message that Colton didn't need any help.

When Colton banked around a corner to climb the stairs, a mass of auburn hair came into my peripheral vision.

Amanda Gelling glided down toward us. "Colton, there you are."

I growled, narrowing my eyes at her.

"Not now, Amanda," he said as he continued to climb the stairs.

"My mom has been trying to get a hold of yours," she said. "She needs to get her signature on the documents."

Colton stopped on the landing. "I'll let my mom know." Then he rounded the corner, heading toward one of the bedrooms.

"What's going on?" Since Mrs. Gelling was in real estate, it wasn't hard to connect the dots. "Are you selling the house?" If so, that meant he was moving. My stomach hollowed.

He carried me into the same bedroom I'd woken up in the last time Grady had a party. "I think so. My mom likes South Carolina, and she feels like she and my old man need a fresh start."

I didn't know what to say as he nudged open the door to the en suite bathroom and set me down on the marble counter. Then he flicked on the light.

"Are you leaving, then?" *Please say no. Please, please, please.*

He blinked, shaking his head. "No. No way. I'm sorry, baby. I'm still reeling from your near plummet to death."

I held back a laugh. He was really shaken up. I guessed I couldn't blame him. That vertical had been as steep as it always was. I gave him a few minutes to process my banged-up knee, which was clotting and fine.

He grabbed a washcloth from behind me, wetted it, and gently wiped the dirt and blood away. When he was finished, he sighed.

"See, I'm good."

His snarl didn't match the smile in his eyes.

"So, if you're not going with your mom, will you stay with Grady?"

"When the house sells, yeah. Grady's dad gave me the thumbs-up. I'll finish school here. I'm not leaving you, Skyler."

I couldn't contain my smile. I did a silent fist pump in the air.

"I should find a bandage." He ducked into the linen closet and came out with a first-aid kit.

"I'm okay, Colton."

He searched my face. "You scared the crap out of me."

I reached up and touched his scruffy jaw. "Falling is part of the sport." I'd said the same thing to my dad not long before he passed. *Skyler*

Lawson, don't you dare shed any tears. Your dad loved seeing you on your skateboard.

"What is it? Does it hurt?"

I stared at a cracked button on his shirt. "Just thinking of Dad."

With the pads of his fingers, he guided me to look at him. "Anything I can do?"

"Hold me."

He was making quick work of bandaging my knee when Georgia's voice trickled into the huge bathroom that I'd only just started to take in.

A walk-in shower built for six was surrounded by glass, adorned with brushed stainless fixtures and brown-and-tan tile, with a separate sunken tub and a skylight above.

"Sky-ler." Georgia slurred my name as she stumbled in.

Colton and I exchanged a surprised look. I probably had more shock on my face than he did. I'd never seen Georgia tipsy, and if she had been the night I'd gotten drunk, I didn't remember.

She swung her arm toward the wall, her green eyes glossy. "What happened? You went sk-ating, didn't you?" Yep, she'd had one too many.

"I was dropping into the bowl and lost my balance. It's Colton's fault." My tone was playful, although I chalked up my fall to the fact that he had taken my mind hostage.

Colton arched his brow. "My fault?"

I gave him a coy smile, but it went unnoticed when Georgia slid down the wall.

Colton's reflexes were quick as he caught her. "Let's get you to a room." He lifted her into his arms. "Skyler, don't move." He gave me the evil eye before he left with Georgia.

"Bye, bestie!" Georgia shouted as she rested her head on Colton's shoulder.

If she remembered anything in the morning, I was sure she would be babbling about how strong Colton was.

Smiling, I hopped off the counter, and my knee buckled. "Ow." I walked around, working out the kinks. A dull pain finally started to set in. I was examining my elbow in the mirror when Colton returned. "That was quick."

"There's another guest room down the hall." He came up behind me, wrapped his arms around my waist, and nuzzled his nose into my neck. "Are you sure you're okay?"

I turned in his arms. "I think so. And with you here, the loss isn't as suffocating. So it's your turn.

What do you want to do?" I was done talking about me.

He caged me in, one hand on each side of me, fingers gripping the counter. His eyes darkened as his thick lips curled at the corners ever so slightly.

My heart tripped once at the intensity in his stare. He raised a hand to my face, his touch as tender as if I was the most delicate creature in nature.

I leaned into him. "I won't break."

He stilled, examining me as though he wasn't sure I was telling the truth.

I closed my eyes, relishing the moment of just him and me. My heart slammed against my rib cage as the anticipation of what would happen next was getting me hot and clammy in all the right places.

His lips feathered over mine.

I whimpered, opening my eyes, and when I did, my belly somersaulted at the sheer lust oozing off him.

Gripping my neck, he pressed kisses on my nose, my eyes, my cheeks, everywhere but my lips. My core went liquid as he continued his assault on my ears.

I stuck out my chest, wanting—no, needing—to feel his body against mine.

Then he pulled away, and I frowned until he tore off his shirt.

I captured my bottom lip between my teeth. He was a god of all gods, with his cut abs, strong jaw, and biceps that I was sure could lift a mountain. But what had me itching to feel him was the prominent V that led down to the stone mountain in his jeans.

When my gaze tracked back to his upper torso, he had a look of sheer satisfaction, like a hunter who had just caught his prey.

32

We stared at one another as the dull beat of the music pounded in the distance. Or maybe it was the pulse wreaking havoc in my ears.

I was ready to throw myself at Colton, but I would probably have fallen flat on my face, which seemed to be my luck that night.

But before I could decide what to do, Colton pounced. He lifted me in his arms and my legs wrapped around his waist as though they belonged to him.

A second later, he was carrying me into the bedroom. Then he set me down on the mattress, seemingly confused, or maybe he was trying to decide what to do next. Maybe he was a virgin too. I highly doubted that. My gut told me he was far from being a virgin. Maybe it was the way he handled me or the way he knew how to kiss. It didn't matter. A whoosh of boldness washed over me.

I grabbed the hem of my tank top. It was time to give him what his eyes screamed he wanted and what his erection needed. I was desperate for him too.

I'd gotten my tank halfway up my chest when he crawled up on the bed. Automatically, my legs fell open.

He grunted.

I shivered at the mere sense that whatever he was about to do would shatter my world in an extremely explosive and awesome way. That much, I was sure of. What I wasn't sure of was how I would react, whether my body would fall in line as if I knew what I was doing or freeze in place.

But my thoughts disintegrated as he lifted my tank top above my breasts, then feasted on my abs until I was writhing beneath him.

I latched onto his long locks, pulling as my entire being was transported to an alternate universe where only the feelings of weightlessness and euphoria were prevalent.

He licked his way up to my breasts, then bit

lightly on one, then the other through the fabric of my bra. I hated that I was wearing anything. But I was afraid that if I tried to strip, I would break the unspoken, tense, and out-of-this-world connection that Colton and I were locked in.

I traded his hair for his arms, grasping his biceps as he worked his way up to my lips. He sucked my tongue into his mouth and tortured it sensually, slowly, lightly, and when I purred, he became a madman. Hands and lips everywhere, he pressed his erection, which screamed he was ready to lose that control he kept barricaded under lock and key, into me.

I was dying to see him lose that tightly wound willpower, ready to feel him on me and inside me.

I flattened the palms of my hands on his cheeks. "Lose control, Colton." I didn't know if he needed to hear it, but I wanted to make sure he knew I was prepared to give myself to him.

He stiffened, tugging on my lip before he let go. "Baby." His tone was an intimate whisper that soaked my panties. "Are you sure?" His eyes darkened with lust so strong, I knew I would never be the same.

I threaded my fingers through his silky strands. "Very sure."

His grin was electrifying as he helped me shed the little clothing I wore.

When I was completely naked before him, he sat on his heels in-between my legs, his chest rising and falling. "Beautiful."

I'd never been naked in front of anyone before. But showing myself to him wasn't as scary as I'd thought it would be. He took me in as though I was a precious stone before touching me lightly.

"I want to be gentle." He traced heated circles around one nipple. "I want to go slow." He switched to my other breast. "I know I won't last." He dragged his fingertips down my stomach, and when he reached the apex of my legs, he sucked in a sharp breath and lifted his hooded gaze.

The hunger swimming in his depths was both thrilling, yet terrifying. My first time, and I was as hungry and desperate to feel him as he was me. My muscles tensed when he dipped his fingers between my folds.

"Fuck" dropped from his lips.

I itched to grab onto something, anything to get my body moving, or else I would be the one who wouldn't last long.

He ran his hands up and down my legs, his gaze roaming like a lion looking for his next meal.

"Please do something. You're torturing me." My voice was strained.

He grinned boyishly, as though he'd just won the race of the century.

Then his fingers were circling that throbbing sweet spot in between my legs—a gentle caress that increased the more I purred and moaned. But when his tongue replaced his fingers, I bucked, moaning so loudly that I was grateful the music was drowning out my voice.

He chuckled, but didn't stop as he took me to places I'd never been before. Even when I pleasured myself, the feeling wasn't the same.

A host of emotions rifled through me—exhilaration, trepidation, lust so strong I was ready to burst, and the one overpowering emotion that hit me so hard, I wanted to cry tears of joy—I was so in love with him. I didn't care how painful my first time might be. I didn't care about anything but him and me and how we could make each other feel. I wanted us to feel something other than pain over losing a loved one.

I couldn't quite explain the feeling, except that it felt like my body was on fire, and at the same time, I was soaring... similar to catching some air on my skateboard, only multiplied by a million.

My breathing was labored. The need to scream was so strong, I thought I would burst, and I did when the overpowering sensation of my orgasm made me cry his name.

Colton crawled up my body, grinning. "Are you good?"

"Can we do that again?"

He chuckled. "As much as you want."

My hand seated on his erection. "What do you want?" I squeezed.

His eyes rolled back in his head before he tickled his lips over mine. "I want to be your everything, Skyler."

My heart bloomed like a budding flower on a spring day. I wanted to cry at the sheer love that was growing between us, at the guy who I had no doubt I would marry one day.

I started to unbuckle his belt until he hopped up. He watched me as he stripped down to nothing but his boxer briefs. Then he removed a condom from his wallet and placed it on the nightstand.

I took comfort that he had thought about protection, because I hadn't been thinking of anything but him. "Colton." I swallowed my nerves, which hit me out of nowhere. "You should know this is my first time."

He resumed his position in-between my legs. "We don't have to—"

I mashed my forefinger to his mouth. "Shh. I want to more than anything."

He leaned down, and his hair fell around us, the ends grazing the skin on my cheeks. "I'll be gentle."

"I know," I whispered. I latched onto the waistband of his briefs, urging him forward.

He gave me a sexy grin before he stood.

I closed my eyes only because I was afraid if I looked, I might chicken out. I knew he was big just from those times I'd seen his erection through the fabric of his clothes. The sound of the condom wrapper tearing made me flinch. I imagined if a mirror was plastered to the ceiling, I would see myself stiff like a corpse.

The mattress dipped, and my pulse quickened to breakneck speed. Mia had told Georgia and me the first time hurt, but only for a minute. *This is it.* I was about to lose my virginity. But that thought was swept away when Colton's voice was in my ear.

"Relax, beautiful."

My eyes popped open. "Is it that obvious?"

"It's okay." He entered me a little then stopped. "Open your legs wider."

I obeyed. He seemed to have done this before with a girl who still had her virtue intact.

He pushed in farther, then stilled again. "Tell me if it hurts. I'll stop." He lifted up, hovering over me, watching me intently.

I bit my lip. I didn't feel much except fullness so far. "Keep going."

Gently, he thrust in again.

I winced.

He dragged the backs of his fingers over my cheek. "Breathe, baby."

I blew out a breath. "Keep going." Mia was right. It was painful, but not as much as I'd thought.

When he was fully seated inside me, he stopped again, seeming like *he* was in pain.

"Are you okay?"

He blinked once. "You feel fucking amazing. I need a minute, though."

I wanted to tell him to take all the time in the world, but my body had other plans when I squeezed around him.

He grunted. "Fuck, Skyler. I'm not going to last."

"Then let go." I didn't care if more pain was on the horizon, I wanted to see his emotions. I wanted to see how I could pleasure him like he had me only minutes earlier.

"Wrap your legs around me," he said.

Once I did, he began to rock in and out. My body naturally followed his.

"Tell me if it still hurts."

"Just a little, but don't stop." Mia had said to work through it, and the more he thrust into me, the less pain I felt, and when we got into a slow rhythm, I was on a new plane of emotions.

I'd thought the pleasure from his tongue was out-of-this-world amazing, but I was wrong. The feel of him inside me, listening to his moans, the weight of him on me, him suckling on my neck and nibbling on my ear as he took me to heights that I didn't want to end... it blew me away.

I latched onto his waist, digging my nails in. He picked up speed, and I followed suit.

"You okay?" he barely asked, his breathing increasing.

"Perfect." And I was.

That one-word statement was all he needed. He rocked faster and faster, sweat beading on him and me. Then he slowed, and without breaking our connection, sucked one nipple, then the other.

I moaned, rocking my hips, needing the friction. "Faster, Colton."

He obliged, and that control he'd said he would lose came front and center as he pounded into me hard and fast, and out of nowhere, a rush of heat blanketed me. As my stomach pitched and rolled and my toes tingled, I spewed noises I'd only heard from an actress in the throes of sex in some movie.

He grunted as he slowed, crashing his mouth to mine like a man possessed. "I'm in love with you, Skyler."

I swore I was about to have another orgasm just hearing those words. Instead, I stiffened.

He dashed away a lone tear that had leaked out as he searched my face. "What is it?"

Why I was speechless, I wasn't sure. It wasn't that I didn't think a guy could or would fall in love with me. But he was the man of my dreams. The one I'd had a crush on for so long had just taken me to places I could've never imagined, and he was telling me he loved me, which rocked my world even more.

I cried softly, smiling at the same time.

He sighed before showering me with the lightest of kisses all over my face. "I am so in love with you. I can't get you out of my head. I go to bed thinking of you. I wake up thinking of you. And I want to be with you all the time."

My watery eyes tracked his as he waited for me to say something. "You've made me the happiest girl alive. I love you hard, Colton." Then the waterworks opened, and for once, I was crying tears of joy.

33

After rubbing the sleep from my eyes, I stretched, feeling the soreness everywhere on my body. I couldn't help but smile so wide, I thought I would scream how happy I was, which I had never thought possible.

The morning light wormed its way through the slats in the shutters, and the clock on the glass nightstand read ten a.m.

I rolled over into a hot blanket of muscle to find Colton staring at me with a grin the size of Texas. "Morning." His tone was husky, eliciting a string of goosebumps along my arms.

I curled up to him. We'd gone rounds two and three throughout the night, and I'd been ready to go for four, but Colton had run out of condoms. I'd never thought my first time with a guy would be so amazingly perfect despite the small amount of pain.

He brought my hand up to his mouth and kissed my fingers. "Any regrets?" I caught a glimpse of momentary fear in his eyes.

"None. You?" I was sure the sudden bout of dread settling in my throat was clear on my face as I held my breath.

He sucked on one of my fingers. "Nope."

I slid my leg between his thighs and scooted closer to him. "So what happens now?" I asked. I'd never had a boyfriend before, and certainly not one who'd expressed his undying love for me.

So much had happened in the span of two days that I was somewhat dizzy with the next steps. Suddenly, my eyes watered as reality came crashing down like a meteor falling from the sky.

"What's wrong?"

I swallowed thickly. "Just thinking of my dad."

"I'm here, Skyler. I'm not going anywhere. I know I said that the last time, but I promise. You come first now. I love you." His husky tone and strong conviction behind his statement massaged my heart and sent delightful shivers skating along my skin.

I would never tire of hearing him tell me he loved me. I wanted to hear him say it a million times more.

"Say it again."

"I love you," he whispered in my ear. "You make me feel alive for the first time since Josh passed away."

I traced a path up and down his abs and chest as silence filled the space between us.

He didn't know how much his love meant to me or how much he was the balm to my shattered soul. I was devastated over the loss of Dad, but I knew without a doubt that I could get through the days, weeks, months, even years ahead as long as I had Colton at my side.

"Are you going to school on Monday?" I asked.

"Yeah. I missed quite a few days."

I had as well, but I wasn't sure if I was ready to sit through classes and see how happy kids were. Maybe being around lots of people would keep my mind from wandering. At some point, I had to get back to some sort of normalcy, and Dad wanted me to graduate.

"I think I will go too," I mumbled as my phone rang.

I was sure it was Nan. Georgia was asleep in a guest room down the hall. She would have been pounding on the door otherwise. Mia, well, she had no reason to check on me.

The annoying piece of technology wouldn't stop ringing.

"You should answer it," Colton said.

I rolled over and snagged it just as the trilling died, only to start up again. My stomach rolled once as an eerie feeling washed over me.

Nan's name flashed on the screen. Since it was Sunday, I wasn't late for anything, or at least not that I knew of. Maybe I hadn't heard Nan when I ran out the day before, all too eager to get in Georgia's car.

"Skyler." Nan sounded panicked when I answered.

I swung my legs over the bed, straightening. "What is it?" I couldn't begin to think what had her spooked, unless someone had broken into the house. That was the only thing that came to mind. Nevertheless, the eerie feeling multiplied.

"Um... you need to come home now. Your Aunt Clara is here from California."

"What? Why?" I knew she would probably want to go to Dad's funeral, but Nan and I hadn't set a date yet. "How does she know Dad died?"

"I called her on Friday night after we came home," Nan said. "She needed to know, since she's family."

"Okay, but why is she here so soon? Dad just passed two days ago."

"Please come home." Nan's plea was strong, and I could sense she was holding something back.

"What are you not telling me?"

"I'll explain when you get here." Then she hung up.

"What's going on?" Colton's hand flitted across my shoulder.

I got up, staring at the blue, empty wall and wondering why she was in town. Dad had changed the trust, letting her off the hook. Unless he hadn't. I dipped into my brain to figure out the time between when he told me he would change the trust and when he was rushed to the hospital.

Colton waved a hand in front of me. "Baby doll, you're scaring me."

I swung my gaze from the wall to him.

A troubled frown cut a path across his forehead. "Talk to me."

"My aunt is in town." I couldn't remember if I'd told Colton about the situation with my aunt, so I explained the trust and guardianship as I dressed.

He slipped on his jeans before trying to tame his unkempt hair. "Maybe she's here for money."

I stopped midway of poking my arms through the sleeves of my top. "We don't have any money." Dad had his 401(k) from his former employer and other savings that I was aware of, but it wasn't like we had a million dollars. Aside from that, I didn't see my dad leaving his sister money. On top of that, she had a job, and I suspected one that paid well, especially given her recent promotion.

I finished dressing. I wasn't about to figure out her motives, not while standing in a bedroom with a shirtless Colton.

I raked my gaze over my gorgeous boyfriend, drinking in every muscle and curve on him from head to toe. I was the luckiest girl on the planet.

He gave me a cheeky grin. "See something you like?" His tone was playful.

I licked my lips, shrugging as I fixated on his gorgeous body.

He chuckled as he threw his shirt over his head.

The doorknob rattled. "Skye, it's Georgia. Open up."

Colton picked up his shoes. "I'll meet you downstairs?"

When he opened the door, they exchanged a good morning before she ambled in, looking like she'd had a rough night—wild hair, bloodshot eyes, and smudged makeup.

She yawned. "I feel like shit. I'll never drink again."

I giggled. "I know the feeling."

She took inventory of the crumpled sheet and blanket as questions started to pile up.

"I'll tell you everything later, but I have to get home. My aunt is here from California."

She stifled another yawn. "For the funeral?"

I lifted a shoulder. "I guess." That was the only explanation I could come up with other than money, as Colton pointed out.

She pursed her lips. "Is she here to take you back with her? I swear, she better not."

"She travels a ton for her new job."

"Maybe she was fired," Georgia said.

"Not helping." I huffed as I started for the door.

"Sorry." She followed me out.

When Georgia and I approached the landing of the curved staircase, Mr. Dyson's baritone voice boomed below.

"I told you not to throw any more parties. Did I not?" Mr. Dyson asked.

Georgia peered over the bannister. "I think they're in the study."

"Let's go," I said. "Colton is waiting for me."

She didn't move. "Um... We have to find another way out."

"Why?"

"If Mr. Dyson sees me, he'll know I've been drinking and he'll call my parents."

"The only thing I can tell is you had a wild night. Besides, he's too busy chewing Grady's ass."

She smoothed her hands over her hair. "I'll meet you outside." She bounded down the stairs like someone was chasing her, but no sooner than she reached the bottom, Mr. Dyson came out with a mean expression on his face.

I held my breath as I climbed down one step at a time.

The air thickened as Mr. Dyson considered Georgia, then me. Fury jumped out of his blue eyes, and I knew he was about to say something fatherly. Instead, he tucked a hand into the pocket of his tan pants. "Skyler." His soft tone belied the terse expression he wore. "Please accept my sincere condolences."

Grady and Colton emerged from the study. Grady looked like he'd been through a hurricane, whipped around and battered. Or maybe it was bedhead.

"See, Dad?" Grady stood next to the elder Dyson. "We were trying to help Skyler take her mind off her dad."

In part, he was telling the truth.

Colton's long legs crossed the room in three easy strides until he had his hand on the handle of the front door.

I hurried toward Colton as I said, "Thank you, Mr. Dyson."

"Oh, and Skyler," Mr. Dyson said. "Please let me know when the funeral is. I would like to attend."

"Yes, sir. I do need to get home."

"Very well." Mr. Dyson gripped his son's shoulder. "Grady, in the kitchen, please." Then he strode away.

The four of us let out a collective sigh.

"Where's Mia?" Georgia asked.

Grady rubbed his neck. "Still sleeping. I need to clean up this mess before I get grounded for a year." He waved his hand around.

Red cups littered the floor and a couple of small tables that had framed pictures and silk flowers on them. *Yikes!* I could only imagine what the kitchen looked like after a night of beer pong.

"I'll stay and help," Georgia offered on a sigh.

"I would, too, but I have to get home." I hugged Georgia. Then I said to Grady, "I'm sorry."

He shook his head. "Colton filled me in. It's cool."

Once Colton and I were in his truck, I blew out a much-needed breath. "That went well. Not."

He started the engine, laughing, a sound that erased the nerves that had settled in my stomach, at least for the time being.

34

The minute I walked into the house, I felt uneasiness in the air. I stopped by the leather couch and inhaled and exhaled a couple of times. That reality that had hit me earlier was back in full force. Dad wasn't there. I clutched my chest, hoping the tightness would subside.

Stella mewled before she emerged from the hallway.

I grinned as she nudged her head into my leg. I'd never been so happy to see her. I bent over and picked her up. "Hey, girl." I squeezed her to me. "Did you miss me?"

She purred her answer.

"I love you too." I stroked her coat. "Where is

everyone?" I wound my way through the house toward the kitchen. "Nan!"

"Skyler." Nan poked her head out of Dad's room down the hall. "We're in here."

Stella jumped down and took off in Nan's direction as if to tell me it was okay. I wasn't ready to go into my dad's room yet. I wasn't sure if I could. Still, I found it odd that Nan and my aunt were visiting in there.

I rubbed my lips together and rolled back my shoulders. *I can do this. Sooner or later, I'll have to anyway.* An onslaught of memories accosted me as soon as I ambled in. Dad's scent was ever present, and I swayed for a brief second as I focused on a picture that hung on the wall directly ahead of me of Mom, Dad, and me at a carnival.

"Skyler, are you okay?" Nan's voice severed my trip back in time, and I turned to my left to find both Nan and my aunt staring at me.

Nan stood near a rolling cart that held the medical supplies we'd used, and her outfit said she had gone to Sunday mass.

I found a spot next to Nan. "Why are you in here?" I swung my gaze to my aunt.

She sat primly and properly on the bed. Her blonde hair was styled in a short cut that reached her ears. She wore a soft-blue blouse that brought out the same color in her eyes behind thin, brown-framed glasses. I could see Dad in her. "I'm sorry about your dad." Her voice sounded as though she'd been smoking since the age of ten, but if she had at any point in her life, her smooth skin didn't show it. It had been a few years since I'd seen her, and even though I wasn't a fan of hers, I could hear the sadness and regret in her voice.

"Why are you here?" I asked as nicely as I could, trying to keep the nerves out of my tone.

"You didn't tell her?" Aunt Clara asked Nan.

Nan's rosy complexion paled as she squirmed. I'd never seen her jittery.

I crossed my arms over my chest. With Nan nervous and my aunt there, I could only conclude one thing. "Please tell me I'm not moving to California."

Nan cleared her throat. "About that..."

I ground my back teeth. "No. I'm not leaving."

She held up a hand. "Don't get ahead of yourself. I'm sure we will work it out."

The room spun just the same.

"Your dad signed the updated forms for the trust and had them notarized since he wasn't able to write well anymore." Nan's voice was shaky. "But apparently Mr. Wilson never received them. We think they got lost in the mail."

At least Dad had signed them. Hopefully, they would show up. *But what if they don't?* "Is that why you're here?" I asked Aunt Clara, willing the nausea to go away.

She clasped her long fingers in her lap. "No. I'd just landed in New York from a business trip when I got Nan's call. Instead of flying back to California, I thought I would stop here."

Okay, not so bad. But I wasn't ready to celebrate just yet. "So what happens now?" If Mr. Wilson didn't have the documents, Aunt Clara was still named as my guardian.

"Mr. Wilson is out of town," Nan said, losing some of the nerves in her tone. "He isn't returning until midweek. His assistant is checking his mail and will keep an eye out for it. In the meantime, we just have to wait until he returns."

"No need to panic," Aunt Clara said calmly. "We'll work through this."

I liked her confidence. The last time I saw her, she'd been snooty to me.

"Dad told me with your job, you couldn't take care of me. Right?" Hopefully, she wasn't about to change her mind.

She smiled warmly. "I really wanted to help my brother. After all, it would only be nine months until you turn eighteen. Still, with my new promotion I'm on a plane six days a week. That means you would be by yourself, and that isn't going to work. Nan seems like a great person to step into the role as your guardian."

"Does that mean you're not going to change your mind?" If we couldn't find the trust documents, I was concerned that none of us would have a choice.

"Let's see what Mr. Wilson advises, Skye," Nan said.

I had to believe we could work it out. "This is my senior year, and I want to graduate with my friends." I figured one last-ditch effort to make my wishes clear couldn't hurt.

Aunt Clara rose elegantly, smoothing her hand down her black slacks. "I haven't slept. Planes are horrible to get any rest. I'm staying in town."

Nan held out her arm. "I'll walk you out. Let's have dinner tomorrow night and chat some more."

Once I was alone, I dropped onto the bed, puffing out air.

I'd hardly had a chance to think when Nan returned. "I'm so sorry, Skye." She sat next to me. "I mailed the documents. I should've dropped them off at Mr. Wilson's office. But I had a ton of things to do that day."

I placed a hand on her trembling leg. "It's not your fault." I couldn't blame her. "What do you think will happen, though?" I examined my nails, deciding which one to gnaw on first. All ten of them were horrible and extremely short, unlike my friends'—they had pretty, manicured nails.

"That the envelope will finally show up at Mr. Wilson's office. I did ask him what would happen if he doesn't receive them. But he couldn't talk. He was catching a flight. He just told me not to worry. So that's what I'm trying to do. I want you to do the same."

My pinky won, and I stuck it in my mouth. "I'll try. You don't think Aunt Clara is here for money, do you?"

She shrugged. "I don't think so. When I called to let her know your dad passed, I informed her of the missing documents. I figured she ought to know just in case. She did ask me if the funeral would be anytime this week. I think she just wanted to see you and pay her respects."

"She seemed sad about Dad."

"She also seems nice," Nan said.

"I'm not moving."

Nan circled her fingers around my wrist and gently lowered my hand from my mouth to my lap. "You won't have any nails left."

Maybe once the situation was resolved, I could get my nails done. Georgia would be more than happy to be my manicurist.

"One other thing," Nan said. "When we speak with Mr. Wilson, should we broach the subject of your birth mother to see if he's located her yet? That is, if you want to reach out to her."

I tensed. "Are you trying to get rid of me?" I was half teasing.

For the second time in a matter of thirty minutes, her skin turned ashen. "God, no. But it's still the elephant in the room, so to speak. I'm just saying it might be a good time to ask him while we have his attention."

"Maybe it's time I deal with it." That way, I could move on.

35

Later that day, I propped myself up with my back against my headboard, holding Dad's computer in my lap. Nan had advised me that if I was serious about knowing more about my birth mom, I should send Mr. Wilson an email. I'd had the afternoon to think, and I'd decided to take the plunge. I knew Dad would have wanted me to meet her—I'd gotten that feeling after he'd dropped the news in my lap. More importantly, I had questions for her, and I didn't want to go through life with any regrets.

The doorbell rang.

I wasn't expecting anyone. Colton had texted me earlier to let me know he would be at the gym with Grady and would check in later. I hadn't told him yet how things had gone with my aunt, figuring it would be better in person, not that I really had any news. Being in limbo wasn't a joyride, though, and I hated to play the waiting game.

Dad's computer screen had just come to life when I heard Colton's husky voice. My stomach somersaulted, and I smiled for the first time in hours.

In less than a minute, he graced my doorway in his gym shorts and a T-shirt. My gaze lingered a bit on his muscled calves. I loved everything about Colton inside and out, but I was learning I had a thing for shapely legs.

He smirked. "See something you like?"

I held my bottom lip hostage. "Hell yeah." I squirmed where I sat.

"Can I come in?" he asked sweetly.

I patted the spot next to me on the bed.

He kicked off his Nikes before planting a wet one on my lips. "Mmm. I've been thinking of tasting you all day."

Stella jumped on the bed, trying to steal Colton's attention.

I giggled as he got comfortable beside me.

Stella wormed her way in and curled up against him. "A Maine Coon, right?"

"Yeah. Stella, and she's spoiled rotten." I gave Stella the evil eye for interrupting us.

"How did it go with your aunt?" he asked.

"The lawyer never received the updated trust documents that my dad signed. Apparently they got lost in the mail. And since my aunt is named as my guardian in the trust, I'm not sure what happens from here if he doesn't get the documents."

"You mean you could be moving?" His demeanor changed in an instant, the happiness in his eyes snuffed out.

I inhaled then released the nervous air in my lungs. "No idea."

He stopped stroking Stella's coat, who then jumped onto his lap and pushed her head into his hand.

I rolled my eyes at my demanding cat.

Colton chuckled as he obeyed Stella, then got quiet as he loved on her, seemingly deep in thought.

A sudden awkwardness charged the air.

"I'm not leaving, Colton." Well, I would do my damnedest not to.

He gave me one of his deadpan expressions,

which told me he wasn't thrilled. I'd learned his blank faces meant he was either angry, brooding, or thinking.

I reached over and managed to pry his hand away from Stella. "I swear, I'm not moving." If the tables had been turned, I would have freaked out. "I'm graduating here. If I have to run away, I will." Maybe I was trying to convince myself.

He grinned at my last statement.

"Talk to me," I pleaded.

He drove a hand through his hair, hard. "I can't lose you. I would... I don't know. I just can't lose you. You're the only reason I'm here."

I thought to counsel him like Nan had me, not to get ahead of things, but that last statement threw me, and my heart skipped a beat. "Explain that last part." I hoped he was referring to leaving town to stay with his friend. Yet I couldn't help but remember him telling Grady that if it hadn't been for me that night he stormed out of his house, he would've crashed into a tree.

Colton locked his dreamy brown eyes on mine. "Many times I have wanted to..." He looked away.

I touched his face. "Talk to me." My pulse tried to punch its way out of my skin. "You don't mean take your own life?"

"I'm not going to lie. I thought the only way out of the hell I'd been in for so long after Josh's death was to join him. But after I had you in my arms on your porch that night, and you told me I was a good person, something just clicked. I can't explain it except you gave me hope."

A ball of fur lodged in my throat. "I love you." I pecked him on the cheek.

But he was having none of that. He set Stella on the bed and then patted his lap. "Come here."

I straddled him while Stella meowed.

Colton chuckled. "She's demanding."

I rolled my eyes again. "You have no idea. But you'll learn I can be too. Now kiss me."

His tongue dove into my mouth, taking everything he could, as if he wouldn't have a chance later on. But I had no doubt he would have all the time in the world to do whatever he liked. Because if I was moving, I was asking Colton to come with me.

We were tangled together until I heard Nan coming up the stairs. Then I resumed my spot with Dad's computer in my lap, as if we hadn't almost stripped each other naked.

"Hey, I'm making spaghetti. It should be ready

in about an hour. Colton, would you like to stay for dinner?"

"I would love to," Colton said.

Nan's face lit up. It was the first time all day the stress had disappeared. "Did you send an email to your dad's lawyer?"

"I'm just about to." I got into his email account once Nan left, and Colton slid down, then turned on his side, propping his head in his hand and watching me.

"Colton, please don't worry. If I know Nan, she will make sure I stay." In that moment, a rush of confidence blanketed me. I had to think positively or I would make myself sick.

"I can't say I won't. But I'll try not to."

That was fair. I had to do the same. "One more thing. Please, please, don't ever think you have to take your own life. Ever, Colton. Anytime you feel like you can't make it through the day, talk to me or Grady or someone. Deal?" Nan had given me a similar message about talking to someone, and Colton definitely needed that same advice. I couldn't lose him.

Stella jumped on his lap. "I promise, baby doll. It was stupid of me to even consider doing something like that. I see that now. You and Grady helped me. My mom did too. And I think to a certain extent, my old man."

"I saw a therapist after my mom passed."

He petted Stella. "Did it help?"

I nodded. "Talking to someone other than my dad helped me deal with her loss. I mean, I was still depressed, but she told me to celebrate Mom and find an outlet. That's when Dad got me the skateboard."

"Is that why you wanted to skate the other night?"

I picked at something hard that was stuck to the computer screen. "Yeah. I know I fell, which was your fault, by the way. But the sport helps me clear my consciousness. And I'm finding you help in that regard too."

He grinned as Stella mewled. "My mom wants me to see a psychologist."

"It can't hurt."

Silence hung between us. He seemed to dive inward, and I hoped he would take his mom up on it. I vowed to help him as much as I could, but I could only go so far. Someone who was removed from the situation saw things differently.

I scrolled through a string of emails between Dad and his lawyer, giving Colton time to think.

One email caught my eye: *Randall, I'm still in the process of finding out more, but here's a recent photo of Skyler's biological mother. See attached.*

Curiosity gripped me, and I opened the file.

Colton adjusted himself so he was looking at the screen with me. "Who are those ladies?"

It was the same pic I'd found one night on Dad's computer screen. "I guess one of them is my birth mom."

I flicked back to the email and finished reading the rest aloud.

"'The woman in the middle is Ashley Perry, Skyler's biological mother. Since we opened up the case, Ashley will be informed. I have an investigator who is digging into her whereabouts. I should have more on her soon.'"

I read the other emails from the lawyer but didn't find any more info on my birth mom, so I clicked back to the picture.

"I see the resemblance." Colton touched the screen, his finger landing on the woman in the middle, who had light-brown hair and eyes to match, along with that cool charm necklace.

I zoomed in on the picture, trying to read the inscription on her necklace rather than the resemblance, which I didn't see. Sure, I had light-brown hair and eyes like her, but that was it. Maybe I took after my biological father. "Where?"

Colton looked at me then at the screen. "Here." He traced the woman's nose. "It's small like yours, and like you, she has a little dimple on the right side of her mouth when she smiles."

Mom had been the one to make a big deal of my dimple when she'd been alive. Since then, no one had commented on it until now. The more I studied the woman in the photo, the more I agreed with Colton. "If my hair was longer like hers, we could pass for sisters. She looks young in this photo."

"I would guess thirty-something," Colton said. "Do you think your mom lives in town?"

"Not sure. I know my parents moved here for my dad's job, and they adopted me after that. So I assume she lives here." She could be anywhere in the world.

"Are you going to find out more about her?"

I chewed on a nail. "I think I'm ready."

He took the computer out of my hands and set it on the other side of him. Then he lifted me up and set me on his lap. Once again, I was straddling him. "I'm ready."

I could feel his growing erection. "Nan is home, so we can't." I lowered my gaze to his groin.

He let out a frustrated sigh as he pouted. "I know, but I've been thinking about something and wanted to talk to you. You asked me this morning what happens next with you and me." He rubbed my bare legs. I'd been lounging in my pajama shorts all day, but I was wearing a bra and stretchy camisole that showed my cleavage.

Intrigue had me biting my bottom lip. "Are you going to tell me or stare at my chest?"

His grin was magnifying. "What would you think of taking a year and exploring the world? After we graduate, of course. After what you just said about finding an outlet, I think it would be good for us to hit the road and clear our heads, so to speak."

My brows hiked to my hairline. "Like other countries?" I'd never thought past Dad or high school. College had crossed my mind, but my grades weren't great, and I wasn't eager to sit through four more years of school. Traveling with Colton for a year sounded freaking amazing. "I don't have money." I didn't even have a job. I did have a trust fund, but couldn't touch it until I turned twenty-five.

"I have a nice savings account with money I made at a job I had when I was at the academy. And I'm planning on finding work here to keep adding to it. We have several months before we graduate, anyway."

The giddiness bubbling inside was ready to burst. "Yes. Yes. Yes. I'll get a job too." I'd never worked because of Dad, but it was time for me to start. "You know, Dad and I took a road trip after Mom died. We had a great time."

"For real? Well it's settled, then."

I threw myself at him, crashing my mouth to his.

As long as Colton was with me, I was ready to tackle anything head-on.

36

The cafeteria hummed as utensils clanged, kids chatted, and chairs scraped along the scuffed tiled floor.

Georgia and Mia sat on the other side of the table, hovering over my phone. "The lady with the pendant is your mom?"

"Yep. I'm waiting to talk to my dad's lawyer to find out more." I'd finally sent the email after Colton had left the night before.

Mia glanced at me. Her hazel eyes sparkled beneath the heavy coats of mascara. "I can see the resemblance."

Georgia pointed to the screen. "Yeah. It's the nose." Then she sat back and studied me. "You're ready to meet the woman who gave birth to you?" Her skepticism came through loud and clear.

I shrugged. "I guess. I'm a little nervous, to be honest. One minute, I get excited. The next, I don't want to deal. If anything, I want to wait until after Dad's funeral—which, by the way, will be one week from today. So mark your calendars." Nan and I had decided that at dinner the night before, barring any hiccups from the funeral home.

"I can tell you're not really sure if you want to open that door," Georgia said.

She knew me well, but I asked just the same, "How do you know?"

Georgia leaned over the table. "You don't light up. And I can see it in your eyes."

"Everything seems like it's hitting me at once. Dad just passed three days ago, my aunt blows into town, and now I find the pic of my birth mom."

Mia slid my phone over to me. "Breathe, Skyler. One thing at a time. And why are you even in school, by the way?"

A heavy sigh shot free. "Distraction. I didn't want to stay home and stare at four walls. And I have a lot of schoolwork to make up if I want to graduate."

Narrowing her eyes, Georgia crossed her arms

over her chest. "We are graduating together, which means you're not moving, period."

I'd filled Georgia in on my aunt earlier. "I'm not so worried about my aunt as much as I'm wondering about the law. I tried to research trusts, but I couldn't find anything specific to my case."

Georgia snagged a napkin off the table and dabbed her eyes.

"Are you crying?" Mia asked Georgia.

Georgia hung her head. "I'm sorry. I can't get Mr. Lawson out of my head. Now Skye might be moving. It just sucks."

I hurried around to her side of the table and hugged her. "You're going to make me cry."

"I'm already crying," Mia chimed in. "I didn't know your dad that well, but he was a good man. And I don't want you to leave either, Skye."

The waterworks opened more because they'd brought up Dad. "As I told Colton, Nan will do everything she can to help me stay. And I didn't get the vibe that my aunt would fight to take me, either." She'd never come out and said that for sure.

"I know," Georgia said through sniffles. "Can I say a few words?"

I giggled softly. "Since when do you ask?"

The three of us huddled together.

Georgia wiped her nose with the napkin. "I want to say a prayer for your dad. I need to get this off my chest."

Georgia, Mia, and I held hands.

"Mr. Lawson, I know you're listening," Georgia started. "I want you to know we miss you terribly and that Skyler is courageous and determined. She has a great extended family with me, Mia, Grady, and Colton. Oh, and Colton will take good care of her. All of us will make sure she's happy, loved, and protected, especially Colton. He loves your daughter, and I know without a doubt that the two of them are destined to marry and have tons of kids. They're the soulmates that many of us dream to have."

"You really believe Colton and I will marry?" My jaw was close to hitting my lap.

"Shh," Georgia said.

"I do," Mia chimed in. "That dude is hopelessly in love with you."

"Shush," Georgia snapped. "I'm almost finished. I love you, Mr. Lawson. I will never forget the fun times we had riding roller-coasters together. I hope you can ride all those roller-coasters in heaven. You'll always be in my heart." Georgia shuddered.

I dabbed my eyes with a hand. "That was beautiful. My dad loved you like a daughter."

The three of us jumped when Grady slid into a chair next to Mia. "Why are y'all crying? Do I need to sever heads?"

Colton skirted the table and sat in the chair next to me. "Did something happen?"

Mia smiled. "Georgia just conducted her first sermon."

Georgia would make a great woman of the cloth if she chose that path. She wanted to help people like her parents, who worked in the medical field.

I snuggled into Colton, feeling ten times better than I had a minute ago.

"My dad is having dinner with an old high school friend who's in town," Grady said. "Why don't we get pizza and kick back at my house later?"

I was still trying to get used to the nice Grady. Mia had certainly changed him for the better.

Mia flattened her hand on his chest. "Did you not just get your ass chewed yesterday for the party you threw on Saturday?"

He tapped her nose, looking all sweet and

flirty. "This isn't a party. Just a few friends, studying and eating."

Colton tickled my ear with his warm breath. "I want to study you tonight."

Shivers slid down my spine. I had just the spot for him to study.

Maybe Georgia was right. Maybe Colton and I were destined to marry, given the love pouring off him. Or maybe I was mistaking lust for love.

Either way, I promised myself one thing: I would live each moment like it was my last. Because tomorrow wasn't a given, and yesterday was gone. So today was all that mattered, and that day, I was with Colton and friends who loved me. For that, I said a silent thank-you.

37

Colton wheeled into Grady's driveway behind Mr. Dyson's Mercedes.

The ocean air trickled in through the cracked window as the faint sound of the waves landing on shore lulled me. The landscape lights surrounding the house highlighted the flowers dotted around the many shrubs and bushes.

"I don't see Georgia or Mia's cars." I'd texted Georgia just before Colton and I had left my house to let her know we were running late, but she hadn't responded. Maybe she was running late too.

Colton cut the engine. "Baby." His tone was full

of dread, and my stomach dropped to the floorboard.

"Why do you look like something bad happened? Is it Georgia or Mia?" Georgia had been as sad and depressed over Dad as I had been. Her little sermon at school that day had warmed me but had also made me want to cry my eyes out.

Still, maybe she'd gotten into an accident and Mia had been with her.

He reached over the console and entwined his fingers in mine. "Oh no. Nothing happened to Georgia or Mia."

I slumped in my seat.

His brown eyes glinted with apprehension in the soft glow of the dashboard lights. "I don't know how to tell you this."

If he was breaking up with me, I would break his beautiful nose.

"Grady called me before I picked you up." His gaze bounced from me to the house then to me again.

My heart couldn't take the anticipation. "Just tell me already."

He took a breath. "Remember at lunch today Grady mentioned that his dad was having dinner with an old high school friend who was in town?"

I nodded jerkily. My erratic pulse was stealing the breath in my lungs as my mind wandered down a road that only led to heartache.

"That high school friend is"—his Adam's apple moved up and down—"your birth mom."

I angled my ear closer to him as I tried to shrug out of his hold. "Come again?"

He gripped my hand. "I don't know the whole story. All I know is Mr. Dyson asked Grady if you would be interested in meeting her. Apparently, your dad's lawyer finally got a hold of her, and then she mentioned your name to Mr. Dyson."

Mr. Wilson was still out of town and would be until midweek, and he hadn't responded to my email yet. I'd checked after school. Maybe he wanted to talk to me in person.

"So we're not here to watch a movie and hang out? You and Grady planned this all along?"

He shook his head vigorously. "No. Baby, please. I just told Grady I would see if you were ready. You said yourself yesterday you think you are."

I stared at Colton's key chain dangling in the ignition. Nerves jabbed at the lining of my stomach. He was right. But I wanted to know more about her first before I reached out. I had been hoping Mr. Wilson could fill me in.

Colton guided my face to look at him. "We can leave. You don't have to do this tonight."

"Why didn't you tell me before we left?" I would've had more time to prepare.

"I was debating how to tell you. Part of me thought it would be easier for you to decide if we were here. Baby doll, I don't want you to move to California. I get we don't know yet what will happen. And honestly, I'm being selfish. Maybe somehow, if things with the trust go south, your birth mom could be your out. She's blood, she might be able to help."

He really does love me. "What if she doesn't want anything to do with me?"

"She's in town to meet you," he said softly.

"Have you met her?" My voice rose.

"No. I'm just the messenger. I'm nervous too."

I was torturing my bottom lip with my teeth. "Why?"

With his free hand, he ran the pad of his thumb over the lip I was gnawing on. "You've been through a lot, and I want you to be happy."

"You make me happy."

He let go of my hand and tangled his fingers in

my hair. "I love you so hard, Skyler. And the tiniest possibility you could move away is killing me. I've been a mess."

I couldn't tell, although Colton was an expert in hiding his emotions when he wanted to. "I'm not leaving you." I tried to infuse as much confidence as I could.

The pounding of my pulse in my ears was all I heard.

After a long, tense moment, he turned the key in the ignition.

"What are you doing?" I asked.

"I was wrong. I should have told you before we got in the truck. I'm sorry." He sounded regretful.

I clutched his arm. "Don't. You're going in with me?" We needed a backup plan in the event Mr. Wilson couldn't do anything to replace my aunt with Nan. Yet I didn't want to use Ashley in that way. I didn't want to give her any false hopes if she had expectations of me welcoming her with open arms. I certainly wasn't ready to do that. I wasn't even sure how I was going to react when I met her.

He nodded. "I won't leave your side unless you want me to."

"I'm nervous, Colton."

"You're also the strongest person I know."

"I'm not. I just have great friends, and the best boyfriend on the planet."

In a flash, his tongue was in my mouth, all gentle strokes and soft kisses.

I moaned, getting lost in him, forgetting for the moment what I was about to do.

He brushed his nose against mine. "I love you. No matter what happens when you walk in there, know that if you fall, I'll be right there to pick you up."

My chin trembled as tears threatened to spill, and not because I was sad. Quite the opposite. "How did I get so lucky?"

His grin was electrifying. "I'm the one who won the lottery with you."

The love pouring off him tempered the trepidation that had been causing my stomach to pitch and roll for the last few minutes.

38

The front door opened before we reached the porch. Grady stood with a hand inside a pocket of his sweatpants. "It's about time. You've been sitting out there forever."

Grady and Colton swapped a manly hug. "Can it, man," Colton said. "This is hard for her."

Grady raised his hands, setting his blue gaze on me. "Sorry."

My mouth should've fallen open at his apology. Grady had never apologized to me. Instead, I smiled at him. "No biggie. Are Mia and Georgia still coming over?"

Grady closed the front door. "Maybe later. My dad and his friend are in the kitchen." He gave me the impression he was nervous too. Maybe he was. Upon closer inspection, a muscle jumped along his sharp jaw.

Colton closed his hand over mine as we trailed behind Grady. With each step, my heartbeat ramped up. If I hadn't been tethered to Colton, I would have turned around and ran.

A light, airy laugh trickled out of the kitchen before I heard Mr. Dyson say, "I miss him."

Grady ambled in, not saying a word, and bee-lined to the fridge.

Three rounded black pendant lights shone over the island, highlighting specks of gold in the marble top.

Mr. Dyson set his wine glass down and re-garded Colton and me. "Skyler. Colton." Mr. Dyson's deep voice penetrated through the shock that had me rooted to the floor. "Come in."

Colton nudged me, but I didn't move. I was fix-ated on Ashley as if she was the most fascinating person I'd ever seen. I was trying to find the re-semblance in the woman who had given birth to me. She had a small nose and maybe similar hair color, but I found her prettier in person than in her photo. Her light-brown hair was thick and wavy, spilling down around her shoulders. Her skin appeared to be smooth, with the right amount of blush to accentuate her high cheekbones.

Colton let go of me, jolting me out of my haze.

"This is Ashley," Mr. Dyson said.

I swallowed a pail of sand.

Her brown eyes locked on mine with an unspoken plea that said, "Forgive me."

I'd had no idea how I would react when I met her, but for some reason a slow, simmering anger deep in the recesses of my psyche took root.

Silence seemed to drop from the high ceiling and splatter down around us. My brain was processing, and with Ashley studying me, I suddenly had no desire to ask my myriad questions about why she'd given me up.

I couldn't get past the expensive dress she was wearing or the diamond-studded earrings that beamed like a beacon in the night. My gaze lowered to her hands to see if she was married, but I didn't see a ring. She gave me the impression she'd done quite well for herself—a nice cushy life, one where she didn't have any kids to support, and one where she'd given up her child for a better future.

That simmering anger bubbled to the surface, and I ground my back teeth.

"Hey," Colton whispered.

I broke free from Ashley's scrutiny. I needed air and a moment to gather my thoughts. I spun on my heel, hurried through the house, and went out to the front porch. The warm salt air hit me like a slap in the face, just what I needed to clear the fog from my head. Inhaling, I ran around the house and onto the narrow, lighted path that led to the beach. The Atlantic was calm beneath the full moon, a stark contrast to the turbulence in my stomach.

I stopped before my feet hit the sand and took in a humongous breath.

"Skyler." Ashley's soft voice only served to fray my emotions even more. "Can we talk?"

I expelled all the air in my lungs. I wanted to tell her no, but my tongue was stuck to the roof of my mouth.

She stood beside me. "I've thought about this moment for many years." Her voice was barely audible over the music of the waves.

Funny, I hadn't. Not that I was complaining or blaming Dad for not telling me. He'd done what he thought was best. *Maybe she did too.*

"Is Mr. Dyson my father?" *That came out of nowhere.* They did look chummy when I'd walked in, and if they'd known each other since high school, it was quite possible Mr. Dyson could be my bio dad. If that were true, I wasn't sure how I would feel about that, and Grady might wig out.

She tensed, hunching her shoulders as a light wind ruffled her hair. "Your father was Mr. Dyson's best friend in high school."

I jerked my head her way. "Was?"

She frowned. "He died in a motorcycle accident in his senior year."

I dropped my chin to my chest, staving off the need to cry for a man I didn't know. *Why do people keep dying in my life?* I knew no one could answer that, but for fuck's sake.

"Skyler is such a pretty name," she muttered, reaching out to touch my hair.

I jumped back, my eyebrows creasing in the middle.

She held up her small hands. "I'm sorry."

"My bio dad dies, and what? You decide to give me up?" My tone was harsher than I intended.

Tears glistened in her eyes. "It's not like that."

"Then what?" I dropped the brassiness in my voice.

She fidgeted with her hands, clearly not knowing what to do with them. "I can see you're not ready to listen. When you are, you can give me a call. Mr. Dyson has my number." She gave me one last long look, then left.

My mind spun, and I just stood there, not knowing how to get past the fact that I'd just met my birth mom or that my bio dad was dead. The latter was messing with my head. Everyone around me died.

Ripples of water ruffled the shore's edge. Maybe dipping my toes in the cool Atlantic would give me some clarity or temper my tender emotions. I kicked off my Vans when Colton's husky voice floated on the breeze.

"Skyler, wait." He jogged over. "What happened?"

I wiggled my toes beneath the soft sand. "Nothing really, except I learned my bio dad is dead." I couldn't understand why that bothered me.

"I'm sorry." He cocooned me in his arms.

"It seems people keep dying around me."

He rubbed my back. "This might make you laugh. Grady thought for a hot second you and he were brother and sister."

"I guess we both had the same thought."

He laughed. "Really?"

I started for the ocean's edge. "They were high school friends. I got the feeling they had a thing back then."

Colton followed. "Grady said it would've made sense if you were related because you two are so much alike."

"I wouldn't go that far, but I guess we do argue like sister and brother."

A wave broke, slithering toward us.

I dipped my toes in the water. "Ashley seems nice enough. But I guess she won't be any help with my guardian situation if we need her."

The water slid over Colton's Nikes. "Well, if you end up moving, I might have to kidnap you," he teased, looking out at the vast Atlantic.

I forced a smile. "I would let you." I knew I would run if I had to, but Nan and my aunt would work things out. I had to believe that.

"Aside from your bio dad, did she tell you why she gave you up?" Colton asked.

"No. She said I wasn't ready to listen. She's right. She seems like she has a lot of money and a good life. For some reason, that rubbed me the wrong way. I wish my dad were alive. I mean, my adoptive dad. I miss him so much. He would know what to do and say."

He turned to face me. "You will, too, baby. I'm proud of you."

"I love you, Colton."

"Baby doll, I can't begin to tell you how important you are to me. I love you hard. You are the calm in my storm. So let me be yours."

I stood on my tiptoes and brushed my lips over his.

My problems began to vanish when he deepened the kiss. Before long, my mind was clear, and my heart was full of nothing but pure, sweet love.

39

The Southern mansion was something plucked out of *Better Homes and Gardens* magazine. Wide, rounded pillars stretched to reach the high ceiling, expensive art adorned the walls, thick fabric curtains gave the rooms a lived-in feeling, and the furniture reminded me of a different era.

Mr. Robert Wilson, attorney at law, had eccentric taste and an office on the first floor of his home.

I bounced my knee as I listened to the *tap, tap, tap* of the keys echoing in the large foyer-turned-waiting-room. A pretty brunette was hard at work at her glass-top desk.

Nan gripped my leg. "What has you so nervous? I told you, Mr. Wilson said we would work things out."

Five days had passed since I'd learned the updated trust documents had never made their way to Mr. Wilson.

"Is Aunt Clara coming?" The lawyer had returned from his trip only the day prior to discuss who would be my guardian. He'd mentioned to Nan how important it was for Aunt Clara to be at the meeting.

She'd decided to stay in town for the funeral and had been very accommodating in assuring us she would help however she could.

"She'll be here," Nan reassured me. "What's got you on edge?"

I bit a nail. "I'm worried about Colton." The rehab facility where his dad was a patient had given the green light for family to visit. Colton had debated about whether to go or not. He had a football game that night and didn't want to miss it, but he couldn't let his mom down. More than that, if he wanted to build any kind of relationship with his dad, he had to show his support. Still, Colton wasn't sure how he and his dad would get along now that Mr. Caldwell wasn't drinking.

"Are you sure it's just Colton?" Nan asked. "You haven't been yourself since you met your birth mom."

I couldn't decide if I was ready to hear why she'd given me up, her excuses or, for that matter, whether I was ready to welcome her into my life as if nothing had happened.

I had advice flying at me from everyone. Georgia, Nan, and Mia insisted that I listen to Ashley. But my emotions were too raw.

The only people who weren't trying to tell me what I should do were Colton and Grady. I didn't expect Grady to give me counsel. He had, however, told me that his dad had a thing for Ashley. I could see that. She was pretty. His dad was handsome.

"I'll be fine. I just want to get through the funeral. Then I'll take the next step."

"Is Ashley still in town?" Nan asked.

I traded one nail for another. "Apparently. She and Mr. Dyson have been having dinner every night."

"Oh." Nan's voice rose in pitch.

"I guess they like each other."

"She's not married, then?" Nan asked.

I shrugged. "I guess not."

A long beep echoed in the room. "Yes, sir," the receptionist said into her phone's headset. "I'll let them know." She looked up at Nan and me, her brown eyes apologetic. "Mr. Wilson is just finishing up a call. He should be done momentarily." She resumed typing.

Nan's phone went off, and she fished in her purse. "Maybe this is your aunt. I'm going to step outside."

No sooner had Nan gone than a door opened behind the receptionist. Mr. Wilson sauntered out, dressed in a dark-green button-up shirt, no tie, and black slacks, holding a folder in one hand. "Carol, can you make sure this gets filed before the courthouse closes today?"

Nodding, she took the folder.

Mr. Wilson grinned my way as his long legs carried him across the pristine, shiny white floor. "Skyler, it's so nice to see you. I'm so sorry for your loss." He scanned the room. "Where's Nan and your aunt?"

I brushed off my jeans as I stood. "Nan's outside. Not sure of my aunt."

He pinched his clean-shaven jaw with his fingers. "Mmm. It's important your aunt shows today. But I don't have an appointment after this, so it's all good. Why don't we get settled? Carol will show Nan and your aunt in."

Once Mr. Wilson and I were in his office, he waved his hand at a small conference table. "Please, have a seat." He went over to his desk. "I'm sorry I didn't respond to your email. And I can't tell you how upset I am at the mail system for losing your father's documents."

I slid into a rolling leather chair. "It's not your fault. But can you do something to switch guardians?" *Please say yes.* Aunt Clara wasn't as bad as I remembered, and I thought we would get along just fine, but my friends, my home, everyone and everything I'd ever known were there. More importantly, I would die if I had to leave Colton.

He sifted through a pile of folders on his desk. "As long as your aunt signs over her rights."

She'd told Nan she would.

Then he collected a large leather binder before heading over to me. "I understand you met Ashley?"

"Yes, sir. Did you talk to her?"

"Briefly," he said. "May I ask how that meeting with her went?"

I hiked a shoulder up to my ear. "It was brief and tense."

He considered me, his green gaze appraising. "First meetings like that usually are. I've seen it many times in my line of work. But maybe when things settle down, you and Ashley can reconnect."

"Do you know why she gave me up?"

"I only know what's in the case file, and it's very thin at best. So no. Besides, it's not my story to tell."

I didn't think he would give me details, but I had to ask. Maybe if I knew ahead of time, it might make it easier to have a conversation with Ashley.

Nan and my aunt came in.

Mr. Wilson set the binder on the table and greeted them. "Please, ladies, have a seat."

My aunt, who wore a sharp blue suit, sat across from me. I hadn't seen her since that morning in Dad's room. She'd been busy with work. I'd learned from Nan that my aunt was working on closing a big corporate account, which kept her tied to her phone and computer. She'd canceled a recent trip to hang back for the funeral, though.

After the introductions, Mr. Wilson started in. "In front of Clara and Skyler is Randall's trust. Since you're both named in the trust, you're entitled to a full copy. However, before we dive into the specifics, I understand, Clara, you would like to relinquish your rights to Skyler. Is that correct?"

Everyone looked at my aunt, who seemed to be fascinated with Dad's trust. She flipped through the papers as if she was looking for something specific. "Did my brother leave me anything?"

Suddenly, Colton's words blared in my head: *Maybe she's here for money.* She didn't seem as though she needed money. I would bet the suit she was wearing had cost a pretty penny, and she'd recently been promoted.

"Do you mean money?" I asked.

Nan's face was distorted. Mine had to have been too.

Aunt Clara moved her finger along the document she was reading.

"Clara," Nan said. "What's going on? You're not changing your mind?"

I held my breath. Surely she didn't want to ruin her new job for me.

She lifted her chin. "I'm sorry. Randall mentioned to me he had some items that had belonged to our parents that he had outlined in his trust?"

A gush of air rushed from my lungs.

Nan sank in her chair as color returned to her cheeks.

"He did," Mr. Wilson said. "If you turn to the last page in the section on personal belongings."

Clara hurried to read that part. When she did, she smiled.

Curiosity had me flipping to that same section. The list included photos of their childhood, a diamond ring that belonged to their mother, an old Rolex watch that had belonged to their dad, and other jewelry and trinkets that I was sure had sentimental and maybe monetary value. What Dad had left her was rightfully hers.

Satisfied with what she'd read, she gave Mr. Wilson her attention. "Again, I apologize. These items are of sentimental value to me. So, yes, I'll sign over guardianship to Nan."

I might have been reading too much into it, but I got the feeling that if she didn't get her parents' belongings, she wouldn't have agreed to sign over her rights. I guess it didn't matter anymore.

Mr. Wilson removed a two-page document from the binder and slid it over to Aunt Clara. "I'll need your signature at the bottom of the second page. You may read through it, but in a nutshell, it says you are relinquishing guardianship to Nan. This document will be binding, and if the original forms that Randall signed show up in the mail, they will be too. Either way"—he considered Nan —"you will be Skyler's guardian until her eighteenth birthday. On top of that, Randall has set up a bank account for monthly expenses—house payment, utilities, food, and such. Skyler will also get a Social Security stipend that will help cover anything else. Any questions?"

Nan, Aunt Clara, and I shook our heads.

One less thing to worry about. All I had to do was bury my dad.

40

———

Guests gathered at the cemetery as we paid our last respects to Dad. His golfing buddies, coworkers, some neighbors, Mia, Grady, Georgia and her parents, and Mr. Dyson were a few who were in the crowd. Colton's mom couldn't make it. She was still in South Carolina, but had relayed her condolences through Colton.

Aunt Clara stood on one side of me while Nan was on the other. Since we'd walked out of the attorney's office three days prior, I'd been a bundle of nerves.

I swiped at a tear then another when a hand landed on my shoulder. Then Colton's voice was in my ear. "I'm here."

I knew he was behind me. I swore he was the only reason I wasn't draped over Dad's coffin. I zeroed in on the priest, who I'd tuned out. I'd been mindlessly staring at Mom's headstone next to Dad's coffin. I'd replayed some of the laughter, love, and good times we'd had as a family.

Despite the time I'd had to say goodbye to Dad, it still hurt like hell to stand there and mourn the best father ever, the man who had raised me, loved me, and taught me so much about growing up. Randall Lawson would always have my heart, and he would always and forever be my hero.

I knew he was in a better place, free from what ALS had done to his body. I prayed that he was talking up a storm in heaven and telling jokes to everyone.

"Go in peace," the priest said as he closed his Bible.

Guests started to scatter. I didn't blame them. Ominous clouds were rolling in as the earthy smell of rain permeated the air.

I didn't move. I didn't want to. The last few hours had been exhausting as people paid their respects. So I hadn't had a chance to be alone with Dad to say my final goodbyes.

"Your aunt and I will meet you at home," Nan said. "Colton is giving you a ride."

I acknowledged Nan with a dip of my head, not looking at her.

Colton slid into Nan's spot and laced his fingers in mine.

I lifted my gaze, and warm brown eyes met mine. "Can you give me a minute?"

He kissed me on the forehead. "I'll wait near my truck."

Once alone, I walked to the coffin and placed my hand on top. "Dad, I know we had time before, but I feel like we didn't get enough of it. I want you to know I'll be okay. Nan is now my guardian, and so far, she's been great. She reminds me so much of Mom." I dashed away a tear. "Your sister is nice too. To be honest, and I never told you this, I always thought she was snooty. I was wrong. She does love you.

"Anyway, I met my birth mom. I haven't talked to her yet but plan to soon. I'll let you know how that goes. I love you and want to say thank you for adopting me and for being the best father a girl could have." I cried quietly as I slid over to Mom's headstone. "You're now with the love of your life, Mom. You and Dad will forever be in my heart." I shuddered, wiping my nose with the tissue I had balled in my hand.

After one last look at Dad's coffin, I made my way to Colton. He looked as handsome as ever in his blue suit, white shirt, and blue tie. His wavy brown hair hung free to his shoulders, his jaw was clean-shaven, and he gave me the most heart-stopping grin I'd ever seen on him.

I almost faltered as I trudged through the soft grass and around headstones. I warmed at how much he loved me, and I loved him. Yet the closer I got to him, a sense of fear set in. All I'd ever known was my parents, who had taken care of me. Now, I was on my own. Sure, I had Nan, but it was different. I couldn't quite articulate the feeling except to say I was afraid of the unknown road ahead.

Colton opened his arms as I approached.

Shuddering, I buried my head into his chest and cried. He was the best thing that could've ever happened to me. He was and would always be the hope I'd been searching for.

41

Halloween came and went. Georgia, or rather her mom, had canceled her plans to have a party. Her parents hadn't wanted kids trampling through their house while they were out of town. Georgia had been disappointed. She'd thought the Halloween party would get me out of my funk, but I didn't care either way.

It had been well over two weeks since Dad's funeral, and with Thanksgiving approaching, I was feeling even more depressed. Dad had loved to cook turkey with all the yummy sides. Nan suggested we do just that and celebrate Dad.

We'd invited my aunt, who had flown back to California not long after we buried Dad, but she politely declined. She was scheduled to be in Australia for a couple of months for her job. I didn't think I would ever see Aunt Clara again. I couldn't say I was affected one way or the other.

Nan and I had settled into a nice routine. We were gradually clearing out the medical equipment and supplies and donating them to the local chapter of the ALS Association and a couple of other charities in need. We'd packed up Dad's clothes and cleaned out his room. I'd hijacked his pictures and hung them throughout the house.

Georgia tapped on the arm of my chair. "Earth to Skyler."

I looked from the sparkling ocean water to Georgia, who was sitting next to me on Grady's deck. We had just finished helping Colton unload his truck. With his house on the market, Colton was moving in with Grady and his dad for the remainder of the school year.

Georgia kicked up her legs and rested her feet on the rail of the deck. "My mom said I could have a graduation party. I think that's better than the Halloween one I couldn't have."

"Awesome." She was all about parties. Granted, she knew how to throw an extravagant one.

"Have you thought any more about talking to Ashley?"

I slanted my face toward the sun. "I told you, I plan to. I'm just not sure when." Part of me was procrastinating. I hadn't gotten over Dad's death, and I was trying to get to a better place emotionally. The last thing I wanted to do was open a wound that should maybe stay closed. After all, as far as I was concerned, my parents were Randall and Candace Lawson. "She went back to Chicago, anyway." Grady had mentioned that Ashley lived in Chicago and owned a printing company. She wasn't married and didn't have kids.

"I'm sure she'll return soon. She's dating Mr. Dyson."

I didn't know how I felt about that, and frankly, I didn't want to talk about Ashley and Mr. Dyson. "I'm going to find Colton." The last I knew, he'd been unpacking in his room. A sudden need to jump his bones coursed through me.

We hadn't had a chance to spend any time together. He'd decided to see a therapist, which I was stoked about. I could see an improvement in him after two visits. He was happier and not as quiet as he had been when I'd first met him. I know I played a role in his healing, but he was working through his father issues and blaming himself for Josh's death. He also had a great friend in Grady, and Mr. Dyson was there to parent him if the need arose. Aside from that, there was school, Colton had football, and on occasion, he would make a trip to South Carolina to visit his mom. And I had my own things to deal with.

"Can you bring me a soda when you come back?" she asked.

I didn't know how long I would be or if Colton was ready to kick back or not. I acknowledged her just the same.

As soon as I crossed the threshold into the brightly lit sunroom, I came to an abrupt halt.

Ashley was standing in the kitchen with her phone to her ear, dressed in casual attire and appearing relaxed and comfortable as she chatted with someone.

I had no clue when she'd gotten there. When I'd arrived with Colton two hours before, Ashley hadn't been in the house or even in town, as far as I knew.

Maybe fate was trying to tell me to talk to her.

When she realized I was in the room, her eyebrows rose.

Colton's and Grady's voices filtered into my

ears. It sounded like they were in the rec room off the kitchen.

She set her phone on the island then glided toward me. "Skyler, I didn't expect to see you here."

I could have said the same. I also didn't know why she was surprised that I was there, given I was dating Colton, who was friends with Grady, and Mia and I were friends. "I thought you flew back to Chicago."

She looked pretty, and her floral-patterned silk blouse brought out the color in her red shorts. "I did. Mr. Dyson and I are on our way to Key West for a conference."

I knitted my eyebrows. "Don't you own a printing company?"

"I do. I'm going as his guest." She stood behind a wicker chair. "I'm so sorry to hear about your dad. Is there anything I can do for you?"

A laugh broke out in my head. I had so many snarky retorts. *You're now asking if you can help when you gave me up?* But I didn't have the emotional energy to deal. I wasn't even sure if I had the strength to listen to her. Then again, if she and Mr. Dyson were a couple, I would be seeing more of her, since Colton was living there now. On top of that, if I wanted to put the past behind me, I knew I should listen. "I don't need anything, but thank you."

"I understand you and Colton are dating. He seems like a wonderful young man."

He was the best. I sat on a wicker chair on the opposite side of the room and sighed with indecision. "It seems like we might run into each other more often."

"Are you saying you're ready to listen?"

I tangled my hands in my lap. "Yes and no. I'm angry and curious." I hadn't gotten over my anger, which was probably one of the reasons why I'd been procrastinating.

She skirted the chair and lowered herself in a matching wicker love seat far enough away that I didn't feel like she was suffocating me. "We're not leaving for an hour. But I don't want to talk if—"

I held up my hand. "It's okay." I was pretty sure it was okay. I couldn't promise how I would react when I heard her story.

She held up her chin. "I had my speech all planned. But as I look at you, I don't even know where to begin. I am sorry, but I know that doesn't help."

"Were you in love with my father?"

She winced as if I'd said a swear word. "No. We were teenagers who got caught up in the moment."

Great. I was a mistake. *Shut up, subconscious.*

I was grateful, though, that Nan had made a doctor's appointment for me, which I'd gone to last week. I was officially on the pill.

"But your father was the hottest guy in school. I was surprised when he noticed a freshman like me. Then before I knew it, I was pregnant." She glanced out the floor-to-ceiling window. "As soon as my parents found out, they whisked me off to a private school out of state. They were the type of parents who prided themselves on appearances and what others thought about them. They couldn't have a daughter pregnant at fifteen."

I swallowed down the shock at how young she'd been, which meant she was only thirty-two.

"That look on your face was the same one I had when I found out I was pregnant. Anyway, I barely had time to tell Jake."

"My father?"

The dusting of blush on her cheeks sparkled in the light. "Yes. Jake Townsend, star quarterback, bright future, a girl magnet." She trailed off as she looked everywhere but at me. "I was so naïve then.

After I told Jake, he wanted nothing to do with me or my pregnancy. All he cared about was football."

"So you got pregnant and decided to just give me up because he didn't want me?" My anger held steady.

She jerked her head, the area under her eyes wrinkling. "Not at all. My parents were the ones adamant about giving you up. I protested until I was blue in the face, but my dad wasn't budging. But in my last month of pregnancy, I convinced my mom to let me keep you. I knew as soon as you were born and she saw you, she would change her mind, and she did." She paused, tears filled her light-brown eyes, and her chest rose. "Then I came home with you tucked into my arms. I'd never been so in love or excited in my life. You were the most beautiful baby I'd ever seen, and I couldn't wait for Jake to meet you. I knew as soon as he saw you, he would fall in love." She lowered her gaze briefly. "Then I came home from school one day, and you were gone. My parents had been working with a local adoption lawyer during the time I was pregnant, and I didn't know. Their plan all along was to give you up. I'd never been more traumatized in my life."

"How old was I?" I was riveted to her every

word as the anger swirling in my gut directed itself at her evil parents.

"Three weeks old. I never got a chance to introduce you to Jake, either."

How sad. I couldn't imagine how she must've felt when she'd gotten home and found her baby gone. I also wasn't sure I was a fan of my bio father for not wanting anything to do with her. My adoptive parents had always taught me to take responsibility for my actions. God, I missed them.

Then a lightbulb came on in my head. *I shouldn't be angry with Ashley.* Maybe at her parents, but in the end, if they hadn't given me up, I never would've met Randall and Candance Lawson. I couldn't imagine my life without them. For seventeen years, I'd had the best darn parents, the most love any mom and dad could give a child, and they shaped me into the young woman I had become. If Mom or Dad had been with me, they would have told me to give her a chance.

Heavy footsteps pounded somewhere in the house, and then Mr. Dyson came into view. "Oh," he said to Ashley. "Take your time."

She scooted to the edge of the cushion. "I'll be a second."

More footsteps clamored behind Mr. Dyson before Grady and Colton appeared.

Colton took in the scene, then prodded me with his eyes, wanting to know if I needed him.

I smiled to let him know I was okay.

Mr. Dyson then waved the guys out of the kitchen and into another room. "Give them some space."

I abandoned my seat and joined Ashley on the sofa. Candace Lawson would forever be my first mom and the woman who'd loved me unconditionally, and Nan was definitely my second mom and would always hold that spot, but maybe having a third mom wasn't so bad.

Regardless, I sensed that opening the door for Ashley and me to get to know each other wouldn't hurt. I figured it would be nice to know my lineage at some point in the future. I also could see how hard it was for her to tell me that story.

"I'm sorry you had to go through that." I really was. "Can I hug you?"

She flung herself at me. "You never have to ask that."

My muscles tightened. I wasn't quite ready to open myself fully to her, but she looked like she could use a hug. "Did you try looking for me?" I untangled myself from her.

She ran a finger under each eye, clearing the mascara that had smudged. "For years. My parents made it so they didn't know who adopted you. They didn't want to know and felt if they did, I would eventually get them to tell me. But a year ago, on my mom's deathbed, she finally directed me to a file my dad had kept on the adoption. But the only thing in that file other than your baby picture was the attorney's name. Sadly, the attorney closed up his practice after a fire gutted his office. I tried to track him down, but I kept running into dead ends. Even if I did speak with him, he was bound by attorney-client privilege, and I wasn't his client."

"Then Mr. Wilson found you," I said.

"Yeah." She flicked a strand of my hair off my forehead. "I like the name Skyler."

"You didn't name me?"

"I did. I'd always liked the name Melanie. But I like Skyler better. The name fits you."

The door burst open and Georgia came in. "There you... oh." She ran over and extended her hand. "I'm Georgia, Skye's bestie."

"Nice to meet you," Ashley said, taking Georgia's hand.

"And you're beautiful," Georgia gushed. "Just like Skyler."

Ashley laughed. "Thank you. You have great friends, Skyler."

I rolled my eyes at Georgia with all the love in the world. "I do."

As if a bell had sounded, Grady and Colton sauntered in.

Colton wasn't the star QB, but he was the hottest guy in school. I hopped up. "Hey."

He encased me in his muscular arms. "Everything good?"

"Everything is perfect."

Maybe Ashley and I would get to know each other, or maybe we wouldn't. Either way, I would be okay. Colton was my family now, and my future was with him. That much I was certain of, and I couldn't be happier.

EPILOGUE

My senior year passed in the blink of an eye. I couldn't believe I was no longer in high school. A lot happened after Dad died and I met my birth mom.

Ashley and I had developed a friendship. I still couldn't bring myself to call her Mom. That title was and would always be reserved for Candace Lawson, my adoptive mother, who had poured her heart and soul into raising me. I wasn't saying Ashley didn't deserve the title. What had happened hadn't been her fault. Maybe one day "Mom" would drop from my lips when I referred to her. She didn't care if I called her Ashley. She gave me the impression that "Mom" would make her day, but baby steps.

"Skyler Lawson, where are you?" Georgia shouted over the music and chatter of people packed into Grady's house. "We need to sing Happy Birthday."

I hid behind Colton. "Shh."

He chuckled as he spun around and pinned me against the counter near the stove. "I'm with Georgia on this. It's your eighteenth birthday and we need to celebrate."

I ran my hands up his chest, not caring if anyone was watching us. "Traitor."

He leaned down and nibbled on my ear. "I have the best birthday present for you later."

I giggled like a crazy schoolgirl. "I can feel it."

Colton and I had been inseparable since we started dating, with the exception of the week after graduation, when he moved his mom to South Carolina. We'd thought his house would sell when they put it on the market back in the fall, but with the new construction of homes throughout the beach town, older homes were harder to sell.

Georgia huffed. "There you are. All I have to do is find Colton and I know I'll find you." She tried to pry Colton and me apart. "It's time to sing."

"Do we have to?" I protested. I was all for a birthday party, but I didn't like to be the center of attention.

"You know it." Then she whistled, and the people who were scattered about the kitchen stopped talking. "It's time to sing Happy Birthday. Gather around." She waved her hands.

Colton moved to my side, giving me a full view of the long island where my four-tiered cake acted as the centerpiece amid a variety of finger foods and goodies.

"Nan, if you'll light the candles," Georgia said.

Guests were coming in and finding spots where they could.

Once Nan lit the candles numbered one and eight, she held out her hand. "Come here."

I slid over to her with Colton nudging me forward.

"Don't look so pained," Ashley said from the other side of the island.

Mr. Dyson, who had his arm around his sweetheart, laughed. "I don't like the attention either," he said to me.

Mia emerged through the crowd, her cheeks flushed, her dark hair messy. Behind her, Grady came in looking like he'd been doing something he shouldn't.

Whether his dad noticed or not, he didn't say a word.

I rolled my eyes at Mia.

She shrugged as she stood beside Ashley.

I couldn't blame her for sneaking away with her boyfriend. I desperately wanted to do just that with my hunk of a man.

I eyed Georgia. "Anytime."

Colton wrapped me in his arms from behind while the guests launched into singing Happy Birthday.

As I listened to the out-of-tune melody, I took a minute to think of Dad. Once he was diagnosed with ALS, eighteen became the magic number. But things hardly happen the way one wants them to. I looked back on the last two years—because it had been close to two years since Dad and I had cried in his bedroom at three in the morning when he told me he had ALS, and I realized in that moment, among family and friends, that each step in our journey had been necessary to get me to where I was.

I was with a guy who loved me so hard it hurt, but in a fantastic way. I had friends who would die for me. I even liked Grady more than I had when he'd stuck his tongue in my mouth in elementary school, and we were on track to be stepsiblings. His dad and Ashley were tying the knot in October.

When the guests finished singing, I made a wish that one day, Colton and I would get hitched. He was my forever, and I wanted to build a future with him. Then I blew out the candles.

Claps resounded, then trailed off as the guests resumed talking or refreshing their drinks. Nan and Ashley began to cut the cake.

"What did you wish for?" Colton bit lightly on my ear. I'd learned quickly that Colton was an ear man. He loved doing things to my ear that made me want to jump his bones. I guessed that was why he did.

"I can't tell you until it comes true."

"I can tickle it out of you," he said.

"You can try," I volleyed back.

"Mmm. I will later, then."

He could do whatever he wanted to me.

Two days had passed since my birthday party, and I stood on the porch, hugging Nan and not wanting to let go. She and I had been crying for the last twenty-four hours, which was crazy—

Colton and I weren't going to be gone that long. But I felt like I was losing a part of my life that I'd come to love with Nan. She'd been the best guardian ever.

"Skyler, let's go." Colton's sexy and impatient voice sent shivers over my entire body. "We're only leaving for a couple of months."

We had to be home in time for Ashley's wedding to Mr. Dyson. I'd agreed to be her maid of honor, and Colton had accepted Mr. Dyson's offer to be a groomsman.

I snarled over my shoulder at the love of my life. "I'm coming." I could almost hear Colton saying, "You will be later when you're under me naked."

I dashed a tear away and smiled. "I should go." I kissed Nan on the cheek. "I'll call you when we get to Columbia later tonight."

Colton and I were headed out on our road trip —not around the world, but across the great US of A. We'd decided it would be cheaper, especially since we never got those jobs we'd planned on getting during the school year.

Both of us had too much going on. Colton had gone to see a therapist to work out his issues with his father and Josh's death. And I wanted to take time to mourn Dad, get to know Ashley, and build a relationship with Nan.

I grabbed my bag at my feet, gave Nan one last hug, then hightailed it over to Colton, who was sizing me up from head to toe like he always did when I walked into a room or toward him, swinging my hips. "I'm ready."

He pecked me on the lips. "Are you sure?"

I playfully punched him in his hard-as-stone abs. "Wherever you go, I go. So let's get a move on. Oh, wait. Did you get my skateboard out of the garage?"

"Of course. I also have your helmet and other gear to protect you," he said sternly.

I rolled my eyes as I climbed into the truck. He freaked out every time I fell. I couldn't blame him. If the tables had been turned, I would have felt the same way.

Nan waved at us, looking forlorn. My heart pinched as though I was losing her, but she would always be part of my life. I owed her so much. I knew that as she grew older, she would need me to help her in some way, and I wouldn't hesitate for one second to be at her side. Great caregivers were super-special people, and in my book, they deserved to be honored and cherished.

Colton slid behind the wheel and started the engine. "Is she going to be okay?"

I buckled in. "She will. It's just hard. We've grown so close." I sighed, ready to shake the sadness and start a new adventure. I pulled out my iPad from my bag. "First stop will be Columbia, South Carolina. Grady and Mia are expecting us tonight. Then we head out to Tennessee to see Georgia at the end of the week."

Our friends chose to attend college, though Colton and I had decided to put off major life decisions for a year. I wasn't in a rush. As long as we were together, I was over-the-moon happy and still had to pinch myself sometimes because I was hopelessly in love with the best guy on the planet. He'd come a long way since that day in the parking lot of the Latte House when he'd hit me with his truck. The mysterious Colton, who had been angry with the world, was as loving and caring as my dad had been.

Colton had been through hardship that I couldn't even imagine. The physical and emotional abuse he'd been through was something no one should ever have to endure, let alone the death of his brother. I would do everything in my power to make sure Colton knew he was loved every minute of every day.

The future was ours to make new memories, and I was sure we would. But for the time being, Colton and I needed space to heal, to shed the darkness that had clung to us for so long, and to have fun and breathe. Regardless of any obstacles thrown our way, our love for one another was all that mattered.

The End

AFTERWORD

I hope you enjoyed Crazy For You and Skyler and Colton's story. This book was my outlet and I wrote it to deal with my own emotions. I've also dedicated this book to my husband.

To my husband of twenty-two years who is the most courageous, honorable, moral, and wonderful man I have ever met. His battle with amyotrophic lateral sclerosis, ALS, has been a challenging journey for the last five years. But through the ups and downs and twists and turns, he always has a smile on his face. He's the love of my life and my soulmate, and I'm honored to call him my hero.

With all the love in my heart.
Susan

Our journey has been challenging, emotional, and often maddening. I've been angry, sad, bawling most nights when Bill's asleep, happy, grateful, and so many other emotional roller coaster rides. And yet, while I would love nothing more than to have my husband back in full health, I can't complain. I've learned so much. I've grown by leaps and bounds as a person and as a wife. You never really know how much you love someone until you're faced with a life-changing situation. Bill always has a smile on his face—morning, noon, and night. And since he lost his ability to speak at the very beginning before he'd been officially diagnosed, I use his smile as a guiding light.

He does communicate with me through his eye-gaze computer. I have a love-hate relationship with that thing. But it has been a godsend.

Everyone who is faced with ALS follows a different journey. However, the average life span is three to five years, and we're heading into our fifth year. We live each hour at a time, and like Skyler's dad, Bill has choking episodes frequently. Those scare me to death. A very dear friend of ours who had ALS passed the same way Skyler's dad did in the book.

Again, thank you so much for reading Crazy For You, and if you want to learn more about ALS or wish to donate to help find a cure, you can check out https://www.als.org/

In addition, I'm inserting some information regarding suicide. Colton had his own demons to slay, but it's important to know that there's help out there.

If you need to talk to someone regarding suicide, please call the American Foundation for Suicide Prevention in the US at 1-888-333-AFSP (2377) or via email: info@afsp.org

ABOUT THE AUTHOR

Bestselling author **S.B. Alexander** is an independent author with over 20 titles to date. She writes paranormal, new adult, and sweet romances that feature hot heroes stealing hearts.

S.B. or Susan as she likes to be called is a navy veteran, former high school teacher, and former corporate sales executive. She's a lover of sports, especially baseball, although nowadays you can find her glued to the TV during football season.

When she's not writing, she's a full-time caregiver to her soul mate of twenty-two years who got a bad deal in life when he was diagnosed with ALS. Her motto: "Life is too short to waste. So live every moment like it's your last."

You can connect with S.B. Alexander in the following ways:

Reader Group: https://
sbalexander.com/sbareaderroom
Author Website: https://sbalexander.com
Newsletter: https://sbalexander.com/newsletter
Email: susan@sbalexander.com

NEVER MISS A NEW RELEASE:

Sign up for her Author App
iTunes: https://bit.ly/sbalexanderitunes
Android: https://bit.ly/sbalexanderandroid

facebook.com/sbalexander.authorpage

instagram.com/sbalexanderauthor

amazon.com/author/sbalexander

bookbub.com/authors/s-b-alexander

goodreads.com/sbalexander

ALSO BY S.B. ALEXANDER

THE MAXWELL SERIES

Upper Young Adult/New Adult Contemporary Romance

Dare to Kiss

Dare to Dream

Dare to Love

Dare to Dance

Dare to Live

Dare to Breathe

Dare to Embrace

The Kade & Lacey Collection Box Set

The Maxwell Series Collection

Dare to Kiss Coloring Book Companion

THE MAXWELL FAMILY SAGA SERIES

Young Adult Contemporary Romance

My Heart to Touch

My Heart to Hold

My Heart to Give

My Heart to Keep

Maiken & Quinn Collection

STANDALONES

Upper Young AdultNew Adult Contemporary Romance

Crazy For You

Unforgettable

Breaking Rules

Rescuing Riley

Holding On To Forever

THE HART SERIES

Romantic Suspense

Hart of Darkness

Hart of Vengeance

THE VAMPIRE SEAL SERIES

Young Adult Paranormal Romance

On the Edge of Humanity

On the Edge of Eternity

On the Edge of Destiny

On the Edge of Misery

On the Edge of Infinity

The Vampire SEAL Collection

Visit https://sbalexander.com/all-books/ to learn more about S.B. Alexander books and future releases.